SIX
OF
SORROW

Books by Amanda Linsmeier

Starlings

Six of Sorrow

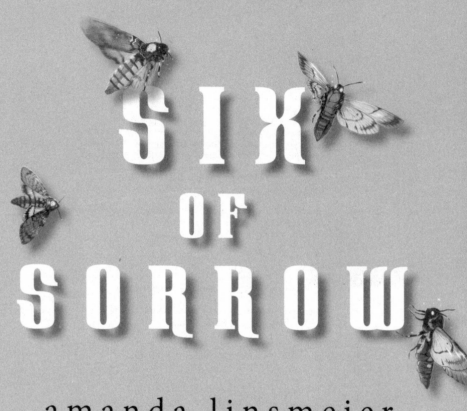

SIX
OF
SORROW

amanda linsmeier

DELACORTE PRESS

Text copyright © 2024 by Amanda Linsmeier
Jacket art copyright © 2024 by Kei-Ella Loewe

All rights reserved. Published in the United States by Delacorte Press, an imprint of Random House Children's Books, a division of Penguin Random House LLC, New York.

Delacorte Press is a registered trademark and the colophon is a trademark of Penguin Random House LLC.

Visit us on the Web! GetUnderlined.com

Educators and librarians, for a variety of teaching tools, visit us at RHTeachersLibrarians.com

Library of Congress Cataloging-in-Publication Data is available upon request.
ISBN 978-0-593-70776-0 (hardcover) — ISBN 978-0-593-70777-7 (lib. bdg.) — ISBN 978-0-593-70778-4 (ebook)

The text of this book is set in 11-point Calluna.
Interior design by Ken Crossland

Printed in the United States of America
10 9 8 7 6 5 4 3 2 1
First Edition

For the friends who feel like soul mates.
Mine. Yours. The ones still here,
those who have gone,
and those who've yet to be.

And for my children.

Has sorrow thy young days shaded,
As clouds o'er the morning fleet?
Too fast have those young days faded
That, even in sorrow, were sweet?
Does Time with his cold wing wither
Each feeling that once was dear?—
Then, child of misfortune, come hither,
I'll weep with thee, tear for tear.

—THOMAS MOORE

It is night and they are running. Tearing across the grass, frightened. But it is far too late for regret. So they run. To safety. To quiet. To their futures. Where they will let themselves forget the details of this evening, their choices. Until one day, inevitably, they will remember again. They will be forced to remember.

CHAPTER ONE

Sorrow was a witch.

Today is named for her—our whole town is named after her—but really, she's just a convenient mythical excuse for people to get drunk and dance around on the beach. This morning I woke early, restless, like a kid waiting for Santa Claus, anticipating something special, something worth believing in. Except today isn't Christmas, it's the Day of Sorrow. It's not the witch I care about—that's only a story. It's because today also happens to be my birthday, but I'm not excited about that. Not really.

It doesn't feel like a birthday if we aren't all together.

As I tug on my plaid skirt and white blouse, into the pinpoint-sharp corners of my memory comes a reel of celebrations: voices ringing out the birthday song, candles on giant cakes, laughter and gifts. Right now, hidden in the back corner of an old jewelry box, a silver spoon ring Georgina gave me—identical to the others. She and I don't talk anymore, but I still have that damn ring. I have other things to remember her by—to remember all five of them by.

We used to be worth believing in.

I shake my head, pushing aside thoughts I don't need to fixate on right now, and I find my tie, fighting the violent urge to fling it off my balcony instead of putting it on. As I loop it under the collar of my blouse, my phone dings. A text, from Reuel, my best friend.

> Happy birthday!! Gonna be late I overslept and can't find my stupid bloomers!!!

With a grin, I type back to her, *go commando*

The dots move, and up pops a sad emoji. A second later: *okay if I just meet you there?*

Dislike, I write, then add, *jk yeah it's fine happy birthday too xo*

I set the phone on my faded patchwork quilt and finish getting ready for school, raking a hand through my blue waves. I pause in front of my cheap full-length mirror with the fake sunflowers Reuel and I hot-glued to the frame, and I slather on my favorite rum-raisin lipstick. My lips are pulled down, and I tug them up, my smile a shade too wide—a Julia Roberts mouth, my mama says. Just like hers.

Even when I'm relaxed, my face ends up moving into a crooked scowl, my eyes naturally narrowing, my mouth telling the world I'm a little bit angry, all the time, even when I don't mean to be. I drop the smile. It is what it is.

I gather my phone and other things before slinging the straps of my bag over my shoulder; then I head downstairs, not bothering to be quiet in my clunky black loafers. I clomp down each step. So what if it wakes her?

In the kitchen, a small pang in my heart as I reach in the fridge to take out a store-brand string cheese and then an apple—red as blood—because just once, why can't I come down to a dozen warm muffins? Some scrambled eggs and butter toast? Something? Anything?

She doesn't know how to cook, she says. A flimsy excuse.

Because don't I remember? Pots of soup and casseroles and cookies spread on a pan?

Once upon a time she took care of me. My belly aches with the memory. Or maybe it's just my bad mood, drifting to my middle, pooling outward. It's my fucking birthday, and my mother is here, but she's not *here*. I shove the cheese in my bag and take a hostile bite of apple as I walk out of the house, banging the screen door behind me and entering the spring morning. I step down from the rickety porch with the peeling sage-colored paint. Leave our old farmhouse and eat my apple as I walk the gravel drive. Through the long stretch of green, green grass, my shoes going wet with dew, before I hit more houses. Through the cypress-thick park, where I chuck the core in a trash can; then I continue past Sorrow's only cemetery, with Reuel's home not far from it, but I don't sidetrack to meet her like usual. This morning I'm on my own.

I swallow any sort of self-pity. I may be alone, in this moment, but I'm not *alone*. I have Reuel, and tonight while our town partakes in holiday traditions—lighting bonfires on the beach and burning wishes—we will ring in our sixteenth birthday together, the two of us.

As I march forward, my mood brightens at the prospect of a half day and then spring break. My wretched uniform doesn't even bother me so much, when I know I can rip it off and change in just a few hours. Birds sing, and the morning air blows against my face, warm and damp, tasting of sunshine and fresh beginnings, and suddenly everything doesn't seem so grim. Nearby, someone is mowing their lawn, the scent grassy, sharp—one of my favorites. I bypass the familiar but slightly longer route through downtown that Reuel and I usually take and go the quicker way. I'm not exactly running on time today, either.

When I reach the brick building of Our Lady of Sorrow High School, I ease past clusters of students lingering, friends walking together, conversation and excitement buzzing in the air—everyone is smiley and full of energy today—and I go in alone. I arrive at my ugly peach locker moments before the first-hour warning bell rings. As I'm putting my backpack inside, a leggy, black-haired girl comes tearing down the hall, pushing past the crush of people heading in the opposite direction, pom-poms clutched in one hand. Reuel. I can *feel* myself lighten at the sight of her. And when she spots me, she grins, like she feels the exact same way. We are each other's safety. Sunshine. Home.

"Hi," my best friend pants as she reaches me, her hair ribbons crooked. "Shit."

"You're late," I warn her, glancing at the clock. "Aren't you supposed to be in the locker room by now?"

"I made it on time. Pretty much. I'm only a little late."

I snort, tugging at my maroon blazer, hating the itchy feel against my skin, against the back of my neck. "Put your stuff in my locker, then you don't gotta run all the way upstairs."

"Lifesaver." Her smile is grateful as she dumps her bag into my locker, shoving it with her foot for good measure, her thick white sock scrunched lower than the other.

I give her cheerleading uniform the once-over. It looks like she just managed to throw it on about five minutes ago. When she bends forward to push her bag in farther, I grab the zipper of her shell, tugging to close the inch-long gap she missed. Her skin is like cream against the red.

Reuel scoots to make room for the freshman trying to get into her own locker beside me, and I ask, teasing, "Find your bloomers?"

She glances at the girl next to us, distracted with her belongings, then gives me a wicked grin and flashes her skirt up. Black undies, not the cheerleading bloomers she's *supposed* to wear.

A laugh bubbles out of me, but it sounds strained. I close my locker door and spin the lock before tugging on her elbow. "Come on, we better hurry. Or you better."

We speed-walk down the hall, and she asks, "What is it? Birthday stuff?" She knows me too well. I shrug and she says good-naturedly, "You better not be grumpy tonight. We're not just gonna sit in my bedroom and watch *Twilight* for the millionth time. It's not even that good."

"Hello?" I raise my brows—*Twilight*'s one of our *things*. "Kristen Stewart makes it good?"

"Okay," Reuel concedes as we jog the last stretch down the hall, carefully weaving around groups of students, teachers. "But, Iz, forget about them." *Them*. She means the other four girls. She pauses just inside the entrance to the gym, and her voice goes softer. "We're still here, aren't we?"

I sigh, feeling like a brat. "Of course."

"Good. And maybe I'll get you to actually have fun tonight. I consider it my personal mission," she says, walking backward toward the locker room, humbly laying a hand over her heart, her black, coffin-shaped nails dramatic against the deep-red fabric.

"Ha," I say, giving in to her charms, nodding. "We'll see."

"It will be," she insists, calling louder, over the din starting as the gym fills up. "And if you decide you wanna go track down a party, I'm sure we can find a dozen options."

"Yeah! Party!" shouts some senior with big muscles and an even bigger voice. His friends cheer, they push each other rowdily. People will use any excuse to celebrate, including centuries-old mythology—not that I blame them. What else is there to do here?

I'm jostled by students trying to get to the bleachers but call good luck to Reuel.

She looks back with a bright smile and yells, "Thanks!" With that she runs off, headed toward the locker room door, where her coach is peeking out, frowning.

"Sorry!" Reuel tells the disapproving woman, and I shake my head fondly, turning away and to the bleachers. I follow the kid in front of me to a spot in the third row and sit, staring around, a little impressed. I think they went even more all-out than freshman year.

A high school gymnasium will always look slightly depressing, but ours has been strung with red streamers and filled with black balloons. The band is enthusiastically playing a Queen song and everyone filing in has a bounce in their step—the cheerleaders literally *are* bouncing now, as they run onto the sidelines into a two-row formation to warm up, Reuel last to hurry over, looking sheepish.

And of course, I can't *not* see Georgina, skipping over to stand beside August. August, legs for days, deep terra-cotta skin, a sparkly bow perched atop her long twists. She could be a model—the next Naomi Campbell, who August used to be obsessed with—if she weren't planning on being a doctor. Or maybe she *isn't* planning on it anymore. I don't know her now, do I?

As I watch the two of them moving to the front row of cheerleaders, all of them ready to pep-rally us into break, I catch myself digging my chipped jade-green nails into my palm. I purposely loosen my hands and exhale, finding Reuel's face in the line. They're not my friends anymore. But she is. She shakes one tinselly red-and-black-and-silver pom at me.

Smiling, I focus on Reuel, refusing to look at who is standing in front of her as they do their sideline routine, warming themselves up before the main event. Why would I? I know they won't look at me.

Someone brushes against my side, and in the space left between me and some other sophomores down the bench, Bridger Leland plops down, grinning. "Hey."

"Hey," I say back at my classmate from art, smiling warmly. His black curls are slightly damp, a faint rosemary smell coming off him.

"Doing anything tonight?" he asks after a moment.

"Not really." I shake my head. "I'm not big on bonfires." My whole life, I've had an unexplainable fear of fires burning out of control, but I don't tell him that.

His brown eyes are warm. Amused. "I mean for your birthday."

My cheeks heat. I don't like to make a big deal about it, now that we're not the six of us any longer, and even before that . . . It *is* such an odd thing, even I can admit that, and I never loved the attention our day of birth drew to us. Besides, I always felt if we didn't share a birthday, we'd be friends anyway, so why focus on that? Now? I realize that even that strange commonality wasn't a strong enough bond to keep the six of us together. I fidget and pull my hair up into a messy bun, finally answer Bridger, "Reuel and I are hanging out, that's it."

She and a nonbinary junior twirl and position themselves back to back and start doing flawless toe touches to the beat.

Reuel's facing us, screaming for our school, our town, our legends. It was a surprise when she tried out, not at all that she made the squad. She looks bold and striking, the edge to her, the sarcastic curl of her cherry-red lips when she cheers, as if she somehow finds it all a great big joke but loves it anyway.

I cup my hands around my mouth and holler for them. Next to me, Bridger claps.

But thoughts about the other girls invade my mind. About today. About what we've lost. Georgina's epic parties, always something amazing to commemorate our births. Sleepovers and spa days and all sorts of fun. Georgina will probably have a party tonight, under the guise of celebrating the Day of Sorrow or not. Of course, *we* won't be invited. Georgina and August are friendly to Reuel, because of cheerleading, or at least they're civil to her. Me? It's like we're strangers now. Like the six of us didn't used to say we were all soul mates.

"What about you?" I ask, turning back to Bridger. His uniform tie is crooked, charmingly so. "Party or something?"

His dark-bronze cheeks crinkle with dimples when he smiles, ever easygoing. "Yeah. Going to the beach with Grady."

Grady. I smile after a delayed moment. "Cool."

"I like the blue." He points to my hair, strands falling around my face. "That's new, right? What'd you call it before?"

"Lavender? Light purple?" I hold back a laugh. For an artist this boy has a shit sense of color. "Thanks. What are you doing the rest of break?"

"Working at the garage."

I nod. I don't know Bridger *that* well, but I know some things. He's liked trains since elementary school. He spent last summer in China, where his grandpa is from, and he's also half

Black. His dad has a garage where he works part-time, and his mom ran off when he was little. We have a-parent-ditched-us in common. Plus art. He's more creative than me, though—I don't even know where he gets his ideas sometimes.

Just as easily as he sat down, Bridger rises, shrugging. "I've seen enough. Gonna go work on my project."

Smiling, I say, "See ya," and watch him climb down the bleachers, slip out of the gym as if nobody else can see him or cares that he's leaving. And it's kinda like nobody can or does. Bridger helps in the office as an aide for a credit, so he's one of the first people you see when you walk in this building, and our school's not even that large—but there are still people who forget his name and face. Bridger could make a *killing* as a jewel thief or something, sneaking in and out of high-security places, unnoticed . . . if he didn't have a moral compass pointed straight north, that is.

Without the distraction of him now, though, it's like I can't help myself, despite my best intentions. I look around. Count us out—even if we aren't *us* anymore.

One. Me. Obviously.

Two, on the next set of bleachers over, I pick out one girl, glossy midnight hair pulled into a stylishly messy updo—Solaina Cruz, sitting with one of her friends from lit club. My mom works at the salon Solaina's mother, Marisa, owns. The two of them are actually close. But not us. Not any longer.

Three, a row from Solaina, a freckle-faced ginger, her virgin ponytail brushing the back of her blazer—Cori Jenkins, who happens to be Georgina's cousin. Cori is cake, sweet and soft.

Reuel (*Four*). The only one I can count on, and of course she'd say the same of me.

And on the court with her, the pair of them, doing their routine in perfect harmony. *Five:* August Archer. And *Six.* Georgina Boudreau. Queen Bee. I could close my eyes and still see her. That smooth, milky complexion, her French manicure— real nails that never, ever seem to chip. The A+ papers, tucked somewhere in her expensive backpack.

Friendships die every day, but ours was never supposed to. The six of us were linked from the womb, fated to be friends, we thought. Once in a while I wonder why we would've been brought together only to be ripped asunder. But ripped implies passion, intent, reason. We fell apart like wet paper, more like. Some of us seem to care more than others.

As if on cue, Georgina gets tossed in the air.

Even if she weren't defying gravity, she'd command attention. A tiny, terrible military general. It's like slow motion, the way she floats down, nailing a flawless landing. In unison, all the cheerleaders hit their final pose, and the crowd erupts in wild applause. The squad spills off the court while the drama club runs out, to a slightly less enthusiastic reaction.

We sit through a skit about Sorrow fleeing persecution and founding this town centuries ago. If you ignore the bad wigs and patched-up costumes, and the fact that it's all just generic regurgitation we've heard a million times before, it's actually not too awful. Then it's the boys' basketball team, doing a series of layups to "Uptown Funk." By the time they finish, the energy in the gym is palpable, everyone buzzing with enthusiasm. I give in to it, yelling right along with the rest of the students and staff. Why not? So what if it's *their* birthday too?

It doesn't make it any less mine.

We stamp our feet and whoop when members of the student council run along the bleachers and toss fistfuls of candy from buckets. A Blow Pop ricochets off the head of the boy in front of me and I stifle a giggle as it falls into my lap.

"You okay?" I tap him, and he laughs it off. I grin, peel off the wrapping, and stick the sucker in my mouth. Sour apple. I don't know why apples are a tradition for today. Nobody in Sorrow even believes in the witch anymore—at least not for the last few generations—but we still partake in the traditions, and we still love it. What's not to love about apple treats and parties and joy? Of course, the promise of spring break might be contributing to the students' feral exhilaration. I'm already anticipating hours lazing about, drawing. Spent with Reuel. Days to sleep in. To be free.

Our principal, Mr. Bruns, with his balding tan head and his tan suit, comes out and gives a speech—an exact replica of the one I heard last year, I think—thanking the band and the cheerleaders, the teachers, the drama club, the basketball team, all of us students. Even his *voice* is tan. Blah. I drown him out until it's clear he's wrapping up the talk.

"As we end our shortened day and head into spring break later, please make sure you clean out your lockers and remove any food items or important things you may need. And, as always"—he pauses, mustering up the most enthusiasm I've ever seen from him, his thin lips turning up at the corners minutely—"let's give a big show of excitement for today! Everyone stay safe and healthy—watch those fires, now. We'll see y'all next Thursday."

A smile spreads on my face. It's not even the things I get to add to my life without the confines of school. It's the things I will get to remove, even if our break isn't even a whole week. Six glorious days with no school and no math. No itchy blazer. No ex-friends. No Georgina.

Exhilarated, I rise with the other students and shuffle out of the bleachers, forming a line to flow, kids dancing their way out of the gym. In the commotion, someone bumps into me and I get pushed out of the line . . . and run right into Georgina.

I take a quick step back before I realize how it looks, how *weak* it makes me look. To put distance between us, I tell myself, not because I'm intimidated by her. But face to face like this, maybe that's a lie. She somehow *looks* more intimidating, more disapproving in her crisp uniform, the V-neck, the hint of flat midriff barely peeking out, sneakers snow white, bloomers hidden under her cheer skirt and probably still ironed. More intimidating, the way she's staring at me. Like I'm drawn with invisible ink. Like I'm being heated into existence and she'd rather I not.

August walks up, oblivious, eyes on her bestie, but her smile falters when she spots me. She looks even better in their uniform, her height and willowy figure carrying it well. As she glances from me to Georgina, her face is uncertain, like she's wondering if she interrupted something. Nobody says anything. The gym is emptying out, students flooding the halls to head to a shortened second hour. And soon the three of us could be alone in here. Won't someone say *something*?

I lift my chin. "Hi."

Like usual, I get nothing from Georgina. Not a smile, not a flicker of compassion or recognition in her gaze. Praline-brown eyes that lack warmth—that actually manage to look chilly. But she's not rude enough to ignore me completely . . . I don't think. I never actually *speak* to her. Just when I'm beginning to wonder if I imagined greeting them, Georgina's lips lift in acknowledgment.

"Blue, hmm?" Her smile is sweet, as sticky and sugary as her voice. She slow-glances at my hair. "How fun. Reminds me of a snow cone."

Before I can help it, stunned silent by her snark, my hand reaches up to touch the crown of my head. I'd describe the color as snow-cone blue too. But I don't want *Georgina* to.

With that obvious win, she gives me one last pointed smile, flouncing away with August beside her, their cheeky bloomers peeking out the back of their cute, swinging skirts. Nothing was said about what today is. Of course not. What did I expect? *Happy birthday, Iz? We miss you, Iz? I'm sorry, Iz?*

Face burning, I follow them with my gaze. Midway to the door, they both pause to meet up with Cori, a curvy Amazonian goddess with golden retriever energy. While their backs are turned, Cori notices me watching, gives me a guilty smile, mouthing *Happy birthday.* It should make me feel better, at least, the acknowledgment. A little bit, it does. I give her a half-hearted nod. *You too.* Cori was always the kindest, but she won't rock the boat too much, won't go against her cousin. Georgina hates me for some reason now. I just never figured out exactly why. Well, fine. I hate her, too.

Impatiently, I turn to find Reuel, who's talking to her coach, nodding along. I can't interrupt them. She's probably getting yelled at for being late. It's not the first time. She sees me waiting and gives me a barely perceptible head shake. *Go on without me,* it means.

Georgina's laugh echoes as the three of them go off together, leaving the gym and me behind. Somewhere, Solaina is with *her* friends, kids from lit club, yearbook staff. We're all happy with our new lives, aren't we?

. Except I remember when we held each other through life's misfortunes. When we laughed so hard, we cried. When we played Barbies in Georgina's basement. Remember when she sobbed in my arms when she got stung by a wasp. When her baby brother was born still. When we were *us*. Remember. Remember. Remember.

But I don't care. I'm *fine*. Screw Georgina. I hope she gets chia seeds in her teeth today. Smoothie-bowl-eating snob. She doesn't miss me. None of them do.

So why do I ache a little? Why do *I* still miss *them*?

I erase them from my thoughts. And I walk on to second hour alone, the fake tart-apple taste cloying on my tongue, choking me.

CHAPTER TWO

We are surrounded by death.

For a breath, we simply pause together, Reuel and I, standing inside the arched gates of Greenbrier Cemetery. The wet air rustles the trees around us, the Spanish moss dripping from their branches, like cobwebs strung from the corners of the night sky, which is so dark it looks like it's been colored with the blackest ink.

"When you said the perfect place to drink . . . ," I start, passing my fingers along the iron swirls of the gate to my right, hooking them against a curlicue edged with rust. I trace the pattern, imprinting it in my mind to draw later.

She grins, motioning ahead. "It's private. And atmospheric. You can't deny it."

"I guess," I say. Nobody will bother us here. The town banned bonfires anywhere except the beach decades ago. Back then there were still enough people that considered this a sacred spot, where Sorrow herself is supposedly buried. Her statue stands to this day, at the very center of the graveyard, built hundreds of years ago, probably about when the tradition of the bonfires started. Even the nonbelievers of today still burn wishes, though they'd rather party on the sandy beaches that border our tiny island than in this old place.

I don't really blame them. Looking around at the decrepit cemetery, I tighten my grip around the neck of the bottle of cheap champagne I'm holding. A second bottle of alcohol's in Reuel's bag. She snagged both from her dad's dust-topped liquor cabinet. He's not much of a drinker.

"Come on." Reuel's dark mouth curves up, cheerleading maroon ditched for her signature head-to-toe black, which makes her look even leaner and longer than she is—she's got four inches on me. "Keep going. We're headed to the top, where the old graves are."

Stepping off the path, I walk beside her in my knockoff Vans. The higher we climb up the hilly cemetery, the older the gravestones become, and the less care they've received, some of their stone broken off in chunks, left crumbling on the ground in a forlorn way. I haven't been here in years, and maybe during the day it's not so bad, but now, even the large tree up ahead is creeping me out, for all that it's loaded with blossoms. It looks like its branches might reach out and snatch us at any moment. It reminds me of the sentient orchard in *The Wizard of Oz*. I shiver a little, staring around us. This is where the ancient slumber, the witch's statue at the pinnacle, just beyond the tree. I ignore the uneasiness that runs along my body, like fingers walking up my vertebrae. Do the dead mind—us being here?

Silly, Iz. It's just a cemetery, in one of the most boring towns ever. Besides, nothing wrong with celebrating life. Dead people don't care.

And I don't believe in ghosts. Or much of anything else, for that matter.

I dart a sidelong glance at Reuel. It was her idea to come here, but I fervently hope it's not gonna make her sad. Reflexively, I turn to gaze down the hill, where the newer graves lie, not that I could see the one from this angle. I'm sure there are fresh yellow roses on it, though. Far as I know, Reuel never misses a week to lay them on her mom's resting place, ever since that horrid cancer took her life, just a few months shy of our thirteenth birthday.

"Here," Reuel says, stopping a couple of feet from the statue, tugging her bag off her shoulder and pulling out an old blanket, shaking it and laying it down. "This is a good picnic spot. I brought snacks."

She takes out a box of skull-shaped cookies and sets it in the center of the blanket with an impish grin. "For the theme. You can't have a cemetery birthday without leaning into it."

"You shoulda been born on Halloween." I smirk as I settle beside her, lifting a bag of neon gummy worms while she pops open the champagne. "And how do these fit in?"

"Oh, that old song." She sings, off-key, *The worms crawl in, the worms crawl out.* Of the corpse, you know."

"Gross." I laugh, make a face as she pours us each a Solo cup. "I'm sorry I asked. But I do love gummy stuff."

"I know. That's why I got 'em." She lifts her drink in a toast, gazing at me affectionately. "Happy birthday, Isabeau."

I refuse to let any sort of sadness touch my eyes—or heart—at her words. I press my red cup against hers and beam. "Happy birthday."

The cicadas chirp, hiding in the areas where the grass hasn't been cut well, whispering to each other like they know something I don't. I watch as Reuel tips her drink into her mouth, the brightness in her eyes, as if, impossibly, the alcohol has already caught up with her a few swallows in. I shouldn't want to want that feeling, but I do. Tonight I do.

I down my drink in one slug. A part of me wants to forget the world and my messy existence in it, my mama's coffee in the microwave, gone cold and forgotten. The fizzy-sweet liquor goes down easily, too easily. And I'm glad.

Reuel says, "Now, gifts." After nestling the champagne bottle into a corner of the blanket, she reaches into her seemingly bottomless tote bag, pulling out a rectangular set of packages, wrapped in azure-blue paper that almost matches my new hair. I wouldn't be surprised if she did it on purpose. She's always doing little things like that, things to delight me.

"Aw, thanks." I smile wide, already feeling warmth bloom in my chest, and I pop a worm in my mouth, chewing as I unwrap the smaller package, pleased to find a new set of pencils and charcoal sticks. The bigger present is a book, but when I see what kind, I cringe at it without meaning to. "Poetry. Great . . . um, thanks."

"Come *on*." She sounds offended on poetry's behalf. "You are shit at hiding your feelings."

I've been told that before. Face like an open book. Laughing, I say, "I love *your* poems, you know that. You're a wonderful writer. I just can't get into the older stuff. And I love the art supplies," I rush out, not wanting to sound ungrateful. I do love them.

"It's important to appreciate the classics, poetry or otherwise. You'd think someone with a *Mona Lisa* print might understand that," she scolds in exasperation, referencing the famous portrait I tucked into the pinboard on my wall, along with other things to inspire my art.

"Fair."

"Older stuff can be really good, Iz. It's not all boring or proper, if that's what you're assuming. Here." Reuel settles more comfortably, cross-legged, flipping through the book.

I take out a cigarette and light it. A nasty habit, but I'm not ready to give it up. I like smoking and it likes me.

"I'll read one of my favorites." Reuel squints, making out the words in the dark. She stops at a page near the middle and says, "Pablo Neruda—he was a Chilean poet—Sonnet Eleven."

I lean into one hand and inhale a long draw of poison into my lungs while I wait.

"*I crave your mouth,*" she begins, words like a shadow, slow-moving, soft.

I blow out a cloud of wispy smoke, listening to her musical voice, the way she enunciates, the way she builds the poem up for me, keeping me hooked, captive even as I try to understand the meaning. She's not just a good writer, she's a good reader. A good orator. Something in the words plucks at my heart, making me *feel*.

"*. . . hunting for you, for your hot heart . . .*"

When she finishes, I clear my throat, the words echoing in my head. "Wow. That was kinda sexy. Intense," I say. "Especially the part about wanting to eat the skin."

"*See.*"

"Okay, you were right," I admit with a half laugh. "Not boring at all."

With a satisfied smile, she folds the page corner over, a forever-dog-earer, despite the oodles of bookmarks I've given her over the years. "Now read the rest. You'll like it. I wouldn't have given it to you if I didn't think so."

"I'll read it," I promise, tucking it, along with the other gift, into my bag. Refill both our drinks, then take another long swallow of the champagne, bubbles popping on my tongue. "Just don't make me sit during the reading tomorrow, okay?" I refer to the event I promised to go with her to in the morning. "I plan to find a comfy chair and spend quality time with a muffin and look at art books until you let me drag you out of there."

"Deal." She giggles, but heaviness has drifted to settle in her ocean eyes.

"What's wrong?" I ask, lowering my cup instead of taking another swig.

"Why would something be wrong?"

I open my mouth, ready to press her. But hold myself back. For now, can't I be content to just be here beside her, the breath of poetry still on the air? She'll talk when she wants to.

Her beautiful face lights up again, all traces of sadness gone. "Now, where's *my* present?"

"Here, bossy." With a huff of a laugh, I hand over a gift bag, which she opens greedily, pulling out the tissue paper like a wild animal ripping through entrails.

"Ohh!" She gushes over the gift card I got her for the bookstore (where she will, no doubt, buy more poetry books or smut Mr. Carson would *die* over if he knew she read) and a new charm for her bracelet. Leaning over, she hugs me quick and tight. "I love it. Clip it on for me?"

I add it to the bracelet, along with the charms she already has: a fox, a dahlia, a feather quill, an angel wing, a moth, a tiny dagger. This one is a crescent moon. I knew she'd love it.

The hours blur together while we laugh and eat junk food, the champagne trickling down the side of the bottle we pass back and forth until it's gone and we open the apple liquor, which is disgustingly sweet, like a melted Jolly Rancher, but we don't mind. The night gets darker yet, the moon brightening, bonfire smoke drifting our way, even this far from the beach. The alcohol has muddled my brain. I need to stop drinking. My mama needs to stop drinking. Is she at home right now, slugging her own bottle? She's alone. My dad left when I was two years old. Middle of the night, snaking his car down the driveway with the headlights off, I bet. What an *asshole*.

"We should do a love spell." Reuel interrupts my brooding with a sudden laugh.

"Funny." I soften my mouth, which I didn't realize I had so tight.

"I mean it."

With a roll of my eyes, I say, "Love spell? Please. Like you need one of those."

It's not that I know *nothing* about romance. I kissed the guy who took me to freshman homecoming. He then moved to the East Coast a week later, like his tongue darting into my mouth for thirty seconds was so awful for him, too, that he had to switch not only zip codes but time zones. It's not like there's been nobody before or since him . . . but things are quiet. I'm open to love, but I haven't met anyone who sets my heart on fire. And apparently, I haven't done that for anyone else, either.

Reuel, on the other hand, doesn't want for anyone being interested in her. It's just that she's picky, or, like she says, she has taste. Which is why it surprised me so much when she started dating goddamn Grady Corbin. Just *thinking* of him has me tensing up.

"Or like you do?" Reuel teases, her wine-dark lips quirking. At my blank expression she gives me a pointed look. "Bridger Leland, your art buddy. That boy's in love with you."

Shaking my head at the thought of my sweet classmate, I shove her playfully, and she falls over giggling. I light another cigarette and talk around it. "He's not. Or if he is, that's his business. Besides, don't you have a boyfriend, Miss Reuel?"

"Yeah, you're right. Forget love spells." She pauses, giving me a funny look. "But, for the record . . . I don't *love* Grady."

"You don't?" I look at her, my mouth falling open so I almost drop my cigarette.

"Have I said I do?" she counters with a shrug, amending, "I like him. He's a good kisser."

He *is* a good kisser. I wish I didn't know that.

Last winter at a party during the holiday break, in a dark corner of a dark room, he pulled me in so that our shadows joined, brought his mouth to mine, laughed hoarsely against my lips even as he kissed me. "I . . . like you, Isabeau," he said after.

The alcohol had dulled my senses, so I didn't pull back immediately. Grady hung out with Bridger; of course I knew him through school and our small town. We'd known each other since kindergarten. But I barely liked Grady as a human—I didn't even know how Bridger could stand to hang out with him. He was an acquaintance, a peer. The guy who tended to say shitty things, then laugh them off as a joke. Who once made a girl cry by teasing her when she got her period and bled through her skirt—it was sixth grade, and maybe he'd matured since then, but *still.* He'd definitely cheated on more than one girlfriend. Thought the world would forgive him because he was—is— model-beautiful, with cut-glass cheekbones and piercing green eyes, hair black as pitch. And it did. It always does.

But *ugh.* Ugh a million times. There was no way he could be anything to me. I shook my head, *Sorry.* I didn't even need to say it. *I don't like you back.*

Grady knew. And his eyes flashed first with the shock, then

the hurt of it. He was embarrassed, his hands dropped from my hips, he took a step back, then another, then another. As if he couldn't wait to be away from me. As if he'd never wanted me to begin with.

A week later, he started dating Reuel. She didn't know about the kiss, about the dark corner, about the look on his face. She doesn't know now, because there's no reason to tell her except to make things weird between them. She doesn't notice how he avoids me, eyes cast down whenever I'm near. How he'll scoot closer to her—to be nearer her or farther from me, I wonder. I'm happy for her, aren't I? It's not even *him*. It's just . . . so awkward.

"I wish you liked Grady," she says sometimes. "We could hang out together more."

"It's not that. I don't wanna be the third wheel," I tell her when she hassles me about it, which is absolutely true. But there's also something about his hands on her that irritates me. Not because I wish it were me. Not at all. But I liked it better before him.

"Is that why you're here with me and not spending your birthday with your boyfriend?" I ask now, half serious. "'Cause you only just 'like' him?"

Reuel grins, digging through the pile of snacks before finding what she wants. She drops a powdery candy skeleton into her mouth. Crunching its sugar bones in morbid pleasure. "Romance comes and goes. Best friends are forever."

She flinches, realizing what she said. An arrow in my heart, I shift my gaze to some random ancient graves behind her. Think about death. Or maybe just the death of promises. The death of love. There were six of us. And now there are two. *Best friends are forever.*

"Are they?" I ask bitterly.

"Yes. *We* are." I feel her studying me. "Come on. Let's burn some wishes before we go to my house." At my hesitation, she adds, "I brought a thing. . . . We don't have to build a fire."

"As if we'd know how." I smile before draining my drink. I don't tease her about wanting to stick to the tradition. It's sort of adorable.

She pulls out a wide can, the label peeled off. It could've held diced tomatoes or something. Then she takes out her green leather journal, angling it toward herself, a secret. She's always secretive about her poems, except when she's not. I'm one of the only people who get to read her work. I know for a fact she doesn't let Grady, which, meanly, makes me feel smug as shit.

"Here," Reuel says, ripping a page, then handing me a strip of it and a pen. "Write yours. Then we'll burn them in the can. Boom, fire contained."

I grip the pen. Feel the blood flood my cheeks. The haze in my brain. It's just for fun, for festivity. But I think about wishes and about our little town witch and about things I wish were true. I lay the slip of paper against my thigh and scribble something on it.

I want to meet him

I write it, then read it twice over before I realize what it says. What my fingers made the pen scratch out. A wish. A secret one, one I didn't even know I wanted. I want to meet my father, the jerk who left us. Who didn't stick around long enough to watch me grow up. It's pathetic, but as I see the wish, my heart thumps a sharp, uncomfortable beat. I *do* want it.

But I hate that I do.

"Done?" Reuel is watching me, waiting. I hastily fold up the paper and nod.

I'd like to ask what she wrote, but I don't for the same reason she doesn't ask me. We may tell each other almost everything, almost always, but right now I can tell she doesn't want to share her wish any more than I want to share mine. She takes my lighter, then shoves her paper in the can and sets it on fire. I toss mine in as well, catching the flame. Our desires burn together. Reuel cups the can in her hands until it grows too hot, then swears and sets it on the grass. Side by side, we watch the fire, plume of smoke drifting up to the stars, ghosts of our wishes within it.

"Oh! The gift," Reuel says. When I give her a look, as if to say *Why bother,* she shrugs. "Hey, it feels weird not to. Anyway, I have more cookies." She procures a small package of raspberry shortbread, shoving it in the can for the sake of ritual—I imagine some old-fashioned person in charge laying out the rules of the day and deciding that one *mustn't* ask Sorrow for wishes without leaving her a gift. Though I suppose that's just manners.

We sit in the quiet, and I fiddle with my lighter, a small, safe rebellion against my own fear. For as long as I can remember I've been afraid, of flames burning rapid and cruel, a blaze consuming everything in its path, including me. I don't do big fires, would rather not party on a beach with bonfires tall as a man; however, I can hold the power in my own hand, flicker a flame over and over again. Can light a candle. Can even burn a wish in an old tomato can.

I stare at the can, the smoky remains of paper hidden beneath the smoldering cookies, something in me hurting and regretful. It's too late to take the wish back. Not like it matters, though, I remind myself. Of course, it's not *real.* We make all kinds of wishes in Sorrow, and old legends claimed that if one burned the right wish or left enough gifts in the ashes—finely wrapped presents, apples, lace, sweets—she (Sorrow) would theoretically return and grant one's wish, which makes her sound more like a fairy godmother than a witch. So we have fun with it, our town, we indulge the fantasy. Requests for cars and new jobs and lottery wins and lovers. Grand desires. Secret ones. Things we'd never tell anyone else, even.

But I hate that I let myself want what I wished, even for a few minutes.

"Hey." Reuel glances at her phone. "It's nine-forty-five. It's official. We're sixteen."

The six of us were all born on the same day, May third. But Reuel and I actually came into this world at the same time, too. We've always said that made our bond even stronger.

"Let's do an oath, too," she says. She roots through her bag, then pulls out the pocketknife her dad insists she carries, just because, holding it up triumphantly. "Like, blood sisters."

"Come on." I scoff as she stands. "What's up with you tonight? Feelin' witchy or what?"

"I'm serious. Look, I'll do it." Reuel flips the blade out, the full moon behind her head giving her the appearance of a saint. She drags the knife down the center of her palm, cutting herself without a word, not even flinching, though her painted lips part slightly, as if she has to let the pain out somehow. Just a breath of it.

"God, Reuel. Don't." I can feel how wide my eyes have grown as I clamber to my feet, dropping my lighter. The night sky is sort of spinning, but this is sobering me up.

When she hands the knife to me, a silent challenge, a silent question, gravestones framing us, I take it. I stare at the sharp edge of silver. I don't like needles. I don't like splinters. The thought of slicing a blade into my skin should make me want to cry. Except, I think of the six of us. What should have been. What if Reuel and I were to part too? How could I survive without her or she without me? Isn't it worth a little blood to keep us together? Isn't it worth it to believe in magic, not as a vague concept or a nostalgic tradition I partake in just because it's the thing to do, but for real? For once?

I push the point into my left hand. I can't even feel anything until the blood seeps out.

"Shit. It stings," I hiss as the pain catches up, as my sobriety reawakens, startling me with its reasonableness. I look at Reuel, try to convince myself. "But it's not so bad. Now what?"

"Hold hands," she instructs, her voice husky. "Say it. Best friends. Forever."

Forever. We agree. But are we promising it to each other or to ourselves? I'm not sure. We drop our grips, blood smearing our palms, dripping down to the earth.

"Yesss." A whisper on the air seems to nip at my earlobe. I jerk, startling even myself.

"Did you hear that?" I laugh nervously. Lightning snakes across the black sky, and I swear, it's tinged blue. Blinking, I ask, "We getting a storm?"

Her brow furrows. "It was just the wind. Shh. Listen."

The breeze gusts, whistling through the trees, and I relax my shoulders, watching how it shakes the branches, how it trembles the leaves. It could almost sound like a whisper, like a word, if you listened hard enough. If you were drunk enough, had a wild enough imagination. And there is no more lightning.

"Yeah. Just the wind." I start to exhale, then narrow my eyes, noticing how peaked Reuel's face has gotten, all the color erased from her cheeks. "Hey—"

She trembles; her eyes roll to the back of her head, whites glossy and webbed red.

With a cry, I dart forward, I catch her by the shoulders as she swoons. We fall to our knees, her dead weight against me. Even as I try to hold on to her, she slumps to the blanket, limbs liquidy. Panicked, I do the first thing I can think of—I slap her across the face. Hard. The sound of my hand on her cheek snaps the air. Her eyes break open and she shudders, but her chest is rising, her breath going from shallow to steady as she stares up at the night sky, coming to. In a broken whisper, I ask if she's okay.

She meets my eyes and a soft, surprised laugh spills from her lips as she looks past me again, at the stars glittering above us. "Yeah. Couldn't be better."

"You passed out," I say as my heart rate finally slows to a normal human pace. "Did you drink too much?"

A smirk curves her mouth. "Maybe I didn't drink enough," she says wryly.

The silence is broken by my giggling, and she loses it too, laughing hysterically, because she's good. We both are. We cackle with laughter until tears run down our cheeks. Until we forget that for a moment, we were afraid of something. We meet eyes, clink our cups together for yet another toast, draining the last of her dad's shitty apple liquor, our palms carved with the promise. *Forever.*

The cemetery is peaceful. And slumbering through our celebration are the dead, in the quiet of the old graves, but the two of us are young, and happy in this moment, and so very, very alive.

CHAPTER THREE

Here we are, the six of us. I hold the frame in my nonwounded hand, standing in Reuel's brightly colored bedroom while she uses the bathroom, studying the picture from back when we were all still friends, when we were happy together. Missing teeth, hair in ponytails, wearing glittery T-shirts. It was the year after August moved to Sorrow—we were nine, and she'd been the last to arrive. Georgina and I were the only ones born in town, but most of our parents were from Sorrow. Though a few of them had moved away, something drew them back to this place.

Roots, Solaina's mom, Marisa, said simply. Roots were what grounded you, and she'd never liked big cities anyway, and so their family returned.

New children in class always sparked interest, especially at our small elementary school, but when you discovered you shared a birthday, that's when things went from interesting to *really* interesting. Of course, as we grew close, there was so much we came to love about each other besides that one big thing we had in common.

Over the years, when asked more about the peculiar occurrence of our births, our parents would shrug, baffled, or even a little weirded out by it. We didn't mind, really, the nonanswers, not that they could give an actual answer. Nobody could. It was just one of those things. We were together, and that was all that mattered. It didn't matter that our parents mostly never hit it off, that we were different in more ways than we were alike. We didn't care about all that.

It was our births that drew us together, and even now, I know the details of each by heart, can still marvel at how wondrous it is that we share the day. Reuel was the only one who came on her actual due date, the rest of us were early or late, by days or even weeks.

Whether it was coincidence, luck, something unexplainable, or—as one great-great-auntie once patted our cheeks and whispered, that we were *blessings from the witch*—the six of us didn't care. We loved each other. It was enough. I thought it always would be.

Reuel returns to her room and I put the frame down, clumsily, placing it on her dresser amid other pictures. Of her mother, holding her when she was about three, before I'd even met her. Of me and her, sitting on the edge of a pool last summer. Of Reuel and her brothers, snuggled up on the couch in striped pajamas a few winters ago, back when Reuel's hair was still light blond, the four siblings all towheaded and blue-eyed.

For a minute I wonder if she'll pretend not to notice I was looking at the picture of the six of us, but she asks, "You think it's weird I still have that? Like, out?"

"Nah," I say. "It's more weird pretending like it didn't happen, us being friends. Like we didn't happen." Except I'm one to talk—I've hidden all the evidence in my closet.

If I had to pinpoint it, I'd say our thirteenth birthday was the final fissure that cracked us all. The first, Cori's parents' messy divorce. The second, Georgina's baby brother, stillborn. The third, Reuel's mama dying. Shouldn't we have grown closer during those traumas? I sometimes catch myself wondering. But that's not how it worked. And then our birthday—thirteen was huge. We were growing up. I shake my head free of the memory, the party. The event that seemed to have ended us. I glance once more at the picture, then back at Reuel, waiting for her reply.

"Yeah," she murmurs. Then she adds, "Georgina, August, the cheerleading thing, whatever. They're fine. And Cori's sweet as ever. But I hardly ever get to see Solaina. I miss her. I miss us, as a collective."

I blink away the sudden prickling in my eyes before I start to cry. Stare down at the funky flower-shaped rug by the bed and settle my emotions.

"You still want me to do your hair now?" I clear my throat. I reach out and touch one tendril of her thick, shining hair; her roots are starting to show. "You wanna keep the black?"

"Do I wanna keep it? It's like you don't even know me." Her teasing voice is light. But I can tell. There's something bothering her. More than just the conversation we had about the girls seconds ago. There's something she's not telling me.

But she agrees, so I get out the supplies I grabbed from my mom's home stash, and then we quietly head to the bathroom to dye her hair the same raven black we used last time.

I'm no painter, but there's something very satisfying about dabbing the mixture onto Reuel's light roots with the brush, bowl of dye going gray in my gloved hand. When the color is done processing, I have her lean over the sink.

Threading my fingers into her inky hair, I rinse out the excess dye, the color swirling down the drain. When I look down, she's staring up at me, eyes deep, full of some unnamed emotion.

"What?" I ask, a little suspiciously. I boop her on the nose with one gloved finger, making her smile. "I got something on my face?"

Reuel laughs. "No. Thanks for doing my hair. I was worried I'd look meh for the dance."

"You could never look meh," I answer, squeezing the last of the conditioner out of her hair, and it's true. Reuel has a self-possessed confidence I've never mastered. She can be in a grubby pair of sweats and still look stylish. Plus, she's gorgeous.

I don't add anything about the dance—Spring Fling will be here in just a couple of weeks, and I have no date, and as of now, I'll be there with Reuel and Grady. I hold back a sigh, then gesture to the mirror. "Look okay?"

Smiling, she nods. "Much better. Thanks for doing it."

While she combs through her hair, I wash out the bowl of color, the biting scent of it catching in my throat, stinging my eyes. I peel off my gloves and follow Reuel back to the bedroom, where I grab my bag. I turn to her and say, "I'm gonna smoke. You wanna come?"

She raises a dark brow, judging how much I've been smoking, but shrugs. "Sure."

We sneak through the house, past her younger brothers' rooms, where it's quiet, but I fondly picture the three rowdy boys drooling onto their pillows. They are a perpetual whir of blond hair and flying limbs, smelling of peanut butter and sweat, piles of sports gear and LEGOs scattered around the kitchen. And I absolutely adore them. I have since the moment the Carsons came into my life, or more aptly, since the boys were born, which came a few years later. Reuel and I were four when we met, and it wasn't long before we were buddied up in preschool. Besides Georgina, she's the one I've known the longest. Then a couple of years later it was Cori, whose mother and Georgina's are twins, Cori's mom urged by her sister to come back and settle down. Then Solaina, when we were six, and lastly August at eight, after her grandmother had a stroke and needed her son to return to care for her.

"Tiptoe," Reuel whispers to me as we pass Mr. Carson's room (he is definitely asleep by now, nursing a nasty cold, apparently knocked out with Nyquil). We go downstairs, through the kitchen, and out the front, to the porch swing. When we sit, it creaks in a comforting way, like it's happy to see us. Though it's dark out, the streetlight casts a warm glow across the block, the faint smoky scent of fires drifting across the island. And dotted all along the beach, people will party into the night, with their bonfires and tons of liquor.

Are the girls there now, celebrating? Except not Solaina. She won't be with the others.

Guilt nips at me. I love Marisa, and I have nothing against Solaina, except didn't she leave me too? If she wanted to be here, she'd be here. I never once told her to go. But isn't that the story of my life? People leave me all the time. Reuel is the only one who hasn't.

"It's chilly tonight," I whisper as another burst of wind hits my bare arms. I pull the big striped sweater I had wrapped around my waist over my thrifted tee, which might've used to be black, and tuck my legs up under me. "Where the hell is spring?"

"Spring is dead," Reuel jokes, words slurred a little, a mix of champagne and tiredness. "Or maybe it hasn't been born yet." She leans against the aqua cushions, damp hair splayed out across the fabric, and pushes off a little harder with her feet. Her second toe is slightly longer than her first. Unlike her fingernails, always done up, her toenails are unpainted.

"Get the other cooler, Tim!" a woman barks through an open garage across the street. We watch a man lug one out of the bed of a truck. It falls off ungracefully at the last second, the lid tipping over, half-melted ice spilling across the asphalt, cans rolling down the driveway and into the street. Runaway beers.

Reuel and I burst into laughter, and the woman's face goes thoroughly irritated at her husband, watching him chase the cans. Without hesitating, we hop up off the swing, tipsy, and run over to help. Giggling, I grab three wet cans, cradling them in my arms, then pad over to the cooler. I tip them inside as the man thanks me.

"Here, Mr. Lee," Reuel says. "I got the rest."

"Thanks, girls," he says wearily, pushing his glasses up on his nose. He smells of smoke and barbecue and salt water, not a bad combination, all in all. He thanks us again kindly, waving us away, back to our spot on the porch.

Is it my imagination, or does Reuel's smile drop too easily once we're alone again? Too quickly? Like maybe it wasn't fully real? Just like in the cemetery. I can't ignore it any longer.

We sink onto the swing again, and in between inhales, I say, "You seem pensive or something. Moody."

"Ha." She jabs a finger into my ribs, but it lacks effort. "I'm a poet. It's part of my thing."

"Mmkay, sure." I hesitate; my eyes drift to a lush arrangement of gardenias in a vase across the porch—even from the other end I can smell their rich fragrance. I push a little. "Is it Jolene?" Her dad's girlfriend. The woman who could never, ever, in her wildest dreams, replace Reuel's mom.

"Jolene." Sarcasm drips from her words. "She's wonderful, he says. But really, he'd rather be with a woman he doesn't love instead of being alone. Or confronting how sad he is."

"Your brothers seem to like her okay, huh?"

"Sure, they like her. She's not always on them to be a lady. You should hear the way she talks to me, the way she talks to her daughters." Reuel raises her voice to a girlish, breathy pitch, mimicking, *"Why, say hi to Miss Reuel, girls, isn't she just so lovely? Y'all know she's got golden hair beneath that black? And what I wouldn't give for a figure like that! Shame she keeps it covered. If I were you, Reuel, I swear I'd be in dresses from sunup to sundown. When I was runner-up at Miss Louisiana, all the girls dressed so pretty. . . ."*

"Gross." I frown, picturing the hair-sprayed horror of a woman. I only met her a couple of times, but I knew from the start she and Reuel would be like oil and water. "Well, you can hang out at my place, you know that."

"Yeah, but it's just a Band-Aid. I can't hide out forever. At some point he'll propose."

"And by the time they get married you'll be off at college."

"Don't talk about that." Her stained lips tug down. She hates to discuss the possibility of us parting, refuses to talk about the future unless we daydream about ending up at the same university, which I only ever admit to myself sounds too good to be a real possibility. With my luck—and grades—I'll be grateful to get into a community college, while Reuel could go off to an Ivy League. If she wanted.

She looks down at her new cut, part of our matching set. Then flips her hand to pick at her nails, distracting herself, like she's either going to cry or tell me something else. Something real, something truer than what she already did. Worry presses on my chest. How up and down she is tonight. Lately. Maybe not to the untrained eye. But I can see it. I can feel it.

My phone dings with a notification, a voice message from a call I somehow missed. I almost swipe it away until I see who it's from. With a grimace, I listen to the drunken recording. Singing me a happy birthday, wishing I were home, wanting to know if she should bake a cake. How hot the oven should be? If I want vanilla, if I want sprinkles? If I want sixteen candles on it? Where the matches are?

"Lena?" Reuel's expression says so much. She knows.

"She thinks she's gonna bake a fucking cake. She'll probably set the house on fire." I chew on my bottom lip, my stomach tight with resentment, the alcohol swirling with too much sugar and not enough carbs. "I was gonna stay."

"It's okay, I don't mind if you wanna get home to her. We're on for tomorrow?"

"Of course. I know how much you're looking forward to the poetry thingy."

"It's not a thingy," she corrects, shaking her head. "A reading and signing, only with the best modern-day queer female poet ever, *the* Montgomery Grant."

I try to smile. I know how excited she is, and I promised. "You'll pick me up, right?"

"I will personally drag my daddy out of his Nyquil haze to be there on time. Be ready, okay? I don't wanna miss the beginning. Anyway, I'm tired. I'll go to bed soon," she says, and yawns at the perfect moment, giving me an extra excuse to change our plans and leave.

I'm already standing. "I hate her sometimes."

"Don't say that." Reuel's voice is soft. She knows what I go through, and she tries to understand, but there's this divide between us now. It's not fair of me to hate my mother when her own is dead. She'd give anything to be mad at hers again, just for one minute.

But hers was good, a hurt part of me reasons. *Better than mine.*

Sighing, I reach for another cigarette, lighting one for the walk home. Screw my lungs. Give me wrinkles. I don't care.

Reuel's face creases up in concern. "Will you be okay?"

I shrug, push back the resentment. Maybe it's not so much hate as disappointment mingled with perpetual worry and another whole complicated layer of love, so much love I think sometimes I'll drown in it. The drinking, how even when my mom rises, she ends up dragging herself down. The way she takes me down with her.

"See. You're mopin' right now. That's my thing, ya know." Reuel stands and stretches her arms above her head, looking even taller.

"Shush." I bump her hip as I pass to step off the porch, her laughter at my back.

As I reach the sidewalk in front of the house, she calls out, abruptly, "Iz?"

"Yeah?" I turn, wrap my arms around myself as I stare at her face, into her eyes. I hold my breath because even the air seems heavy, this anticipatory breath loaded. Kinda like when she stared up at me as I did her hair. What is it?

After a hesitation, she finally, simply says, "You better go fast. Just in case she gets into trouble. Be safe. Text me when you get home."

"I will," I agree, like always. Sorrow's so boring you almost wish something would happen once in a while. It'll be rowdier than normal, with the holiday, but I'm not afraid to walk alone in the dark, and my house is not that far.

Reuel leans against the banister of the porch, waving once as I go, watching me slip into the shadows of the streets. I feel like she left something unsaid and I fret over it the whole way home. What else could be bothering her?

When I get home, I find an open bag of flour on the counter in the kitchen, a bottle of generic vanilla extract tipped on its side, spilled, and the oven is hot, but my mom didn't get much further than that before remembering she doesn't know how to cook, let alone bake. No candles were lit. No houses were burned down in the making of this noncake. In her first-floor bedroom, she's passed out on her bed, curled into a ball, sleepy smile on her flour-dusted face.

Angry but too tired to do anything about it all, I leave the mess she made, besides shutting off the oven, and I leave her to her dreams, trudging up the stairs to my room on the second floor. I remember to set the alarm on my phone so I don't over-sleep in the morning. They'll be picking me up by eight, Reuel's text reminds me when I let her know I've gotten home safe. I strip out of my clothes and fall into bed, my fingers stinking of smoke, my throat raw, apple flavor clinging to my tongue, liquor churning in my belly, a sickening whirlpool.

Maybe it's just the nostalgic feeling in the air, the sense of specialness today, the knowing that people are still burning fires only a few miles away, but while I'm staring up at my spinning wooden ceiling, strung with fairy lights and decorated with a few posters, the myths run through my mind.

The old tales say our little island used to be part of the Louisiana mainland, but some centuries ago it split and drifted away to settle into Black Bay. Though that makes no sense. That's not how islands form. They say the witch made it happen, of course. She left the mainland following a series of ignorant attacks from those who didn't understand her power, and when she stepped across the ocean, she took this land with her. Making a life for herself, one full of love and magic and all sorts of good things. Those are the stories that were handed down, anyway.

I don't believe all that. Maybe there was a woman named Sorrow once upon a time—we even have a seventeenth-century portrait of an old lady hanging in our library that's supposedly her. Maybe she dabbled in the unusual. Maybe she even did start this town (magical parts not included—obviously the island already existed). Still, there is something nestled deep within my heart. A kinship, even if Sorrow's simply the heroine of a fairy tale meant to spark some sort of pride in our town, meant to give our history meaning. We share this day, whether it means shit or not. Maybe I'm too tipsy to deny it now, the sentimentality hiding inside me, because for much of my life, this date also celebrated me and my friends and the love we had for each other. There's a longing I can't ignore now either, because it will never be like that again. Except it's not the witch's fault—she's just a story and I'm just a lonely girl searching for some sort of connection. Try as I might, as I remember the wish I made with Reuel, as I drag my finger along the broken skin on my palm, I can't blame anyone else. I can only blame myself for getting caught up in a fantasy.

I *don't* want to meet my father.

I *don't* miss my old friends. Good riddance.

That's my last thought before I sink into dreams, which are all in black-and-white.

A girl standing with her back to me, hair curling to her waist, soot black in the monochrome world. She turns just enough that I make out her profile, tiny mole to the side of her lip. She is nowhere near as pretty as Reuel but somehow reminds me of her anyway. She laughs and twists away, running, and something in my heart lurches. Now I am chasing after her, but I can't catch up, no matter how fast I go. Somewhere, in a dark space, I stop running. I bend over and spit out a whole apple core. Then reach up to the sky with trembling fingers, peel back the gray, warmth pouring from above and then from *me*, coloring the world red. *Paint,* I think. Then the paint has turned to blood. My hands slick with it, my dreams becoming nightmares. Of my mama stumbling before me, slurring her words, crying that she doesn't know how to make the cake. That she's *Sorry. Sorry. Sorry.* Of flames flying out of the oven, creeping up the stairs to get me. Of something licking at my hand, my oath wound scarring green and turning infected. Of a big cat prowling the streets of Sorrow, a beating, bloody heart between its sharp teeth.

Of Reuel, blocks away, crying quietly in the night, my name echoing from her crimson lips.

I'm going to be late, *damn it.* They'll be here to pick me up any minute.

I pull my wet hair off my face, my temples pounding, and twist it up in a towel before hastily drying my body. My left hand stings, the small cut crusted over with dried blood. I look at it a little shocked, remembering the way I drew a knife down my palm. It's tender now. Why didn't Reuel and I wrap them last night? Why did we even do it? The memory of it is cloudy in the light of day. I force myself not to think about other things.

Like foolish wishes scratched onto paper and lit on fire. Wishes about deadbeat fathers.

I manage to find some antiseptic and a strip of gauze in the medicine cabinet that never gets restocked until after me or my mother gets sick, and even then, only with bandages and the cheapest off-brand cold medicine I can find. I dab on the cream and wind the gauze around my palm in a hurry. Next I get dressed, throwing on a cute-ish oversized T-shirt, jean shorts, and silver earrings, and I tug the towel off my head and pull my waves into the quickest French braids of my life. When I run down the stairs, bemoaning my hangover, I come face to face with the last person I wanna see right now.

"Morning." Mama eyes me, cup of coffee in her hand, her pale sage-green flowered robe drawn loose around her frame, an Anthropologie clearance find many years ago. "Where you headed in such a hurry?"

"Reuel and I are going to a poetry reading in the city. They were supposed to pick me up like five minutes ago to make the ferry." I look at the time. "Or ten."

She nods. "Well, I'm glad I caught you. I have your birthday present."

"Thanks?" I rush by her and fill my water bottle, giving up on the idea of breakfast entirely. My throat is dry and scratchy. I definitely smoked too much last night. I don't bring up the disaster she left for me in the kitchen. Glancing around at the mostly clean counters, I see she took care of it. "I'll have to open it later. They'll be here any minute, and we can't miss the ferry."

"I was hoping you'd be home last night." Disappointment hangs on her words. Her amber eyes search mine, one eye flecked with more gold than the other. "I got home from work early to be with you. I didn't even hear you come in."

"I walked home late. You were asleep." *You were passed out. You were drunk.*

"What time?"

I throw up my hands. "I don't know. Elevenish?"

She manages to look upset. "I didn't know you'd be gone all night."

It wasn't even that late. Without answering her, I pack my water bottle in my tote, double-check I have all my stuff for the day trip. Cheap portable charger. A granola bar. Money in case we can talk Mr. Carson into letting us stop for lunch or if I want to buy an art book.

"And you drank?"

"So?"

"You're too young." More disappointment.

"Don't act like you care," I say meanly.

Her mouth goes taut. "Izzy. I do care."

I pull my tote over my shoulder, sighing as I check my phone. No answer from Reuel even though I've texted twice to see what's taking so long. "Look, I think it's a little late for this, okay? You're having a good morning, I'm happy for you. But don't start playing the role now."

I look up in time to catch pain flashing on her face. "I may not be a perfect parent, but I am yours. On the good days and the bad. I have a right to an opinion about your behavior."

"Yeah, well. I sure have opinions about yours," I fire at her. "Thanks for ruining my night, by the way."

"What?"

"Nothing. You wanna drive me to Reuel's since it looks like they're running late? Or are you shitfaced right now?"

In the moment after the comment shoots out of my mouth, I'm not sure if she'd like to burst into tears or slap me, or maybe both. I can tell she's sober, and I only said it to be a snot, obviously. But she does neither, not that she's ever laid a hand on me. Instead, she sort of sucks in a slow breath, cupping her slender long-fingered hands a little more around her mug, pulling it to her chest, covering her heart. Then, seeming to have decided something, she abruptly sets the mug down, her milky caramel coffee sloshing onto the counter, and reaches into her messy purse, pushing aside her rumpled black work apron, rummaging for something.

She hands me her keys, mouth a grim line. "Here."

I stare. "I don't have my license yet," I tell her, as if she didn't know. That hasn't bothered Georgina (or her parents) at all; I've seen her driving her silver SUV all over Sorrow for a while now. I don't mind breaking rules, but this must be a test. "What are you doing?"

"Well, you're so grown-up, aren't you? You know everything. You don't even need me. Right?" She lifts her chin, her overbleached hair falling away from her face. She has freckles. They make her look too young for those hurt, tired eyes.

"How will you get to work?"

"I can take care of myself," she answers, sharp, but her chin wobbles.

I picture her scooping sugar into a bowl, trying to read the measuring cups, spilling the vanilla across the counter. Think about her trying and failing over and over again. Something in me hurts. And I hate her for it.

My head throbs too much to argue, to make up with her. I'm not sure I even want to. "Fine," I say flatly, closing my hand around the keys. I walk past her, head out the door, something in me burning, my cut stinging, my anger, too. Or maybe I'm just mirroring her disappointment. In her, in myself, in this life and relationship we've built together and torn back down dozens of times. Hundreds of times. Thousands.

I drive as slow as I reasonably can while still rushing. Reuel doesn't text me the whole time, and I feel awful, imagining the crestfallen look on her face when I have to wake her, tell her she overslept, she missed the event, her favorite author won't be signing any books for her after all. I push the pedal down harder, speeding now, risking it. If we rush, we can still make the Saturday ferry, which leaves every couple of hours. We've got at least twenty minutes to make the first run. We can get there.

When I arrive at Reuel's house, I jog up the sidewalk and the steps of her porch, then rap on the dark wood door once. Twice, before it swings open and Mr. Carson is on the other side, his nose swollen, his eyelids puffy and pink.

"Isabeau," he greets me with a weary nod. "Morning."

"Hi." I pause, eyes catching on the giant plant over in the kitchen. Green and healthy just last night, it's now dead, brittle and yellowed, leaves scattered on the floor around the pot. Frowning, I look back at him. "I thought y'all were picking me up. . . ."

"Huh? Reuel's not here," he answers, then sneezes, wincing like it hurts.

"Well, when will she be back?" I ask, peering at my phone, confused. No new texts to explain why she'd be late. This is her thing. "We're supposed to go to that poetry reading, remember? She got tickets weeks ago. . . ."

He frowns. "Oh, right. I forgot about that, sorry. I've been sick. But why isn't she with you? She slept at your place last night."

My eyes go wide. "She didn't sleep at my house. I went home

alone, and she stayed here. Didn't she?" Even as I say it, I think, *Shit, I've blown her cover.* But why would she lie?

He makes space so I can ease past him and run up to her room. Empty. She's not here. I turn to find Mr. Carson coming up the stairs after me, his face red. I shake my head at his questioning eyes, taking a step back. Together, we check each room, upstairs and down, searching for her.

The boys are watching TV in the den, giant mugs of cereal in their hands.

"See your sister?" Mr. Carson asks in a mild-mannered way, like he's trying not to worry them.

They shake their heads, distracted, spooning Froot Loops into their mouths.

Mr. Carson turns back to me in the hall, takes out his phone. "That girl better have a good reason for this," he says gruffly.

But I can read the emotion behind his brusque tone—he's not only irritated, he's worried. He calls Reuel, and when she doesn't pick up, he leaves a message asking where she is, if she's with that Grady boy, if she slept at home last night, and if not, where in God's name did she sleep?

I text her again. *Reuel where are you?*

There's no reply.

Reason tries to explain—she probably did sneak out to be with her boyfriend. Maybe she really *did* want to spend her birthday with him, I realize, sick feeling in my belly. With him . . . and not me. She probably didn't want me to feel like she was ditching me. Didn't want to hurt me. So she stuck with me, and when I left, made her way to Grady.

Except. Why would she miss the event today?

Reason says now, less patiently, she just overslept. She's probably curled against Grady's side, hiding in the shadows of his room before they're caught by his strict, churchgoing mother. That's it.

But reason is driven out quickly when we get in touch with Grady—Mr. Carson even speaks to his parents. She's not there. She's . . . nowhere. The minutes blur together, becoming hours. Hours full of fear and desperation. We talk to the police—they say I'll need to see them later, give an official account of my time with Reuel last night, make sure we're not missing anything important. We must be . . . but what?

I call my mom to tell her what's going on. She answers, breathless, and I explain, teary-eyed, almost reluctantly.

"Reuel is missing?" Her voice cracks over the line, and there's a deep fear clinging to her words. I picture her hand gripped around the phone, knuckles white, her knees buckling as she sinks into a chair in the staff room at Marisa's salon.

I numbly recount the details of what I know—almost nothing. And tell her the police want to hear from me about the last time I saw Reuel, that we're supposed to go this afternoon to speak with them if she can get off work. Tell her I'm fine. But I'm crying as I whisper it.

"Be home by three." She ends the call with a final, stunned request. "I'll work it out so I can go with you to talk to the police."

"Okay," I say before we hang up. I hope the police can help, but there's so much we don't know. What we do is very little: Reuel disappeared somewhere between that porch swing and when I arrived this morning. Her shoes by the back door—just where she kicked them off when we got in from the cemetery. She's gone.

Over the next few hours people arrive. Jolene, the hair-sprayed horror. Close relatives: Reuel's sweet grandparents;

aunties bring a pack of young cousins along, who are a blessed distraction for Reuel's little brothers. The children are sent off to play in the den. We wait all morning. Calling, praying, crying. She's still gone.

After a lunch where nobody eats, the adults shoo me out to talk privately. I can't bear to go home, so I wander back up to Reuel's room.

I look around, as if I'll find something, some clue as to where she might've gone. The bed, made up, her closet hanging open—black clothes spilling out, some puddled on the floor, hangers still attached. Her school stuff crumpled in a corner, though her cheerleading uniform is hung nicely. I touch one pom-pom, laid out on the bench at the foot of her bed, and close my eyes, remembering to breathe. When I open them again, my gaze lands on Reuel's desk, stacks of poetry books haphazardly placed across it. And on top, half hidden beneath the pages of her open journal, something I missed before—her phone. I swipe it open to find all my texts, her dad's missed calls, Grady's. New voice messages. The volume is off, which explains why we didn't hear it. But now my throat is all lumped up. Where would she go and not take her phone?

I glance at her journal, open, a pen even left atop it. Like she was in the middle of writing and forgot to close it, forgot to put it back in her bag where I saw it last. Leaving it open, vulnerable like this, is not like her. I hesitate, leaning closer. It's not like she hasn't let me read her stuff before. I don't know why I'm so scared—what do I think I'll find? A suicide note or something ghastly?

Reuel is missing. She wouldn't be mad at me for looking at her journal, not if it could help us find her, bring her back. I lift the book to read her messy writing.

I dream up a love, your hand in mine, my fingers
trace your jaw, I dream us happy, dream the words
I can finally say, dream myself brave, dream your
striking eyes, dream you, as mine.

I lower the book, fighting back irritation at finding a love poem to her damn boyfriend. Striking eyes. Grady does have stupidly beautiful eyes. She told me she didn't love him, but maybe even though I've tried to hide my dislike of him, she can tell how much I would quietly disapprove if she took that big leap forward in their relationship. Or maybe she isn't ready to admit it to herself. I'd hate it if I loved that jerk too. I swallow the bitterness bubbling up, and gently set the journal down, leave it be. What matters is where she is. How I'll get her back. Not some lovey poem about her boyfriend.

I back up, away from the desk, out of the room, finding it difficult to breathe deeply. Make my way down the stairs, with Reuel's phone in hand, to tell Mr. Carson about her leaving it behind, a revelation that clearly unsettles him. After, I step onto the porch, to get a breath alone, leaning against the painted column holding up the porch ceiling. I don't even feel like smoking. I just stand, mind racing. The vase of gardenias on the wrought iron patio table gives off a mulchy, rotted scent, the flowers drooping. I step forward, reach for the largest flower, my fingers catching on a petal that nearly crumbles under my touch. I frown, my stomach turning.

Immediately, I go back into the house, trying not to hear the fear in the adults' voices rooms away, grateful the boys are distracted with doting grandparents and cousins.

As I walk around, searching, I soon realize what else is wrong here. Reason can shut the hell up. The Carson home is filled with plants, and it's not just the one in the kitchen that's died. Not just the gardenias on the porch that have rotted hours after they were vibrant.

Every plant in their home is dead.

Dead, overnight.

I sit down before I fall over.

My heart racing. My hand burning.

It is night. First, they make a circle. There is salt and there are herbs. A fire. They hold hands. They don't know what's coming. Don't know what's been. They don't know what's waiting for them.

CHAPTER FOUR

Istay at Reuel's all day, helping, or at least trying to help, though I mostly feel like I'm in the way. Finally, at ten to three in the afternoon, I drive myself back home in my mom's car, I step into the house. She's already here, sitting in the kitchen in her black work clothes, smelling of mousse, her dye-flecked apron flung over one chair as she picks at her fingernails, ripping the cuticles to shreds—one of her nervous habits.

"Any news?" she asks, jumping from her seat, almost tipping the chair over.

Her presence jars me out of my brooding thoughts. I swallow. "No." I pause. And even though she said she'd come with me to the police station, I voice my doubt aloud: "I wasn't sure you'd make it home?"

"I left early so we could get there in time. You said four, right?" When I nod, she adds, "I only had one color this afternoon anyway. Marisa took it, and I got a ride."

I close the front door behind me. I sniff, catching the scent of something. "You cooked?"

"I didn't know if you'd had lunch, and we might be gone through dinner." She flushes. "It's just frozen pizza. I know you cook better than me."

Because I had to learn, I think, again mean. I was sick of eating ramen and eggs. But I'm too drained to start a fight or even finish the last one. I step out of my shoes on the way to the living room and flop onto the couch, wincing when it squeaks in protest. "Great, whatever."

"So?" She opens the oven and pulls out the pizza, setting it on the counter on the cardboard circle, swearing as she flings the oven mitt off. It's wearing thin in one corner, and I always catch my thumb the wrong way, burning it. But pot holders are low on the list of priorities around here. Mama inspects her finger for a second before looking up. I can't quite read the expression on her face. It's like a mixture of fear and guilt. She asks, "You okay, Izzy?"

I cringe, feeling so scared I might shatter. I shake my head. "I just wanna find her. There's a search tomorrow morning, her family is organizing it."

"When?" The contents in drawers rattle as she opens and shuts them, looking for the pizza cutter.

"Left one, next to the oven," I say wearily. "And it's at eight at the Scouts club."

"I'll come." Sadness tinges her voice. I find myself surprised by her admission, that emotionally she'll be able to handle that. She lifts her eyes and asks, "How many pieces?"

I come back to reality. The pizza. I wave the idea away. "Later. I can't eat now."

"Okay." She squeezes her hands together, as though to keep them from trembling. "I'm sure they just want info, in case you can be helpful in finding her. Don't be nervous, honey."

But as we make our way up the steps to the police station an hour later, *she's* the one fidgeting, nearly tripping over the threshold, even though she's stone-cold sober. I grab her elbow to keep her steady and she finds my eyes with her own, her smile troubled, forced. We are led into a stuffy room with three chairs and a small table.

"Sorry to make you wait," a reedy stalk of a man apologizes cheerfully as he comes in, shuts the door. "Coffee or water?"

We both shake our heads.

His shiny umber forehead is damp, but his tone is smooth, easy. Like he isn't in the middle of solving the case of a missing girl, or at the beginning of it, actually. "I'm Detective Warren. Thank you both for coming. Yesterday was Friday, of course, the last time you saw her, Isabeau. We just wanna get a basic rundown of the day. Were you with Reuel the whole day? From school till you went home last night?"

"I saw her at school—we have lunch and biology together— but after, I walked home."

"Alone?" He scratches something on his notepad.

"Yeah, I was alone." I fidget in my seat, uncertain.

"Relax, Isabeau." He peers over at me, face calm. "You're not in trouble, okay? I know y'all were drinking yesterday—we found the empty bottles of liquor. We're not issuing citations, although the parents might have some words about that. This is bigger. We just wanna find your friend, all right?"

I loosen my stiff shoulders, set my hands in my lap. "I went home after school, ate something, and watched a show. Then I got ready and went to the cemetery to meet Reuel."

"You walk there or get a ride?" He glances from me to my mama.

"I was working," she interjects, looking over at me. Eyes sad.

A hint of shame, even. Is she thinking of our fight this morning? It seems like centuries ago.

"I walked," I offer, turning back to the man. "Sorrow's not so big."

He cracks a smile. "You got that right. Now how 'bout the rest of the night?"

I tell him the highlights from our birthday, how we sat at the cemetery before finally going back to Reuel's. How I walked home, my mother in bed, asleep (I don't mention drunk). How I went right to sleep (passed out) and woke up this morning, waited for Reuel until I went to her house. I tell him, "That was it. When I left last night, she was on her porch."

"Neighbors confirmed they saw you both there and saw you leaving a few minutes after you helped them clean some stuff up." I nod, picturing the runaway beer cans, and he goes on, "Have you noticed anything else, not just yesterday? Anything might be a lead. Anyone bothering Reuel lately? Anything upsetting her?"

"No," I say, except I falter.

He pauses, pen midair, brows raised. "Yes?"

"It's nothing, really," I say, recalling our conversation on the porch. "I think Reuel's been having some trouble adjusting to her dad's girlfriend. She's been distracted lately, dealing with that. Her mom died a couple years ago, so things have been hard for her, getting used to this new normal."

He notes this down and then waits for more. I shake my head. "I'm sorry. I really don't have any other information. I just want you to find her. Find if she was taken, who took her—"

"Us too, young lady. Us too. But so far, we're not finding much. No signs of an abduction," he admits, more to my mom than me. "It's looking like a possibility she could be a runaway."

"Really?" My mom sounds as shocked as I feel.

"How can that be?" I ask accusingly. Runaway. "Reuel may have been sad—a little—but she's not unhappy. She has a boyfriend, her family, her writing. She has *me*."

"Sometimes it's the ones you'd least expect." He skims his notes, and I bite the inside of my cheek so I don't scream. "We'll check with the ferry company, see if anyone's seen a girl of her description heading off the island. No other leads, really. Boyfriend's got a solid alibi . . . cried like a baby when we told 'im about her."

Is he supposed to be revealing this all to us, anyway? I resent him suddenly, the entire police department, everyone, because are they doing everything they can to find her? Or doesn't it matter so much? No big deal. There's other things to do in Sorrow. Like parking tickets. Lawn citations. Petty crime. And if they think she's a runaway, how much effort will they actually put into finding her?

He and my mother converse politely for another couple of minutes while I stare out the window, arms folded in anger. When they rise, he shakes both our hands. I thank the man, but I can hear how shrill I sound. Still, his smile is kind, and I only have one person to be angry at now. Raging at. The person—or people, I correct—who took Reuel. They're the ones who deserve my wrath. Because there's no way she would just *go*. And if she didn't go, doesn't that mean she was taken?

The whole drive home, Mama doesn't speak a word, I think she's just too upset. Now that the distraction of the detective is gone, her agitation seems to come back fully. She's tapping her finger against the wheel, not to keep time with any music, but in an annoyingly nervous way. Of course she's nervous. She loves Reuel too.

I stare out the window. Breathe in tingly, stuttered breaths, as if I'm scared to inhale too deeply. As if the minute I relax something else bad might happen. I pray Reuel's name the whole way.

After a hellish array of nightmares and far too little sleep, I somehow manage to be out the door and waiting at the Scouts club twenty minutes before eight a.m. Word of the search party has spread fast and wide. Despite her promise to come, my mother's door was shut tight, her room quiet when I left—she's probably still asleep. I try not to be so irritated by it, that I'm by myself—but I'm not really. I stare around, something in my chest tight and aching, at the people here for Reuel. I shouldn't be surprised at the turnout but I somehow am, the sheer number of people already milling about outside the club, wearing subdued and serious expressions. I spot Grady and Bridger, the former's eyes tinged red (stoned or post-crying, possibly both); the latter gives me a somber wave, which I return. I don't move closer, since we're about to start getting organized. A flurry of wind blows my hair in my face. I tug it back into a low knot, then button my jacket, my fingers numb—from nerves, though the air is chilly for May. The sky's gray—it looks like it might storm.

An aunt of Reuel's—a loudmouthed and capable woman—is the one to split us off, and I'm put in a group with my science teacher, a woman I've seen behind the counter at the bakery, and a girl from my gym class, plus her older sister. We nod grimly at each other before we set out, to the east side of town to search a section of beach there, in case Reuel wandered out that way toward the fires, maybe to join a party spontaneously, maybe for some other reason. We scatter all along the shoreline, to the areas beyond. The scent of burning sticks bundled up with rosemary and dried apple slices—Sorrow's traditional combination—is fragrant. Some bonfire pits still smolder, gifts for the witch left to blacken and burn, the smells of salt and herbs, apples and beer, tequila and pot, all surrounding us, making the air heavy. My heart is heavy.

I have never had to search for a missing person, and it's as horrible as it sounds. Every step I take, I can't help wonder, will Reuel's body be lying up ahead?

Will I find a foot? A hand? Her blue eyes staring up at the sky?

I force myself to clear the thoughts, the horrible, horrible thoughts.

"Reuel!" Mr. Dawson, our teacher, calls, side-eyeing me sympathetically. We yell her name with him, I scream it as loud and desperately as I can. Our group moves along the shoreline, curls around the edges of our verdant island. Still nothing. We push on, even as a misty rain begins.

It's about two hours until we return to the Scouts club, dampened, tired. Inside the big room a table is overloaded with food for us all. Someone has brought in Nescos of corn casserole and fried chicken. Beans and sticky rice, biscuits with honey butter, bowls of barbecued shrimp, and sandwiches, too. There's hot coffee and ice-cold beer, and bottles of water and Gatorade nestled together in a cooler. Church ladies and kindly mawmaws have made pies and pastries, tortes stuffed full of Cool Whip and gelatin and Red Dye #40.

There's no way I could eat, so I step past the food and drinks and make my way to a table, sinking into a chair. A second later someone sits beside me. I look up in dull surprise at Georgina. *Georgina.*

Georgina Boudreau. Sitting next to me. On purpose.

"What?" she asks primly, like she's got every right to be in that seat. Like she never left my side. "I'm here for Reuel." In the space of the quiet, she adds, eyes level, "And for you."

Frozen by her explanation, I'm unable to speak, but manage to move my head into a jerky nod, or something resembling it. I fight the urge to pinch myself, to wake myself up.

"The others are on their way," she tells me. "We got split up in the search groups."

For the first time I realize how rosy her cheeks are. And she's wearing a rain jacket. Mud on her Hunters. She was out looking too. There were so many people in the search party, no wonder I didn't see her.

"Thanks . . . ," I say cautiously. *The others?* She can't mean the other girls . . . can she?

"Of course. I still love her," she replies, as if it's that simple. "I still care."

If I wasn't so bone-tired, so full of fear, I might fall out of my seat at her admission. Before I can even formulate a reply, more chairs at the table are being pulled out, squeaking against the floor.

Here they are. The others.

August tips her chin with a bleak smile. Solaina has a pained look on her face. Cori leans down; she enfolds me as I sit, struck silent. I manage to raise my arms around her and squeeze, her messy red ponytail tickling my cheek.

Nobody speaks. Nobody asks what the hell is happening. How it's happening.

We know why. Logically, I know why. They're here for Reuel. A shock as I realize, recalling what Georgina already said. They're here for me, too.

Cori releases me, and she and the others fall into their seats, shrug off jackets, remove rain-drenched hats, close umbrellas, which I wasn't wise enough to bring. A glance at a phone, a text sent, a water bottle opened and a sip taken, though none of them have gotten food or make any effort to, even as people start forming a line and grabbing paper plates. The room fills to the brim, the chatter louder. Reuel's littlest brother, Bentley, runs in from somewhere else in the building, cookie in hand. Her other brothers are surrounded by relatives, being smothered with affection and sugar—the boys weren't out searching, I know. Mr. Carson wouldn't allow it. I'm not sure where he is, Jolene, where anyone else is right now. All I know in this moment is these girls surrounding me, and how both right and wrong it simultaneously feels. If we're gonna make up after all this time—which is hard to believe is possible, and just because they're here doesn't mean it might lead to *that*—Reuel should be here too. We can't be six without her.

A sob escapes me, unbidden. And a hand covers mine, skin a couple of shades darker than my own. Fingernails purple. I look up into Solaina's solemn nearly black eyes, eyelashes sooty and spiky. She whispers, "They'll find her."

Nodding, I push down the fear. My search party didn't find a thing. But there are still people out there looking. Maybe the next group will hear something. Or the next.

Maybe someone will make an announcement soon.

Maybe maybe maybe maybe.

"I can't eat," August says, standing, fidgety. She throws her coat back on, then shoves on a bucket hat, hesitates. "You guys wanna go get some air? It's stopped raining. . . ."

We look around at each other, silently contemplating her question, I think—at least I am. Not because we've all had plenty of air. But because it's one thing to be here, for me, for Reuel's sake, but leaving this table feels like entering the real world, somehow. A world where I wonder if it's possible that we're all friends again.

Everyone is waiting for my lead. So, numbly, I murmur agreement. We push our chairs out, rising, the smells of all the good food wafting in the air, mingling with the scent of rain. With the stench of trepidation. *Reuel Reuel.* I blink away the tears.

We've neared the hall that leads to the side door when Georgina—at the front of us—stops, holding up her hand. She looks back, heart-shaped face screwed up, finely arched brows knit together in confusion.

"What—" August starts. Her voice trails off as we stare down at the end of the hall, beyond Georgina. At our mothers. Well, some of them—Solaina's, Georgina's, August's.

Mine.

They're arguing, voices low, faces taut, except Georgina's mother. Ms. Kate's back is to us. I can tell she's upset, though, her fist squeezed around the handle of her umbrella, her head shaking.

There's a furious look on Marisa's face. She throws her dainty hands up. "—denial! That poor girl. You're not listening," she hisses, voice dropping off in frustration.

A frown is etched into August's mom's smooth face—Ms. Camille. "I thought we agreed already."

My mama lets out a pitiful little cry, a whisper—broken, and I catch my breath.

The women stop arguing to embrace her, surrounding her, cooing at her, patting her back, Marisa's anger fades as she grips her tightly. Ms. Kate is the only one who doesn't step closer to comfort my mom. She turns her head, lifts her eyes, across the hall and right at us. Her mouth clamps shut, and she goes still.

The mothers' gazes find us. They let each other go, dropping their arms, stepping back from each other. Like they were caught doing something they shouldn't.

The tension thick, the questions palpable.

After a second—a long second—Ms. Kate smiles, but it's strained. "Girls. We were just . . . talking about everything." Brighter, she asks, "Where you headed?"

We don't answer.

Quieter, Marisa says, staring at us, "You're . . . together."

They all seem to realize it at the same time. Eyes flooding with questions.

"Yeah," we say in unison. Just like old times. We used to finish each other's sentences. Used to say the same things, not meaning to. We stand, five facing four. Waiting in the tense stillness. Do we need to explain? We are here again together because of Reuel. Because, for all our differences now, they knew I needed them. It doesn't mean I forgive everything. But they're here. That counts for something. It counts for a lot.

But why are *they* together? They've never liked each other—most of them. I never saw them hug in my life. Never saw them talk so intensely, either. They've sure clammed up now.

My mom hasn't said a damn thing. Her eyes are bloodshot—like she was crying, or drinking, I can't tell. When we move forward, heading outside as planned, she reaches out. Her hand flutters across my rain-damp hair.

"Izzy, wait." She tugs a beanie out of her purse. "I brought you an extra."

Crying, then. If she were drinking she'd never worry about my soggy hat.

"Thanks," I say slowly. The four girls and I exchange a look again; the women don't move. They stand there silently while we go on, down the hall, out the door.

Once outside, I turn around, staring through the glass.

They are still there. Watching us. When they see me, they scatter, separating. It looks suspicious. It makes my stomach hurt. The look on their faces. Like paranoia. Wariness.

"That was weird . . . ," Solaina mutters, moving around a low-hanging crepe myrtle branch to settle into a wrought iron patio chair. Nodding, I feel my hands itch for my cigarettes, but I know Ms. Kate won't approve. Then I decide, Reuel is missing, so I'll smoke. I don't give a shit what anyone says. Who's gonna stop me? I light my cigarette and take a long inhale, sitting at a chair opposite her, leaning my elbows into the round tabletop, even though it's wet with rain.

Georgina eyes my bandaged hand but doesn't ask. I lower it, embarrassed. It's nobody's business but mine and Reuel's what we did in that graveyard. And . . . it feels sad now.

"I thought they hated each other," August says, first frowning at me as I blow out a cloud of smoke, then shaking her head, pondering; you can see her mind working through her greenish-brown eyes. She adds, amending, "Some of them."

Her own mom is friends with Cori's and Georgina's (the twins). And mine and Solaina's are friends. Who knows if Reuel's mom would have fit in somewhere, had she lived. But they don't speak, not like this, together.

"Hate is a strong word." Cori shoves her hands in her pockets, shifting her weight from one foot to the other, nervous. She stares upward, at the gloomy sky, thick with clouds.

"I never thought they hated each other. Disliked, maybe. Or just never got to know each other . . . despite us," August says softly, then adds, "What do you think that was about?"

"Maybe they're just upset about Reuel—because it is horrible. But it's unusual to see them like that, talking."

I murmur, "Arguing. And hugging."

"But what do you think they were arguing about?" Solaina says. "Reuel?"

The others shake their heads, uncertain.

"I don't know," Georgina answers, a pensive look on her face as she buttons her red jacket up to her throat. "But it felt like whatever it is, they don't want us to know."

Part of me doesn't want to agree with her, but it's true. That is what it felt like. Almost like they were keeping something from us.

CHAPTER FIVE

hen my mom and I get back home at the end of the night after helping clean up at the Scouts club, I brush aside her offer of food, her encouragement to get me to eat something. "No," I say with a shake of my head. "I'm gonna go to sleep."

"Already?" She darts her gaze to the window, the night outside, then to the clock on the stove. "It's barely nine, and you didn't eat anything at the club, probably all day. Besides, you don't have school tomorrow. Not until Thursday. You could even stay home then, if you want. I can take a few days off to be with you." But she bites her lip. We need the money.

"I'm just tired, Mama." I don't say it with spite. Just honesty. "And I'll go to school when break is over. The girls . . . maybe we'll talk. It helped being with them today, I guess."

"You're suddenly friends again?" she asks, her face flashing with some emotion. Apprehension, maybe. I'd like to think it's her concern over me getting hurt again, but I'm not so sure.

I shrug, too tired to hold on to any suspicion. It doesn't make any sense anyway. "I don't know. I don't think it's that simple."

She comes closer, but hesitantly, as if she's worried I'll lash out. Reaching out a tentative, gentle hand, she smooths the frizzy hair off my face. It takes all my strength not to lean into her palm, to throw myself into her arms. But I hold back because I'm afraid if I fall into her, I won't remember how to stand on my own again. Her eyes meet mine, full of love, and she says, low, "I know she'll be okay, Izzy. They'll find her. Don't worry."

But there's something in her voice that breaks through the sincerity she intends.

It's doubt.

"Okay." I let her hug me and then I turn robotically and head upstairs, so exhausted I can barely lift my feet, but I don't think I could sleep now if I tried, despite how much my body wants to.

I set my stuff on my dresser and bring a cigarette to my lips, opening my balcony doors and drifting outside, along with the cloud of smoke.

It's dark, apart from the moon. The rain stopped hours ago, and it's quiet. Too quiet.

So quiet it's like the night itself is holding its breath. I stare out at the land, at the trees, at the secrets hiding in the deep-green shadows and among the fragrant jasmine twining its way up the lights near the shed. When the breeze picks up, a wooden swing strung on one of our trees starts to sway. As it moves in the wind, the ropes cry out. Somewhere in the dark a branch snaps and I jump.

My skin prickles and I lower my cigarette, looking down more carefully at the yard.

The hairs on the back of my neck rise, and my stomach drops at the same time my heart goes up into my throat, my body ringing alarm bells for . . . something. I hold my breath, studying the land.

The trees bow their heads together and whisper about me; the night knows all my secrets and some I don't even know, some I won't even say. The world seems too big all at once, too wide, too dark, too frightening. Goose bumps run down my arms, and I grip the rail tighter with my free hand, worried I might black out as things flash through my mind, images, sounds, smells. *A slow trail of red running from someone's nose. A plate, full of smoky meat, coarse vegetables. The spoon clattering to the crude wooden table. A scream. The perfume of apples.*

Blinking as my mind clears, I slowly lower my hand, my fingers having smashed my cigarette. Unclench my jaw. Remind myself to breathe. Just . . . my imagination running away with me. That's all.

It's only a squirrel or something, I tell myself, shaking off the fear. Still, for a moment it seemed like there was someone there. I felt like I was being watched.

Someone whispers my name and I shiver. Now I'm just scaring myself! I'm fine, I remind myself. I'm safe. But Reuel might not be.

The longer I stand here, let the crumpled cigarette burn down, the more it's obvious there's nothing out there, nobody watching me. My muscles relax, the alarm easing. I flick the butt into a coffee tin full of sand I keep beside my balcony chair. Go to the bathroom and brush my teeth and wash my face, then get into a tank top and boxers and climb into bed, but I lie awake, mind reeling. Where could Reuel be?

She's all right, I tell myself, wrapping my body in the covers as if that could protect me from the fear of losing her forever. I peel back the bandage on my hand, touch the skinny, crooked scab.

Even though I know she can't answer, I grab my phone and tap a message. *I'm so scared. Please come back.*

I draw down prior texts, snapshots of history on one little screen. GIFs and funny memes, and selfies of us and jokes, so many jokes. Things about silly crushes on kids at school, advice, both serious and not. Snippets of Reuel's poems, one-liners she would send me when I'd push her to share.

> I never meant to be tamed
>
> This is the way the sun
>
> feels when the clouds part
>
> I have nothing to write about
>
> if I don't write about you

When I'd asked her about that last one, she'd finally, reluctantly, confessed it was Grady Corbin. I'd teased her relentlessly for months. She'd been embarrassed because he was—is—kind of a douchebag. Who unfortunately is just her type, tall and dark, sharp cheekbones. But her feelings for Grady didn't pass, and it was while she liked him that he kissed me. Even *if* I'd wanted to kiss him back, I could never do that to her. And months later, she's still writing love poems for him. She's happy with Grady.

I look through our pictures, my gallery full of them. Stare into her eyes. It could be her grief that's at play here. Maybe she went back to the cemetery alone, thinking of her dead mother, coming off a conversation with me about mine, ready to cry over her grave. Maybe she drank more alone. Maybe it was just bad timing, bad luck, that someone else happened to be there too. Maybe she went off with the wrong person. Except Detective Warren's word repeats in my mind. *Runaway.* Could he be right? Did she run away, without a word? Without her phone—so she couldn't be reached? I don't want to believe it, but maybe the oath she made with me was a hint.

A goodbye.

I finger the line on my palm, breath ragged, and try not to cry.

A new text comes in. My heart leaps into my throat until I realize it's not Reuel.

> It was good to see you today even though the reason is bad. I missed you.

Solaina. I slowly type in a reply. *I missed you too.*

It's a start. Maybe we can be friends again. Maybe, some-how, we always were deep down. I set my phone aside, and I close my eyes, finally giving in. Letting my body take over my mind, letting sleep blot out all my thoughts.

All my questions. All the things I can't explain. Not even to myself.

My eyes open.

Sleep slips off me like a silk coat from my shoulders. I'm awake and something is . . . not right.

I swallow and keep still, letting the dark settle around me, trying to figure out what it is that woke me.

A sound . . . like someone chewing.

Puzzled, hazy with confusion and sleep, I dart my gaze around. The moon is waning but still generous with her light tonight. It only takes a moment to see someone standing over my bed. Fear leaves as quickly as it arrived, and I shriek with gratitude as I realize who it is.

"Reuel?" I shoot upright, scrambling out of my covers to grab hold of her arm, tears already pouring down my face. I run my eyes down her, her lank hair, the smudge of mud on her chin. She's still wearing the clothes from our birthday, and they look dirty, damp, her feet bare. Her face is bone white.

I shake her a little to get her attention, to get her to speak. "Are you okay?"

In the silence, she looks down at me and smiles.

I drop my hand from her elbow as I stare at her. My skin goes cold with chills.

She swallows, then lifts something to her mouth, her jaw working.

My mind is slow to understand. It was her chewing, that sound. I watch in horror as she takes a handful of my cigarettes and eats them—like French fries.

"Stop!" I cry, pulling at her wrist, yanking her hand away from her lips, scattering the rest of the cigarettes on the floor. "You'll get sick! What are you doing?"

She doesn't answer me but sinks down on my bed beside me, that strange, terrible smile, her eyes unfocused. She reaches out to touch my face and I shrink back.

"Where have you been?" I ask, chest heaving. "What the hell is wrong with you?"

"It's fine. I'm fine," she says, that smile fading, voice a bell, clear and delicate. Her shoulders start to shake and tears spring to her eyes. "Really, Iz. I'm fine," she repeats.

"Are you hurt—"

"I—" She breaks off into a moan, shaking now, her whole body.

"Hey, deep breaths," I whisper, frightened for her. "Let me get help."

She jerks away, then freezes for a second. Bending into herself, she takes a deep, rasping breath, body shuddering, a sob loosening from her chest.

I lay a hand on her burning-hot forehead, brush her limp hair away with the pad of my thumb. She slowly turns her face, her eyes meeting mine. My lips part at the glassy look inside them. The nothingness. My voice is hoarse, tight. "Reuel . . ."

"I'm fine," she repeats, louder, brighter. "I'm fine!" she scream-laughs, her face breaking with a painful-looking smile, the vein in her forehead dark, raging, as though it might split her skull.

Horrified, I sit frozen, unsure if I should comfort her or be afraid. But it's Reuel, my best friend in the world. My fingers tremble as I reach out again, take her shoulder under my palm. Her teeth are clacking together, like she's cold. But her skin is on fire.

I try to stay calm, the fear sickening my gut. She's not fine. She's hurt or something, maybe she's been drugged. "Stay put. I'm gonna wake my mom up."

"Okay." Her whisper is hoarse. She stops shaking all at once, and then she opens her mouth and vomits all over the floor, her feet, my rug. It's thick and dark, congealed. I stare at it as it spatters, foul-smelling.

"I'm sorry," she tells me weakly. Before she falls back, slumping into my arms.

The wind comes in through the open balcony, chilling my back, the moon spilling light from behind, making us into monstrous shadow shapes on the wall.

CHAPTER SIX

They say Reuel's sick.

"A bad fever," it's explained as. Some kind of virus that caused her temperature to spike, made her hallucinate and wander off, disoriented, to black out more than once—eventually, of course, in my own bedroom. But she's back. She's here, alive and well.

Or, she will be well. Once she recovers.

Georgina is the one who calls us all together, finding a way to reshock me. Are we truly all friends again, or are we just temporarily held together, like a craft project stuck with hot glue that never quite sticks once it's cooled off? But she puts her foot down and has Ms. Kate get us a pass to visit Reuel all at once—sidestepping the strict family-focused visiting rules. There is no question of me going alone to see Reuel. We're all on a group text and everything. Like nothing ever went wrong. We don't talk about it. Yet.

I'm almost too stunned to be grateful, and a part of me resents how easily I let myself fall into this rhythm again. And it is easy. I can barely muster up any caution, as if I weren't hurt deeply, as if I couldn't be again. The five of us have silently made a truce, like they know how much I needed them, how much I still do, even though Reuel's back.

Just a day after she returns, we walk, three and two, holding hands, as we clip down the hallway in two rows. The hospital smells of antiseptic and lemon-scented cleanser and sickness. I keep thinking I can catch the faint, metallic odor of blood underneath, but of course that's just my nerves. My hands tremble, and I have to stop myself from reaching for my cigarettes. Obviously, I can't smoke here, and it wouldn't help anyway. Nothing will help until I see Reuel, make sure she's really all right.

She's here and she's fine, I remind myself for the hundredth time. But I don't know that I'll ever be able to release that image of her in my room, how she looked. What she did.

"Oh." Cori lets out a wisp of breath and squeezes my hand when we round the corner to find three tousle-haired boys playing on tablets outside one room. Reuel's brothers.

They look up from their screens when we come closer, Bentley's face lifting in a smile when he sees me. I wonder if he remembers the others? Three years ago when we were still friends, he was only three. But he knows me well.

"Hi," I say, moving forward on my own, leaning down to wrap my arms around the three of them. Bentley sniffles into my ear. I ask, "What are you doing here?"

The oldest, Colton, shrugs as I release them, trying to look tougher than his twelve years. "We wanted to see her."

"She'll be okay," I reassure them, keeping my voice confident. At my side, behind me, the girls echo my sentiment.

"I know." Colton juts out his chin. In the middle, sandwiched between his brothers, is Lennox, the shyest, who looks down, nodding to himself. Colton adds, "They said her tests look good. She can maybe go home Wednesday, or even tomorrow, if she keeps food down."

I sigh a breath of relief, but something in me is afraid to hope.

Not until I see her, not until I talk to her, not until I can hold her.

"I thought you weren't friends anymore," Colton says, looking over my shoulder at the other girls.

I bite my lower lip, unsure what to say. August answers for us all. "We are now. Again." Georgina and I meet eyes, and in hers is something that says, *I dare you to argue.* The corner of my mouth lifts a little. She smiles in return, and I think, *This is the Georgina I know. The one I loved. Not the Georgina that made fun of my hair.*

I realize it a second later—the last time she and I were here together was when we were born in this very hospital.

"Your dad in there?" I turn back to Colton, nodding to the closed door. Room 373.

"Yup. And Jolene." He makes a face before he catches himself.

I let out a half smile and scuff him on the shoulder. Maybe the boys don't like her as much as Reuel thinks.

The door swings open, and their tall, broad-shouldered brick of a father walks out, face ruddy and lined. "Hey, girls. Y'all can go in and see her but keep it brief. She's still tired and a little confused. They had to sedate her to get her to rest."

"Yes, sir, of course." Georgina sails past him, and the others follow. He watches them with an unreadable expression. It really must be odd for our parents to see us together again.

I've always found Mr. Carson intimidating. Too big, too solid, too loud, hollering at the boys, or laughing with them. But he's liked me the most of all Reuel's friends, or maybe he's just had to get used to me because I'm the one who stuck around. Even though he must be worried still, he manages to smile briefly as I pass.

I go slowest, following the others inside Reuel's hospital room. Why? I must want to see her more than anybody. Apprehension grips me, because what's she going to look like? That terrible smile flashes in my mind. The way her skin burned under my fingers. The certainty of her being . . . wrong.

When I walk into the room, I stop short, my eyes drawn to the small-looking figure on the bed, covered in a white sheet and a white blanket. She's asleep, or I guess just sedated. There are needles in her arm and a pulse oximeter on one finger, machine at her side beeping the pattern of her life. It all rushes over me as I take in everything, finally noticing Jolene leaning over the bedside. I freeze as she swipes Reuel's pale face with a fluffy brush.

Blush. Like Reuel is off to a pageant instead of lying in a hospital bed. Aware of us girls now, waiting awkwardly, Jolene straightens, sniffing. She opens her purse and drops the makeup and brush inside. "Such a relief, isn't it? I was just beside myself with worry."

I didn't even *speak* to her when she was at the Carsons' the day Reuel went missing. But now I hear myself asking, accusing, "You're putting makeup on her?"

Jolene snaps her watery gaze to me, her hair-sprayed auburn locks barely moving, her cheeks going sharp pink. "Young lady. I'm just seeing she looks her best, because when you look your best, you *feel* better, don't you know that?" She dabs at her eyes as she says, almost to herself, "It's a miracle she survived, being so dehydrated and ill. Another day or two out on her own and they woulda found her body rotting in a ditch."

August sags at the graphic description, and at her side Solaina mutters a curse.

"Can you just go?" I say to the woman; my words sound strangled, even as my voice rises. "Reuel would not give a shit about her face right now. Besides, she looks beautiful. She always looks beautiful. She doesn't need that. She doesn't need *you*."

Jolene looks shocked. "How dare you speak to me with such disrespect?"

"Isabeau." Mr. Carson peeks in the door; he must have heard me. "Keep yourself together," he says mildly. My face heats at his gentle reprimand. "Jolene, come on. Let's go get a bite downstairs. The boys are hungry, and you told the girls you'd call them, remember?"

She tightens her purse on her shoulder, lips pinched, and moves past without seeing me, perfume too strong, too stifling. *She's* stifling. No wonder Reuel doesn't like her.

As the door clicks shut, the girls are watching me. Georgina serious, while sympathy is written on August's face. The others, I can't look back at. I don't know how to act now or how to feel or what to say. A twinge of regret and embarrassment flush through me; I meant what I said to Jolene. I just maybe shouldn't have said it now. I stare at Reuel, at the fake rosy glow on her ashen cheekbones, and ball up my fists, wishing I had something to wipe it away.

"Come on, Iz." Solaina steps to my side, takes my hand, grounding me. "Breathe?"

Silent, I nod, squeezing her hand back, the girls studying me before looking at Reuel. I wonder, briefly, what it is they're thinking.

The machines beep and my best friend is lying there, and I can't help feeling a rush of guilt. If I hadn't gone home that night this probably wouldn't have happened. I wasn't drinking as much as Reuel. I was watching her, because lately aren't I always watching her? Always watching to see if she looks happy? I'm a light sleeper, I would've known, even in my champagne haze, if she'd gotten up, sick and disoriented. I would've known if she'd tried to slip out of the house, wouldn't I? If she'd been hallucinating from the fever, which is what they think happened. I could have followed her, stopped her, been there with her, protected her, brought her to the hospital myself for fluids and tests and whatever.

But I didn't and I didn't and I didn't.

I don't realize I'm crying until Cori hands me a tissue, passing the box around, because I'm not the only one who needs to wipe tears away.

"Is she gonna be okay?" I ask. I need someone to tell me *yes.* I need to hear it again.

"Of course," Georgina answers with total confidence, patting Reuel's still hand. "She'll be right as rain soon. They're taking good care of her. And she looks a little better than you said . . . yeah?"

My nod is jerky. Anything is better than that night. The girls know, even though my description was probably nowhere near as vivid as the real thing.

"But . . . the cigarettes." I frown, bringing it up again. They already know.

"Hey, remember in health we learned about pica?" Cori brightens with an idea.

Solaina frowns. "That thing where pregnancy makes you crave shit like Tide Pods?"

"Language . . ." Georgina chides, lightly.

We ignore her, looking at Reuel.

It feels like someone kicked me in the gut. She can't be pregnant. She can't be. She hasn't had sex with Grady . . . has she? She would've told me.

"But her fever." My voice sounds a little strangled.

"Right. High fevers can make you feel really off, can make you feel confused." August smooths a spot on the bed and sits near Reuel's feet, looking at her with concern. "It seems far more likely that's why—even the doctors said so. And Iz said she was acting weird."

"You're right." Cori nods. "It just popped into my mind. This whole thing is so unusual." She reaches over and puts one warm hand on my shoulder. "But she'll recover fine. Remember what Colton said? She can maybe go home tomorrow!"

I smile at Cori, feeling more settled now with that reminder.

I blow out a breath. Reuel is gonna be fine. And I can't imagine the look on her face when she finds out about the other girls. When she realizes we are *us* again.

Our visiting time goes too quickly, but in the end, before we are kicked out, Georgina slips Reuel's left hand into her own, and I take her right. We circle the bed, all linking up. We look down at Reuel, and around at each other, realizing what might have happened. What we might have lost. All because of reasons that seem so, so childish now. Reasons I don't even understand. Maybe never will. Silent understanding passes among us.

"Never again," Georgina says fiercely. She meets my eyes.

We don't say *sorry* yet, we don't provide explanations for why we grew apart, we don't ask questions. But we promise each other—we promise Reuel—never to part again.

I believe we mean it.

* * *

The first day back at school is nearly unbearable without Reuel—still stuck in the hospital, although *possibly* getting out today, later than they expected—and with the near-constant rumors floating around about her, and even about *us,* the eyes on us, at our backs. Mostly people leave us alone, the five of us. At lunch, August disappears into the arms of her longtime boyfriend, Louis. He is all easy smiles and too-good-smelling cologne that makes even me wanna inch closer, though I keep a careful distance so I don't nudge against the cast on his recently broken leg. Throughout the day, I manage to keep up in classes, but am grateful when it's time for me to head off to seventh-period art in the basement—where all the coolest electives are held—though none of the girls are in my class. The last time we created art together was in middle school, making papier-mâché animals and watercolor self-portraits and shadow boxes out of cereal boxes.

As I walk into the large room, Mrs. Jean's cup of green tea steams the air with a grassy fragrance. She gives me a friendly wave but doesn't ask about my break (she obviously already knows it was shitty), her sepia-brown fingers clad with silver rings, enough to fill half a jewelry box. I wave back as I pass her desk. It's probably unfair of me to secretly think I'm one of her favorites, but she's one of mine. Moving forward, I spy Bridger across the high-ceilinged room, already seated on his metal stool, and I smile a little. Dropping my book bag, I set up my space next to him, like usual.

His eyes meet mine. "Reuel's okay?"

I can't find the words, the gratitude lumping up in my throat. I manage to say, "Yeah."

"I'm glad."

"Thanks," I say, admiring his landscape formed from paper

scraps—garbage. Gum wrappers, and tiny pieces of foil, a piece of green mesh from a bag of limes, more. "Yours is even better than last time I saw it. All that texture you added is really interesting."

He smiles crookedly and continues working as the room fills with other students. Mrs. Jean puts on Jimi Hendrix, the low sound of it drifting through the speakers she has tucked into the corners of the room. One girl walks around in her stocking feet—shoes are always optional in Mrs. Jean's class, especially for herself. Though we're stuck in god-awful uniforms, the school is lax on what we put on our feet, apparently, so long as it's not distracting. Next to me, Bridger keeps his classic Pumas on, tapping his toes off-beat to the music.

I turn to my paper, trying to focus even though I can feel stares drilling into my back. People know what happened to Reuel, or they know a distorted version. They know I'm her best friend. Thankfully—and shockingly enough—like in other classes, nobody meddles. The silence is loud enough, though; the blank page stares at me as well, waiting. I lift my hand, moving the pencil hesitantly, as an image comes to me, a gift from the muse, the dark-haired girl I saw running in my dreams the night of my birthday. They were mostly nightmares, really, but *she* didn't scare me. I sketch in the outline of her body, her long, long hair, spiraling to her waist.

My hand falters as I try to remember what she wore. And her features—I only saw a three-quarter profile of her face. Was her nose long and elegant or tipped up at the end? She had a mole . . . didn't she? Or was it a scar? I sigh as the inspiration slips away. Even though it's made up, even though it came from my literal imagination, I'm afraid to get it wrong, somehow. My confidence in this piece lessens the longer I work on it, but it's too late to start over without a plan or I'll have wasted the whole class and I'm already behind on this project, so I force myself to draw on, shading the curve of the girl's cheek, sketching out a background of trees, humming under my breath in the way I tend to do when I'm lost in my work. But I'm not really lost. Not today—not in a good way, at least.

As I draw the girl's dark eyes gazing off into the distance, I remember Reuel the night she returned, the bruiselike shadows on her skin, remember her crying, laughing, the murky stains on my rug now, impossible to get out no matter how much I've scrubbed at it since. I remind myself again and again, and again. *She's found. She's alive. She's okay.*

Despite the comfort of this room, this space, the boy next to me, all period long something in my belly feels spoiled, sick with anxiety. It's not until after school when I get a series of texts from Reuel that my mood lifts.

> I was discharged—home now. Feeling much better. Have to sit out from cheer for a few days tho . . .
>
> I love you. Thanks for all you did for my family. My daddy appreciates it so much.
>
> I get to go to school tomorrow!! Can you believe I'm missing it? Excited to see you.
>
> I heard about the other girls being around . . . uh wow?? i have a million texts.
>
> Call me.

I dial Reuel immediately, kicking off my loafers in the kitchen. Her voice is hoarse when she gleefully says my name. I smile through my tears.

"So, what exactly happened?" she asks, sounding slightly weak. "Big reunion while I was out or what?"

"I have so much to tell you," I say. "But I'm dying to hear about *you* even more. I'm coming over. Do you mind?"

"I'll be mad at you if you *don't*." Her laugh is soft, fond.

I change into street clothes and head straight out, stopping on my way to buy Reuel flowers, even though I can only afford a cheap bouquet from the dollar store. When I get to her house, I run up to her room, where she waits sitting in bed, and I hug her as hard as I can without crushing her still-fragile body. As I lean over her, I give the desk a sidelong glance. Her journal is gone. Hidden away. I push Grady from my thoughts, focusing in on the present. Reuel's here. She's safe. Who cares about that dude?

Bouquets from friends and family scent the air, and there's so much color in this room, like always, but it stands out even more now. From the floral arrangements to the jewel-toned pillows on her bed to her prints tacked above, so much *life*, it makes the dead spider plant on her shelf look even deader.

She catches me staring at it and frowns. "All our plants died while I was gone. My dad must've been so worried about me he forgot to water them. . . ."

I clear my throat. Remembering how quickly it happened. That's not why. But I smile, nod. Then settle in next to her on the bed, making sure I don't crowd her.

"So?" I don't finish the sentence. She knows what I mean. *What the hell happened?*

"You left, I remember," Reuel starts slowly. "I went inside soon after that. Had a glass of water in the kitchen. Then I came up here and went to bed. The room was spinning and I started feeling sick. Well, we drank a lot, you know? I think maybe I got up to puke."

"And you don't remember where you went?"

"No." She lifts her hands helplessly, the charms on her bracelet clinking together. Tears spring to her eyes, and I can only imagine how she's feeling. "I don't even know where I was. All I remember is I woke up in the hospital—but I don't know how I got there."

I picture her standing in my room. Her smile. How delirious she must've been to eat cigarettes. The ambulance picked her up at my place. "So you don't remember being at my house?" I ask tentatively.

A lost look crosses her face. "They said that . . . but I don't remember how I ended up there. I don't remember seeing you. Did we talk?"

Swallowing hard, I manage to put an easy look on my face—I hope—and say, "Yeah . . . We talked."

There's no point describing that night. I would rather focus on the now. I reach over and take her hand. "Are you sure you're feeling okay?"

"I'm sure. And you feel normal, right? No symptoms?"

"None," I say, shaking my head. "I guess I didn't get it."

"Good. I don't want you to go through what I did." She smiles through tears, adding, "I'm *so* glad to be home, Iz. You have no idea. Now. *Your* turn."

I catch her up on everything with the girls. Seeing her laugh, her brows rising with wonder, is almost enough to erase the concern over her that lingers, because she still looks pretty rough, her skin pale and dry, her eyes tired. I *try* to ignore the rest: the way she doesn't remember a thing, the way we can't account for any of her missing hours. The way something keeps nagging at me as I stare at her. Remembering how sick she was. Reminding myself she's so much better now.

I *try*.

CHAPTER SEVEN

Friday—finally. Reuel's well enough to return to school, and before I know it, it's lunchtime and we are walking in together. The cafeteria is loud as usual, bustling with starving teenagers and drenched with the overpowering smell of garlic and oregano. Mostly, nobody pays much attention to us. This morning the whole building seemed to go quiet as we came in—their eyes on Reuel, whispers about what happened, if she was still ill—then that word: *contagious.* To her credit, she didn't let it faze her. She's braver than I am, that's for damn sure. Having anyone stare at me makes me wish the floor would open up and swallow me whole.

But now, here at lunch, the other students are distracted with their own meals and friends, and they pay us no mind, and maybe Reuel's disappearance and miraculous return are old news by high school standards. And anyway, everyone is already tired of being back here and ready for the weekend. I'm one of them. Reuel and I grab trays and sit, greet everyone.

Usually, the two of us eat together, squeezed at the end of a table full of random people, untethered by a larger group. But not now. Now it's not even just the six of us girls, like back in middle and elementary school—there's also Georgina's boyfriend, Jesse, and Louis, grinning as Cori draws a smiley face on his cast—*her* girlfriend off in Germany for a study abroad trip, otherwise she'd be here too. I don't know any of these extras well, but of the two boys, Louis is the better catch. Jesse has had his nose in his phone the whole time. He's underwhelming, at best. A cardboard boyfriend I suspect Georgina keeps because he's eye candy and that's all. But maybe that's mean of me.

I can't help but smile though, watching August lean into Louis, snuggling against him, content in their very small world.

My smile wavers, then drops as Grady sidles over, closing the gap between Solaina and Reuel. I narrow my eyes in the couples' direction, not wanting to watch him kissing all over Reuel, who's not recovered enough to be *manhandled,* for God's sake. And he looks disgustingly beautiful today, his tie charmingly loosened, that jawline, that black hair hanging over his striking (gag) eyes, almost matching her own long locks. Two ravens, two dark angels. They look good together.

They look fucking great together.

I lift my gaze from them as Evan Watts skulks by. "Hey, birthday bitches!" he crows, slowing down to mock us, just missing stepping on a runaway meatball on the floor—damn it. I let my imagination take over—picture him slipping on it and falling on his ass. In reality he snickers, looking us over. "Y'all back together, huh? Needed to be relevant again?"

"Jealous, Watts?" Georgina asks sweetly, tossing her chestnut blowout off her face, dainty diamond studs winking in her ears. "That you were hatched instead of born?"

We bust out laughing, and his pale face goes burnt sienna

at the cheeks before he stalks off. Grady snorts, wrapping his arms around Reuel and nuzzling into her neck. She smiles, but it's tight. Shadows beneath her eyes, blood vessels still broken in the delicate area there. She doesn't eat a thing, just moves the spork around, picking apart her lunch as everyone else talks, distracted.

"You okay?" I say to her, low.

Her mouth is a line, full lips pressed together. She answers, "Fine."

I'm fine, I'm fine, the way her laugh screamed through the shadows of my bedroom that night she miraculously came to me.

She avoids my concerned, searching gaze now, and shrugs a shoulder, as if Grady is a pest and she wants him off her. But he doesn't get the hint, kissing her along the jawline.

"Hello? We're eating here," Solaina grumbles, but it's more of a fond exaggeration than real annoyance. She flicks her black-winged eyes behind me, a wistful look on her face. I twist my neck to follow her focus, zeroing in on a boy she used to have a crush on, way back in eighth grade. I'm guessing that crush never died. I nudge her knee, and she looks at me, blushing in confirmation. I marvel at this quiet moment—we're sharing secrets again. Just like before.

"Speak for yourself," Cori says, glumly picking through her spaghetti, dropping a noodle on her blouse, which immediately leaves a mean orange stain. She half-heartedly dabs at it with her napkin. "This is gross."

"Shoulda brought your own lunch, like I always say." Georgina stabs a bite of romaine before dipping it into her fancy lemon–olive oil dressing—her meal is made up of greens (probably organic) and lean protein and fruit. She doesn't approve of

PDA and glances at Reuel and Grady, but stays quiet, focusing her attention on her meal. She's been softer now, since we reunited, but I know we all need to talk. I just don't know when to do it. We are walking a tightrope now, I worry. What if we take one wrong step and go falling again?

Snow cone. I push aside the insult. I want this to work out, this dynamic—minus the plus-ones, which I could do without, to be honest. I'd like it to be just us girls. I'd especially like a *certain* boy to go. . . . I take an aggressive swig of my chocolate milk, trying not to let Grady's presence get to me. Reuel is back. I am grateful for that. I'll never stop being grateful. And a thought cheers me—now that the other girls are friends with us again, I won't be the third wheel for Spring Fling anymore. We can all go together.

With a sharp inhale, Grady stops kissing Reuel, pulling back an inch and looking at her neck. He runs a finger along it, grimacing. "God, Reuel. What happened?"

There's a huge bruise I didn't see before—I don't know how. It eats up the skin on her neck with its brutal color, climbing out from the collar of her blazer, probably dipping down beneath it. My mouth has opened to repeat his question to her when she rises.

"I'm not hungry." Reuel drops her utensil and tugs Grady up beside her, his elbow in her trembling hand. "Let's go talk."

We stare after them as they leave the cafeteria and go stand in the hallway. I can just see Grady's back. A glimpse of Reuel's face. Her hands moving as she talks with them.

"She's breaking up with him," Georgina says before turning back to her meal—one neatly segmented blood orange goes into her mouth.

"Maybe not." Cori's smile is optimistic. "Maybe they're just talking."

We all look again. Reuel gestures, pointing from him to her chest. Her heart.

"Nah, they're breaking up," I say.

Solaina gives me a *look*, eyebrows quirked together. "You sound happy about it."

I realize how bright my tone was. I shake my head guiltily. "I'm not happy if she's *sad* about it. I only . . . Things are weird with him." Hesitating, I look at everyone, including at the two boys. And I take a leap. "What is said at this table stays at this table, right?"

"Of course." Georgina prods Jesse, who is staring at his phone. He nods absently, not even listening. Louis leans in to hear along with the girls. He likes gossip, I take it from his eager expression.

I lower my voice and explain, "Grady kissed me . . . right before they got together."

"Oh, shit," Louis says, thick eyebrows raised.

"And you like him?" August asks, her olive eyes full of sympathy.

"No!" I emphatically answer. Then, softer, "No. I rejected him, and definitely hurt his feelings. I'm sure he doesn't like me now—and it's uncomfortable. He never even looks at me. I'll be glad if he's not around, but of course I'm sad for *her*."

"Doesn't look like she's too broken up about it," Solaina says dryly, jerking her chin in their direction. Then she sobers, leaning forward to ask in a concerned whisper, "Girls, what the hell happened to her neck?"

Wordlessly, I shake my head. It's not just her neck. The dark shadows under her eyes. The doctors let her go home—her fever was gone, her tests came back just fine. She's obviously cleared to return to school. But she still looks ill. And that bruise . . .

We turn to watch Reuel walking back to us, a lightness in her step. She sits and licks her lips. Smiles, all casual. "What'd I miss?"

"What did *we* miss?" I ask.

She starts eating, finally. In between slow mouthfuls, she says, "We're not together anymore."

"Why? You don't like him now?" Cori asks, darting a glance at me. I feel like everyone looks at me—even, shockingly, Jesse—they all must be thinking about the kiss.

Reuel considers Cori's question, swallowing. She sets her spork down and crumples her napkin up on her tray after only two bites. "I don't wanna be anyone's girlfriend right now. And no. I don't like him like that." She adds, "Not anymore."

Solaina pats her hand, comforting her. Solaina's wearing her spoon ring from Georgina, I notice. Should I get mine back out from my jewelry box? Should we all be wearing ours again?

"So." Georgina smoothly changes the subject. "It's Friday. Sleepover at my place?"

Everyone agrees, Reuel's face lights up. Her smile returns. I watch her talk and laugh, but not eat. I should be (selfishly) happy she's free of Grady now, but I feel a little sad, and I'm not sure why. I stare at that terrible bruise on her neck. I wonder how she got it. I wonder again where she wandered off to. What happened to her while she was gone. What's still happening now.

* * *

"Hey, Isabeau." Mrs. Jean smiles when I get to art. I greet her and walk over to Bridger, already in his usual spot. He must've worked through lunch, since I don't remember seeing him then. I say hi and set up my space, clipping my giant piece of paper on my easel, staring at my progress so far, biting my lip. Pencil ready. But my hand doesn't move.

Mrs. Jean walks over. "I love how you made the subject looking off like that, just a hint of her face, and such good shading already. *In a Dream.* Fitting title. It does make me think of a dream, for some reason. That's what good art does. It makes you stop and wonder."

"Yeah?" I cock my head and study the portrait, trying to put the worry about Reuel out of my mind. "I wasn't sure. About the whole thing, really."

"Be more confident in your choices." She pats my shoulder, whispering conspiratorially as the room fills with other students. "You're too good not to be."

Bridger, at my side, nods, then goes back to his piece, gluing a used sucker stick to the canvas, eyes fixed to his work, a piece of foil stuck to the back of his hand.

I say thank you, and Mrs. Jean gracefully eases away, barefoot again, her toes polished verdigris green, making the rounds about the room before going to her wide desk, turning the stereo up higher, static pushed aside by a song by the Mamas & the Papas she plays a lot. I can pick out a lot of old music now, because of her.

"Iz!" Someone taps my shoulder and I look over to see Solaina, grinning at me.

"Lost in your work or what?" she jokes at my startling, then almost seems to catch herself, how *easy* this all feels, just us, one-on-one, and her smile wavers. She blurts out an explanation: "I had to run down here to get some poster board for my lit project and thought I'd see what you're working on." Looking over my picture, she twists her mouth, thinking.

"What?" I ask self-consciously.

"Is she famous?" Solaina tilts her head.

I look back at the portrait and shrug. "No, I dreamt her up. Why?"

"I don't know. She's familiar, I guess—I feel like I've seen her in a show or something. Anyway, you're still so talented," she says in shy approval, her eyes sparkling with warmth, the hesitation slowly melting.

"Thanks." I duck my head, smiling, sure my face is flushed at her praise. "I guess it's going okay."

"More than okay," she whispers, before she darts off to go grab her poster board, leaving as quickly as she arrived. But it's enough, between her and my teacher, to boost my confidence.

"Bridger," someone calls across the room, "want my condom wrapper for your project?"

A few kids laugh, and Mrs. Jean dryly replies, "You *wish*, Kai. Now get to work or you can grab the mop and start cleaning if you have nothing better to do than be obnoxious."

I laugh. Bridger laughs too. Kai grins good-naturedly.

"Now, everyone." Mrs. Jean calls us to attention. "I know you're still working on the pieces you started before break."

Ruefully, I stare at the girl on my page. I started late. I'll have to take the portrait home to catch up with my classmates.

"But," she goes on, "before class is over, please grab one of these old yearbooks for the weekend. By Wednesday next week, I want you to have the materials ready to start our next project—a collage, but with a twist. I'll explain everything in more detail then. For now, you should know I want you to go wild. Rip as many pages out as you want—whatever draws your inspiration—and go ahead and recycle whatever you don't want to use."

Our class looks to the stacks of yearbooks piled up on the floor in the corner. "Really?" a girl in the back says. "We can take whatever we want? Aren't some of those super old?"

"They were donated and are extras, so they're free to destroy," Mrs. Jean explains. "Or, as I like to say, 'make art out of.'"

A guy standing nearby grabs one off the top and flips through. He laughs and tips the page toward Kai. "Bro, look at this guy's hair."

"Ah, that was called a bowl cut," Mrs. Jean says cheerfully as she looks over his shoulder. She adds, "The nineties were something else. My personal *second*-favorite decade. So, everyone, please take a book."

The guy pushes the yearbook toward me to grab a different one. I shrug and set it off to the side. I'll look through it later. I don't care what year I get. One thing at a time.

I grab my pencils and I pick up where I left off, shadowing the lines of the girl's half-shown face, edging her into existence.

CHAPTER EIGHT

Georgina's home is that stately white house you always see in movies, at the end of a long block, with perfect landscaping, and a huge garage, and gentle lighting with a dimmer switch in every room. It's her and her parents and that's it, in this giant house that's been in their family for decades. Ms. Kate had a stillbirth four years ago, and that was the last time I saw Georgina cry, when she told us about her baby brother.

I push myself forward, suddenly uncertain, having to come here alone—and late at that. I had to retake a stupid math test after school, then go home to get my stuff for the sleepover. I step closer, thinking about turning points and changes, staring up at the Boudreaus'. The shutters in pale French gray framing the taller-than-me windows. There's a deep, rectangular pool, though it's not visible from the expansive, gated backyard, which is thick with grand magnolias that give off a sweet, lemony scent. The little white playhouse where the six of us played make-believe, the courtyard garden already lush with greenery and perfectly kept spring flowers. Kept by a gardener, of course.

There, the front door. Twenty feet ahead. Ten. Five. I walk up the few steps to the blue-ceilinged porch, hung with ferns, and then my hand is on the knocker. I lift the cool brass dragonfly, antiqued by time. Hit it against the wood with a couple of satisfying thuds, the breeze—finally the heat has been born—blowing against my back. I shrug off my plaid shirt and tie it around my waist, sweat starting to bead on my upper lip, but I'm thankful for the warmth.

The seconds drip slow like molasses. The door swings open and there Georgina is. She's changed into street clothes, as have I. She stares at me for an unreadable moment, her hair perfectly arranged against her candy-pink top. On a sweeter-looking girl, it would read demure. On Georgina, it has sharpened all of her. Her nails. Her face. Her mouth melts into a smile, her voice surprising me with its welcoming softness. "Hi. Come on in. Everyone's here."

Her smile widens and she waves me in impatiently. I follow her into the air-conditioned house, so cool I can't help but shiver, and on into the large and familiar kitchen, each step practiced, natural. I know this home almost as well as my own. That hasn't changed. There's a crystal bowl on the massive island, still kept full of lemons, I see. The smell of shrimp étouffée hangs in the air, but I know without a doubt it's from a restaurant. The last time I saw any cooking done here it was a platter of pb&j sandwiches with the crusts cut off. Like my own mother, Ms. Kate doesn't cook, but unlike me, Georgina doesn't either. This house is premade gourmet meals, food delivery, and going out for dinner two or three times a week, if I had to wager a guess at their habits being the same now.

Ms. Kate sits at the granite-topped island, glass of pink wine in her blue-veined hand. Her ever-expanding lips pull up at the sight of me. I stare in surprise—why, I don't know. I shouldn't be caught off guard seeing her. I've seen her in town, shopping with Georgina, at school functions. Hell, I passed right by her at the Scouts club the other night. But this is more intimate. More real.

"How are you, chère?" Her eyes are bigger than I remember. Her forehead smoother. Her body bonier, folded around me in a hug. I could snap her wrists in half. She pulls away, smiling. "It's good to have y'all back here."

"It's good to be here, Ms. Kate." It's ridiculous how formal I sound, how stiff. I try to relax, but I find myself running a finger down the tiny scar on my palm. A comforting, nervous habit I've quickly adopted.

A brown-haired man comes into view, rounding the corner from the back hall. Mr. Boudreau—Georgina looks so much like him it's uncanny. He glances over, waves vacantly without really seeing us before slipping up the staircase and going to his office, as usual. Probably to be buried in paperwork, or, as I suspect, simply hiding. I used to think he was a little afraid of us girls, the shrieking laughter, the messes we made in Georgina's huge playroom (which was eventually renovated into his wife's walk-in closet/room), the space we took up. Georgina doesn't seem to notice his quick escape, or mind, but then again, she's used to it. We all are, or used to be. I've seen the back of his head more than I've seen his face. To this day I wonder if he even knew all our names.

But Georgina's mom has always been so welcoming to all of us, so *nice*. Georgina once told us she had a really rough life until she got to high school, whatever that means. You wouldn't know it by looking at her, though. And between her and Marisa, I sometimes forgot to feel sad about my own situation. So what if *my* mom was never anyone's favorite?

Shamefully, I think, *Not even mine.*

"I ordered cupcakes for you girls. Red velvet. I'll bring 'em down later."

"Thank you," I say with a genuine smile.

"You're welcome, Isabeau." She turns to her daughter. "Georgina Rose. Not too much to drink, now." She doesn't seem to mind, so long as we're subtle about it, I guess.

Georgina's lips tug into a smirk, but she doesn't bother making a sarcastic comment about her mother's attempt to take control (an impossible goal)—and she flings open the basement door, ushering me down, closing the door behind herself.

The girls are all sprawled out along the massive white sectional—new since last time I was here. Everyone greets me with eager smiles, a bright chorus of *hello*s, and Georgina asks around, "Anyone want a shot?"

"Ohh, yes, please." August beams with a toothpaste grin, folding her long legs under her, smiling down at her phone. Louis, I'd bet a million on it. There's something I deeply love about their love for each other. She catches me looking at her and her eyes positively twinkle.

I smile wider at her, making my way to the couch, plopping between Reuel and Solaina. The three of us meet eyes. This has to be as strange for the two of them as it is for me. But it's a good strange, being back. The air smells the same here. Subtle cleaning products and expensive candles. I take a ruby-colored shot Georgina hands out, down it, heat flooding my belly. Cori turns up the playlist she has going on, singing along to the happy-girl music, dancing (semi-badly) in her sherbet-colored I ♥ BUGS T-shirt, and the mood in the basement lifts even more, feeling positively celebratory. We're together.

Solaina reaches forward to grab a handful of chips and laughs over a video August tips to show her on her phone. Solaina's done her hair up into a French twist, and her leaf-shaped earrings dangle almost to her spaghetti-strapped shoulders. I forgot the little birthmark on her right shoulder blade, but there it is.

Humming under her breath, Georgina sets down a tray of even more shots, then takes a ladylike seat on the chaise while we all talk, laughing, being silly, getting into the rhythm of the evening. After we've settled, Georgina fills up the snacks and then flips on the giant-screen TV to scroll so we can choose a movie. Cori isn't a drinker at all, I learn, and Reuel doesn't take anything alcoholic, which is probably for the best. I narrow my eyes at the shadows on her face while she talks to the other girls. What is she thinking about under all this casual banter? Worrying about? After all, I've known her for centuries, so isn't it normal to worry about her worry? I can tell there's something on her mind. Is she regretting breaking up with Grady?

"You're good?" I ask her under my breath, even as I realize how annoying it probably is that I keep asking.

"I'm good," she agrees, looking away before I can assess her too closely.

"*Slasher movies?*" August groans. I gaze up to see her, wrinkling her nose at the saved watch list Georgina has pulled up. "I'm not watching those," August tells her.

"Really?" Georgina tilts her head, blinking. "As an intellectual I'd think you'd know how beneficial horror movies can be for the brain and nervous system. Plus, if you're thinking of being a surgeon you better get used to blood. Anyway, you know it's all corn syrup."

August snorts. "Yeah? Well, it's still nasty." I, for one, agree with her.

"Let's watch *Cinderella*," Solaina suggests, face lighting up.

Cori flashes a big smile as she claps her hands together. "Ohhh, yes."

"I think we're too old for cartoons now." Georgina laughs, showing off her perfectly straight smile, which cost her parents a fortune. She used to have a snaggletooth. I run my tongue along my own slightly crooked teeth. At least it gives me character.

"I meant one with real people, the *1995* one," Solaina says, as if we should know. She goes on, impassioned, "Besides, nobody is too old for cartoons *or* fairy tales. You know the original Grimms' tales were actually written for adults. Some of them can be gory, like Cinderella's sisters getting their eyes pecked out and their feet cut off." She grows more excited as she goes on, "In their version of the story, I mean. Obviously that doesn't happen in the movies. Regrettably."

"You're still into all that, huh?" Georgina teases, but the way she's looking at Solaina tells me she's genuinely interested. We all are. In many ways, we are relearning each other. A lot changes from thirteen to sixteen, after all. Not just our bodies, but our minds, our interests.

"Yeah." Solaina nods. "And we're doing a big project in lit club, stories from our own cultures, so obviously I'm doing Puerto Rican and Portuguese tales. The club is a blast." Then she admits, almost to herself, "Well. The people not so much. But the topics, yes."

"I thought you were friends with them all?" I can't help my curiosity. "I used to see you together all the time."

Her freshly glossed nectarine lips twist, like she's trying to keep from smiling, when she says, "I mean, yeah. They're my friends-*ish*. But I also can't stand them."

Georgina cracks up, and I find myself laughing along with

everyone else as well. But there's a fine line I think we are near to crossing—talking about friendship. About what happened to us all. About what is happening now.

When? When? When will we say it? Ask it? Discuss it?

We exchange a look, a brief and weighted one. I *know* each of us knows what the others are thinking. But the moment passes, and Georgina gestures to the television, unbothered. "Whatever, y'all choose then, since you're so picky. I'm gonna go change." She walks away and heads upstairs for at least her third wardrobe change of the day. When we were really young she used to like this movie from the eighties—*Dirty Dancing*—and every time the main character changed her clothes, Georgina would find an outfit close to it and change too.

Solaina eagerly snatches the remote up, asking around once if we all care if she picks. We collectively agree, it's fine. *Cinderella* it is.

I adjust on the couch, and my hand brushes against Reuel's. I suck in a breath—it is ice-cold—and then I pull up one of the furry throw blankets that are rolled into a basket near the coffee table. I cover her as best as I can. Damn air conditioning. It's not even *that* hot outside.

"Thanks?" she says, questioning.

"You're freezing," I say, trying to smile through it, keep my voice light, so nobody else will look over and get worried about her too. The last thing she would want is anyone making a big deal of it. Only I can't really help it.

Reuel shrugs, picking at her nails, looking away from me. I'm on the wrong side of her to see how that bruise on her neck looks. I stare at her profile. Surely she can see me looking at her. But she doesn't turn to me. It takes all my effort not to reach over and—I'm not even sure. Feel her forehead? Check her pulse? Shake her by the shoulders and demand she tell me if she's feeling bad?

After lowering the lights, Georgina settles back on the couch just as Solaina pauses on the opening credits, and I turn away from Reuel, to stay present in this moment, with everyone here. Reminding myself. All is well now. This is what I wanted for so long, even if I didn't want to admit it. Solaina presses play, and we snuggle in for the movie, passing snacks and pizza, red velvet cupcakes thick with cream cheese frosting—*For a belated birthday thing?* I wonder but don't ask. Georgina doesn't eat sweets, but she downs another shot and offers us all more too, and for the sensible ones, bottles of Evian. Reuel takes a water, but she doesn't even open it. I know, because I think I watch her more than the screen—even though Solaina made a good choice. There's something vaguely familiar about the movie—I wonder if she made us sit through this when we were younger.

Tulle ball gowns twirl in shades of lavender, lilac, plum, periwinkle, teal. Girls in satin gloves, one in glass slippers, her pale blue dress a foamy delight, diamonds at her elegant brown neck and in her tiara winking, her teeth white as pearls. Even Georgina seems to enjoy the fairy tale, laughing at the foolish stepsisters, saying the prince is hot, which is true, but he also looks a little like Bridger's dad, which is weird for me to be reminded of because Bridger looks enough like him too, and Bridger is good-looking, but I do *not* think of him that way. But maybe there's something wrong with me. He's sweet and cute and likes me, I can tell.

So why can't I like him back?

"Reuel?" August whispers, passing a cupcake to her casually. Everyone else's attention is on the movie. But I watch Reuel hesitate—can see the concern flit across August's face. Because she and I both know Reuel hasn't eaten a thing tonight.

But Reuel takes it, unpeeling the wrapper, defiantly keeping her gaze forward on the movie, where Cinderella is going head to head with the cruel stepmother. Reuel takes a bite, eating, her face going paler with each mouthful. Her jaw moving slower. Her throat taking longer to swallow. The cupcake growing smaller.

It's dark, the lights are low, but I can still make out the tears running down her face.

"Reuel," I breathe. "What's wrong?"

"What's going on?" Georgina asks in alarm as she turns the lights bright again.

We all stare at Reuel, her chest heaving and heaving. Her eyes, those tears. Her hands are trembling.

"Are you sick?" August takes the last bit of cupcake from Reuel's hand before it drops.

"I'm not sick," she answers. But her face is too white. Going green.

Warning bells ring in my head. "She's gonna barf. Quick, get up, Reuel," I say, hauling her gently from the couch. She looks like the walking dead. Her skin ice-cold.

Fumbling to the bathroom just steps away, she gets to the toilet in time with my help. The other girls watch at the door, whispering under their breath. About what to do with her.

"Shhhh," I say, patting Reuel's back. I gather her hair up loosely in my fist. She pants and heaves again, emptying her tender belly of the red velvet cupcake, and by the looks of it, not much else besides bile. The water in the toilet bowl is a disturbing crimson.

"Georgina went to grab her a Gatorade," August says, easing into the bathroom.

Nodding, I turn to Reuel, rub at her back some more. Now

she's dry-heaving, body shaking. In between gagging, she whispers, "I thought it would stay down—"

"It's okay," I tell her, shushing her. "You don't have to talk right now."

When she's through, I get her a cold washcloth to press against her face. Watch her rinse her mouth, wash her hands. After, Solaina and I guide Reuel to the couch. August unscrews the bottle of Gatorade and hands it over to her.

"Thanks, Doctor." Reuel gives August a grateful, teasing smile. August smiles, but concern is still shadowing her eyes. Just like the rest of us.

"One sip," I tell Reuel. She hesitates over the beverage, and I demand, "Take one."

I don't say the *or else.* Or else we'll call your dad. We'll call the doctor. We'll get you help. Because you shouldn't get this sick over a few bites of dessert.

She lifts the bottle to her lips, swallows, wincing a little— her throat surely raw. She pulls the bottle back, complaining that it's too cold—that it hurts her teeth. But I sigh, satisfied, set it on the coffee table. She drank some. Now she just needs to hold on to it.

"So, now what?" Cori asks, mouth quivering.

"I'm tired," Reuel answers Cori, as if that is an answer. She burrows into the fur blanket, looking so small. Peeks up at me. "Can I sleep now?"

"Call the nurse line, shouldn't we"—Georgina is saying in the background, Cori muttering something back to her cousin—"at least text Mr. Carson?"

"I just threw up—it's not a big deal." Reuel frowns.

"But . . ." I stare at her. Not *just.* "You got, like, *aggressively* sick."

"No, please, Iz," Reuel implores, like I'm the only one who

will take her side. "Please don't make me go. I wanna stay here with you. I promise, I feel better," she insists.

"Really?" I ask, hoping I don't sound as doubtful as I feel. I sit beside her on the couch, feel her forehead for real. Cool, a few degrees lower than my hand. Feel her wrists, for her pulse, a little self-conscious, with doctor-hopeful August watching me. But I know enough. Reuel's pulse is steady. Her breath is calm. Her color seems better—not as good as it was pre-disappearance. But better than moments ago.

"I *promise*," she answers.

"If you start feeling bad again, we're calling," I say to her. "No ifs, ands, or buts."

She smiles, thanking me. Closes her eyes. Lids thin, veined blue.

"I'll watch her," I tell the others. "Maybe she's having a reaction—the antibiotics or something."

"We'll all watch her," Georgina says, finally exhaling for almost the first time, I think. She lays a hand on my arm and squeezes.

I twist to look up into her face. We speak without words. I don't even know what we're saying. But I know it's full of love. Forgiveness.

And fear, for Reuel. For what's happening to her. She got violently ill just from eating a cupcake—she didn't even drink tonight. I recall what her brother said at the hospital—that she could go home if she kept food down. But why is she sick again now?

August murmurs to no one, unfolding her blanket for sleeping. She grabs her toothbrush and a satin bonnet from her bag, heading to the bathroom to get ready for bed. Reuel is breathing deeply already, exhausted. Almost asleep.

Under my breath, I tell the others, "I'll take first watch." I reach for my stuff, slip out of my shorts and into sweatpants. Nobody argues with me. We are quiet as we get into pajamas, drink water. In her sweet baby-doll nightie with the ruffled straps, Georgina dumps the rest of the shots down the wet-bar sink, the party mood soured now. She tucks the cupcakes we didn't finish under the glass dome of the cake stand in the small basement kitchenette, which is nicer than my full-time kitchen. Pulls the Roman shades down on the basement windows. Plugs her phone into the wall beside the sectional, turns off all the lights, apart from one night-light in the room that flickers in a comforting way. She settles in for sleep with her pink floral pillowcase and a teddy bear, which might just be ironic. I'm not quite sure.

Before I know it, Georgina's snoring softly—something she always insisted she *does not do*—and Solaina and Cori are both shifting restlessly but look asleep. Perpendicular to me, August is text-good-nighting Louis with a lovestruck grin on her sleepy, freshly washed face. I know she'll pass out in a minute too. I don't mind not sleeping. I'm not even tired.

I rest my fingers on Reuel's wrist. Keeping the beat of her heart well into the night. Even when August wakes up to a low alarm for her turn. She reaches over, feeling for Reuel, checking her steady breath. Satisfied, she sits up, watching over her. Her eyes finding mine in the dim light of the room.

"You're up, Iz?" she whispers to me, not sounding surprised. "I've got her."

"Thanks, August," I say, but still, I don't sleep.

I watch Reuel.

I thought she was asleep, but somehow, in the dark, her hand finds mine. Her fingers lace into my own.

Neither of us lets go.

It is night. Their mouths taste of liquor and laughter. Somewhere, music plays.

In this moment, they are happy. Unaware of what they'll have to give up.

Unaware that one day, they will regret everything about this night.

It is night, and they pull out a book.

CHAPTER NINE

"Turn off your alarm," August grumbles, voice thick with fatigue.

The incessant ringing drills into my head and I groan a little. I must've fallen asleep well into the morning hours.

"So annoying. Solaina." I lift my head and wipe the sleep from my eyes when she doesn't answer. I repeat her name in a soft plea, *"Solaina."*

"It's not mine," she mumbles, her face half hidden under her blankets. "It's Georgina's phone, I think."

"Sorry. Georgina?" I push my toe to nudge her across from me on the chaise part of the sectional. When I don't feel her, I peer over.

She's not here; just the form of her body imprinted in the pile of fluffy blankets left behind, her teddy bear flopped over. I glance across the room to the bathroom. Door open. Light off.

"Ugh, what's she doing?" August reaches over, fumbling for Georgina's iPhone and swiping the alarm away.

"Maybe she's upstairs? Getting breakfast?" I offer, then

yawn, smile. I almost forgot that about Georgina—it's the kind of thing she'd do. Go upstairs and fix up a tray full of croissants, fresh fruit, tiny yogurts in glass pots, individual bottles of orange juice, bring it all down for us complete with a flower in a bud vase. I assess the other girls as my body and mind wake up fully. Reuel, I find first, of course. That's when I remember.

Last night. I push myself upright, nervous, but there's no need to worry. My body relaxes. She's still sleeping, facing away from me, one arm flung over her head; her breath rustles, her back rising and falling gently.

"She seems okay, right?" I point at Reuel. She moves just to the side, enough to reveal the pile of strands of hair on the white pillow.

I lean closer, focusing in on a bald spot at the back of her scalp. I stare at the black hair on the pillow, uneasy. Why is she losing so much all of a sudden? I had my hands in her hair the night of our birthday—it was so healthy then, thick and shiny. But not now. Not since she went missing.

"Her breathing is steady, I think." Cori doesn't notice the strands, and her observation settles me—it's true. Cori bounds off the couch with the energy of three girls, finding her glasses, hair every which way, her pajama shorts highlighter yellow, matching her happy vibe. She's used to getting up early for swim practice. She smiles brightly at me, Solaina, August. Cheerfully says, "It's so nice to be back here all together, isn't it?"

I don't have to hide my happiness. Not here, not with her, or them. Not anymore. I rise and stretch, pushing aside the concern for Reuel—the hair loss could just be another side effect of her medication or the stress of dehydration and illness. That's probably it. I kick aside my bundle of blankets, agreeing with Cori, "Yeah."

Solaina swears under her breath, but it lacks fire. "Why are we awake already? What time is it, like five?"

"No, Grumpy." I get up, walk over to the closest window to lift the shades, washing the room in buttery light, but I keep my eyes on Solaina, throwing her a teasing smile. "The sun is up—can't be too early."

She begrudgingly returns my smile, yawning. "Well, I'm tired. Had nightmares all night. Some creepy voice . . ."

"A voice?" Cori asks, going still, her smile falling. "Saying what?"

We all look at her and she says slowly, "I had nightmares too—someone was trying to get me to *do* something. . . . I just don't remember what."

A shudder ripples through me. "Solaina?" I say.

She shakes her head. "I don't really remember either, but I feel, uh, like a little weirded out."

The sun is shining in my left eye, blinding me, and I glance outside, actually looking this time, and let out a gasp. I go up on tiptoe, lean closer to make sure what I'm seeing is real. "Oh my God . . ."

"What?" Cori is beside me before I can answer. We clutch at each other, wordlessly, even as August and Solaina ask, rush over, look out too. Reuel stays on the couch, still sleeping soundly. Four of us stare out, in shock.

"Are they . . . dead?" Solaina breathes.

We gape at the Boudreaus' pristine green lawn and thriving landscaping. And littered across the grass, birds, fallen out of the sky. Necks twisted at odd angles.

It's like with Reuel's houseplants, but ten times worse.

Robins. Blue jays. An oriole. A finch. Dead.

August whirls away and runs up the stairs, calling for Georgina, her voice shrill.

"What happened?" I ask, gaping at the deadness of things.

"Look." Solaina points, tapping her oval fingernail against the glass. Terror drips from her voice. "Look at the neighbors' yard. No birds."

We crane our heads to peer over that way, to the right, then to the left.

The land on either side is untouched by whatever did this.

It's only the Boudreaus' that is tainted with death. Wrong.

Cori is crying silently by my side. I take her hand and hold it tight, giving her whatever strength I have while taking on some of hers. Fear is a kick in my gut. "This is bad," I whisper.

Bad might be an understatement. Dead birds. Dead plants. Reuel's hair falling out. What else—

"Georgina's not here," August calls from the top of the staircase. "Her parents are sleeping, but the side door is wide open. Get up here. *Now*."

One breath, shared. One look.

As I turn toward the couch, Reuel rolls over, still sleeping soundly.

There is dried blood, crusted from her nose.

Solaina swears again, darting over to her, checking her, waking her, while I stand, panicked, like a coward.

Reuel sits up, bleary-eyed, throat raspy. She rubs at her eyes, swipes at her nose. She looks like a hot mess . . . but she's here.

Georgina is gone.

CHAPTER TEN

Soon after the police arrive at Georgina's house, they send us girls away—as family, only Cori is allowed to stay, wrapped in her dad's arms, her own mother clutching Ms. Kate's hand as she sits, in shock. Mr. Boudreau looks wooden, too stunned to even blink. There are looks of concern, whispers I catch as the girls and I gather our things to go. If Reuel had an illness, a virus, does that mean Georgina got it too? That she's hallucinating right now? Blacked out somewhere, feverish and lost? Could we all catch it, since we've been spending time together? There is talk about making a list of symptoms, putting something up on the school website for students to watch out for. I walk out the door with this last thing ringing in my ears.

Only, I can't help thinking that it's not as simple as an illness, despite Reuel's obvious symptoms. And if that's the case, then what in God's name happened to those birds?

Reuel's dad picks her up immediately, shaking his head, tight-lipped. I don't ask them for a ride home. Reuel throws me a stricken glance as she climbs into his car, her face paper white, all traces of that bloody nose gone. But I can tell—she feels like shit. It's not hard to find the space to worry for her, even though Georgina fills up so much room. Will Reuel throw up again when she gets home? Will she tell her dad what happened last night?

My mom doesn't answer her phone to get me, so I get a ride with Solaina. She insists, but Marisa barely speaks as she drives, her hands clenched around the steering wheel, actually passing the road to my house because she's so spaced out.

"Mama," Solaina says in a small voice, thick with emotion. "You missed the turn."

Marisa shakes her head a bit, as if coming back to the present. She looks up, meeting my eyes in the rearview mirror. Silent tears streaming down her face. "I'm sorry," she whispers in anguish, to both or neither of us—I'm unsure.

"It's fine," I tell her. But she only tightens her hold on the wheel and does a U-turn. We drive the rest of the way in silence. I sit in the backseat, leaning my head against the cool leather, their car smelling like coffee and hair products, Marisa's black apron folded neatly next to me, the tiny logo face up: MARISA'S BEAUTY BAR. I know how many years she worked to get that salon, and pride fills me on her behalf, even alongside the pain of Georgina's disappearance.

By the time they drop me off, all I want to do is sit on the porch and smoke a cigarette in my misery, but my lighter won't work. I push open the front door to grab a different one from the junk drawer and I'm greeted by a burning smell. I run through the kitchen to find my mother passed out on her bed, her curling iron sitting on her dresser left on, singeing a scrunchie too close to it, almost, almost catching it on fire. She could have burned herself and the house up, and I would have come home to the charred bones of it all, and then I would have been really,

really alone. I have to force myself to breathe. To not lose my mind at the what-ifs. *A fire, a fire, eating her alive.*

I hate her ten million thousand arrows in this moment. A horrible part of me thinks if she hadn't been drunk the night of our birthday, I would never have left Reuel's house.

I yank the cord out of the wall and toss the scrunchie in her bathtub, opening the window to clear the space with fresh, humid air. And then I slump to the floor and lay my head against my knees, and while my mama dreams off her liquor haze, I think about Georgina. Her laugh, her red dresses, her perfect hair and perfect nails and perfect skin. I keep thinking about how I hated her a little for the last couple of years, and how I only just got her back, and don't want to lose her again. I think about the smell of glue and new pencils. About her shining hair when she sat in front of me in seventh-grade English, how she would twist in her seat, prim little smile on her face, before turning around, refusing to talk during class. I keep picturing her driving around town in her silver car, sunnies on. I cry, and it hurts my chest. But Reuel came back. Won't Georgina?

August calls all of us to hang out at her place on Sunday afternoon, while we wait on plans to find Georgina. Or for news. I feel like I'm drifting through a bubble, a dream, a nightmare, as I ease my way up the steps to August's fine house. This is surreal, it's not even happening. It can't be. Georgina is missing, just like Reuel was. How could she go missing too?

When Louis answers the door, I nod up at him. "Hi."

"Hey." He reaches out, leaning down to hug me, his good cologne and boy scent enveloping me. I follow him inside as he strides on his crutches.

The house is warm, Ms. Camille in the kitchen in her white-and-walnut-striped apron as she pops some kind of batter in the oven, looking troubled. But who wouldn't be troubled right now? She doesn't even seem to notice us as we pass and go into the living room.

August, crumpled tissue in one hand, is wrapped in an older-than-her blanket her grandmother Mimi crocheted many years before she passed away. Solaina is slumped on the floor with her head in her hands. Reuel just sits there in an overstuffed green chair, like she's numb. But when I come into view, something in her seems to break open. She lets out a cry and her face shatters. I go straight to her and clutch her to me, and she shakes in my arms, her body feeling slight and wispy, like she could blow away. I pull away, staring into her shadowed eyes. The skin below them is purple, bruised-looking. Her cheeks hollow.

"You throw up more?" I ask in a croaking voice.

Reuel shakes her head. "I'm okay."

But her lips are chapped and her skin is drier than it was yesterday, looking patchy and rough. It's so unlike her normal, dewy complexion. I want to offer her lotion. ChapStick. Electrolytes. A hot meal. Something rich and butter-laden. Shrimp and grits. I want to take care of her.

August blinks rapidly, trying not to cry. Louis doesn't move from her side but strokes her back, an A+ boyfriend. Jesse is nowhere to be found, not that I'd expect him to be with us.

A phone rings in the kitchen, and we all jump. Ms. Camille goes to answer it, turning away from us to hiss into the other end. "Stop it! I said no. Quit calling me." She hangs up abruptly, and when she meets my eyes she pauses. "Spam caller." Then she calls out thickly, "Sterling, come on, help me with this food, please?"

August's dad passes through the den, wearing a familiar and

beloved Saints T-shirt, pausing to kiss his daughter's head and give us all a grim smile before he joins his wife in the kitchen. He gently sets his hand on her denim-clad hip and leans down to whisper in her ear. She shakes her head, upset, and I turn away to give them privacy.

I can't force down any of the food they eventually bring in, unable to swallow with this fear clogging my throat.

"This is so stupid." I run my fingers through my tangled hair, agitated. "I hate not knowing where she is. Or what really happened—is she sick like you were?" I ask Reuel, mentally tacking on: like you *are*.

"I'll just say what I'm thinking." Solaina frowns. "Could it be something worse—a kidnapper, maybe? Taking teenage girls and drugging them or something to *make* them sick—and it's just a strange coincidence that it happens to be two of our friends who've been targeted?"

Louis shifts nervously, his hands protectively holding August tighter, and the rest of us exchange wary glances.

"There weren't drugs in my system . . . ," Reuel says slowly, but there's an uneasiness on her pale face.

August's phone rings, and she shrieks, fumbling to answer it.

By her expression I know. It's Cori. August presses the speaker button, and we lean in, collectively holding our breath—if anyone would have an update on Georgina, it would be Cori. She's been at the Boudreaus' all night. It could be info on a search party—surely we'll do that for Georgina. Surely the town will come together once more, like with Reuel. Someone already even mentioned calling in hounds to track her.

Except—

Cori crying on the other end. Fear climbs up my throat. Snatches my words in its claws. I hold my breath, bracing for bad news. Louis grips August to his side like she'll wilt if he lets go. Beside me, Reuel is shivering, her teeth chattering.

She's dead she's dead. Just like the birds. The plants. Dead. Dead—

"They found her," Cori sobs, barely articulate over the line. "She's alive."

I find a breath. My voice. I cry, grabbing at the girls around me. "Thank God."

In the other room, a soft thud. We turn to find that August's mom has fainted from the relief.

Georgina is released from the hospital following monitoring and an IV drip, and on Tuesday, we head over to her house after school—except Solaina, who had to stop at the salon and do something for her mom first. Reuel, Cori, August, and I gather in Georgina's bedroom, a room I didn't even see last time I was here. It looks mostly the same as when we were thirteen—a large, tidy rectangle with vintage-style wallpaper dotted with tiny rosebuds. White canopy bed made up with fluffy bedding, but now it's been upgraded to a tasteful taupe duvet instead of the rainbow stripes I remember from three years ago. There's the same huge French-style full-length mirror. Closet stuffed full of pretty dresses and expensive jeans. Books—almost strictly historical romance and nonfiction—organized by author, her desk with a computer, iPad, paper trays for keeping schoolwork neat. A linen pinboard, new since last time, which reminds me startlingly of my own—though hers is much more *aesthetic*.

I turn to Georgina, waiting. We all wait. Who will ask first? She didn't even have to stay that long in the hospital, and she'll be back at school tomorrow, but she still looks like hell. And . . . and . . . I force myself to keep my eyes on her puffy, strangely oily face.

Instead of elsewhere.

She sits in her bed, propped up on the pillows.

"So you don't remember *anything*?" August asks, her uniform unrumpled even after a full day of school, the blouse ultrawhite, her black stockings embroidered with vines, her heeled oxfords shining.

"I remember the sleepover," Georgina answers thoughtfully. "I remember all that. Then we went to sleep."

"And then?" Cori nudges gently.

"Then nothing," Georgina says. She meets Reuel's eyes.

Reuel nods, voice gravelly. "Same with me."

I already knew that. But it's still disconcerting to hear. I start, frustrated, "But—"

"Honestly, I don't wanna talk about it. It was bad enough that it happened," Reuel says, adding, quieter, "Twice." With a weighted look at Georgina, she pushes off from the side of the bed, folding her arms across her body. Shivering again. Reuel's always cold now. Ever since that night of the burning fever.

"I mean," Georgina adds thoughtfully, "not *nothing* nothing. I woke up before the hospital once. . . . Everything else is like a black hole in my memory. But it's crystal clear, this part, anyway. I remember opening my eyes and staring up at the sky. Smelling the ocean."

A jogger found her on the beach, caked in sand, her little nightie damp with salt water, the skin below her eyes bruised and shadowed. And her hands . . .

I say, a little hesitantly, "Solaina mentioned the idea of,

like, a kidnapper. Is it possible it could be something like that? Someone who *took* the two of them?"

"The police said no signs of abduction." With frustration pulling her mouth down, Georgina says, "You can stop talking about Reuel and me like we're not here. *We're here.*" Indignantly, she adds, "And I think I'd remember if I were taken. I wasn't taken. Don't you think you girls would have woken up if some stranger snatched me from my own house?"

She's so impassioned, so sure, it gives me pause. It does make sense . . . that she left on her own. But still. What about the rest of it?

August bites her lip. "This is freaking me the hell out, and I'm not the only one. My mama isn't sleeping, she's so worried. I caught her wandering around the kitchen at midnight, trying to make tea—the kettle wasn't even on."

"Mine's been hovering like you wouldn't believe," Georgina says, with slight scorn. "Surprised she's not up here now, in bed beside me."

"She was scared for you," Reuel points out. "We all were."

"I know." Georgina sighs, softening. "But I'm all right. It's just a virus—"

"I know that's the easy answer, G, but I don't think you were both just feverish, and happened to wander off," August says, almost apologetically—like *she* doesn't even want to believe there's an alternative reason. She addresses the rest of us. "Do we really think they're *just* sick?"

An involuntary shudder when I remember Reuel in my room that night she returned from wherever she'd been. That unsettling smile on her face. The way she threw up and threw up and threw up, until I thought she'd turn herself inside out. Her eyes unfocused. I peer out the window, which faces the backyard.

Stare at the pool, the stillness of it, the unmoving trees, dotted with magnolia blossoms. The dead birds have all been cleaned up, but I still see them in my mind. I hear myself finally say, "No, I don't think that's it. But they do seem sick, too."

"I feel fine," Georgina insists as I turn around, her smile too bright. Full of denial. She pulls her blanket up a bit, then flexes her bandaged fingers atop it, as though daring us to mention them.

"I mean, if Reuel caught it first, then Georgina got it from her," Cori offers. "My mother was hesitant to even let me come here." Her cheeks grow red and she mumbles, "She thinks y'all will give me the illness or something or—"

"Girls." Solaina darts in, almost tripping over the threshold into the bedroom, her hands visibly shaking, her car keys clinking together.

"What's wrong?" I ask when she sinks into a chair, blowing out a breath, putting her head between her knees.

"Uh, Solaina?" August is watching her with a look of concern.

Solaina pushes her wild curls out of her face and looks up at us.

"This is gonna sound crazy . . . ," she starts. "But I almost drove into a fucking curb."

"Solaina—" I say, startled.

"That's not the crazy part. It's that I kinda, like, blacked out while I was driving. And I saw stuff. Stuff I don't recognize. There was a dark room, and I could smell a fire burning, and a bunch of papers, scattered on a table. I looked down and saw some shit on the floor, like, those grasses or whatever they used to cover floors in the olden days."

"Rushes?" The word pops into my head. My voice sounds raspy. "You had, like, a vision."

"A vision." She jerks her head in something resembling a nod. "Yeah."

"I—uh—I had something like that, the night Reuel came back," I whisper, watching their eyes all widen degree by degree. "I didn't say anything. It sounded too weird."

Georgina opens her mouth, then closes it.

"You had a vision too?" Solaina blinks. "Of what?"

Flushing, I explain as best I can about the flash of images I got while I was on my balcony. Then I ask, "Anyone else? August?"

She shifts from foot to foot, nervously smooths her skirt down, as if she needs something to keep her hands—and thoughts—busy. "I didn't see things like you guys. I had a bad dream on our birthday, is all. It didn't seem like a big deal, you know? Just a dream."

I glance at Reuel. She meets my eyes and I wonder how she could look even worse than she did five minutes ago. Her face is too pale and drawn with confusion.

"Anyone else?" I ask, almost afraid to hear the answer. There are varying degrees of agreement on the nightmares. Both Cori and Solaina had one the night of the sleepover though only Solaina and I had "visions." But two seems like two too many. What's happening?

"August is right. This doesn't feel like a sickness," I say out loud. "This feels like something bigger."

"I think y'all are reaching," Georgina says, looking at each of us in earnest. "So what if we had some bad dreams? That night, I just slipped out. Obviously I was ill. And my stomach has been bad . . ." She trails off, placing a gentle hand on the swollen mound beneath the covers.

"Okay, G." Solaina stares at Georgina. "But how do we explain that?"

We purposely don't look at Georgina's hands. But we know what she means.

August lets out a somber whisper. *"Oh."*

I turn to see what she's looking at. Reuel, now. Sitting in front of Georgina's old-fashioned wooden vanity with the round mirror, raking through her dull hair with trembling fingers, a clump of strands woven through her hands. Falling on the floor, dozens more than what fell out on her pillow at Georgina's. Hundreds more. Laying part of her scalp bare. She is crying, tears trailing down her pale cheeks, her face shattered.

I move to her side, take her wrist. Softly push it downward, unthreading the strands from her cold fingers. She doesn't resist. Boneless now. Frail.

"Something is wrong with me," she whispers into the mirror. Her eyes filled with terror. "And I'm so hungry . . . but I can't eat. My throat is burning like fire."

"You're okay." I sweep back her hair from her cold forehead. Push a clump of it on the floor away with my foot. It can be swept up later. "You're okay," I tell her. Will her to be. I glance behind me at Georgina. She isn't so calm now, gripping the duvet, holding her breath as she watches Reuel, frightened.

"Water," Solaina says, handing Reuel her sticker-covered aluminum bottle.

Reuel tips her chin slowly, taking a sip. When she closes her eyes and exhales even more slowly, I look at our friends, staring at us, wide-eyed and afraid. I channel some bravery I don't have. Stand up straighter, pressing my hand against Reuel's back, anchoring her.

I lock eyes with Georgina.

Don't look at her hands. Don't look at them, I tell myself, even as Georgina releases her covers to clutch at her belly, like she's in pain.

The raw stubs of her fingers, bandaged up to cover where her fingernails were ripped out. Clawed out. Fallen out. We don't know.

We know almost nothing.

But we are all terrified. I know that much.

Back home, I grab my phone and burrow into my bed to retreat into my despair even if it's only six o'clock or so. I forget all about schoolwork, all about the laundry I need to switch over before it goes sour in the wash machine, all about everything I should do besides wallow. I've been scrolling mindlessly for close to two hours when a notification dings. Too eagerly, I swipe up my phone for messages, but it's Solaina, not Reuel.

> I need to talk. Can I call u?

> Of course

When the phone rings I answer right away.

"Isabeau?" She sounds panicked.

"What's wrong?" My tone rises an octave, automatically, and I push myself upright.

"I . . . sorry, I'm safe." She seems to be calming herself, breathing slow and deliberately. "But I think someone was following me."

"What?" I ask sharply. "What happened? Where are you?"

"Nothing *happened.* I've been home for a while. I just went to get the mail and I felt someone out there, watching me. I turned around and nobody was there. But someone *was*. I could feel it, the hair on the back of my neck stood up and I got chills. I've got them now thinking about it."

Even as warm air blows in from the open balcony doors, goose bumps erupt across my skin. I remember that feeling. The night Reuel came back, when I'd smoked on my balcony, I was convinced there was someone out there in the wild dark. Someone coming for me. I brushed it off, but I don't think I can anymore.

I don't think we *should* brush it off. "So . . . ," I start, then falter. What now? "What are you thinking about all of this?"

"Honestly? I'm wondering if it's all connected," Solaina says. "The birds, the plants, Reuel and Georgina, sharing visions . . ." Her pause is weighted. Her voice goes softer when she continues, "And whoever I felt watching me tonight, they didn't feel friendly."

"Yeah," I whisper, not wanting to believe it. Except I pull up that feeling I had as I stared out from my balcony into the night, and the fear returns, making me shudder involuntarily. "It felt . . . ominous."

Hungry, I don't say.

I pick at a loose thread on one of the patches of my lavender quilt and bite my lip, hating how scary this all sounds. "We've gotta figure out what's going on, but in the meantime, what do we do?"

"We should tell everyone not to go off anywhere without a buddy. That goes for you too, Iz. Quit walking your ass alone all over Sorrow, got it? Call me if you need a ride—I know you still need to schedule your road test, but I've got my license now. I'll borrow the car if my parents don't need it."

"You got it." A ghost of a smile touches my lips at her caring.

After chatting for a few minutes, we say goodbye. I sit for a long time, settling my nerves before I get up from my bed and go lock my balcony doors. Heat lightning streaks the sky. It's going to rain soon. The humidity is thick, heavy. I peel off my overshirt and pull my staticky hair off my neck, then take out my cheap lightning bolt earrings, which I've had on all day. My earlobes feel sore and itchy. I nestle the earrings in the empty brass seashell dish on my dresser, beside my cigarettes, and then go downstairs.

In the quiet kitchen, I make myself tea to ground my body, skipping honey and milk like I usually take it. I microwave a macaroni and cheese dinner—all I have the energy for now— which is surely, *at best,* a five out of ten, but I jazz it up with shredded cheese and extra butter and pepper. I take it and the tea back upstairs, to have dinner alone in my room—which is somehow less lonely than having to eat at the kitchen table by myself. I pause at my open door. Hesitantly, I peek around my doorframe, like someone might jump out and get me, but I'm alone. I shake my head as if I can remove my anxious thoughts, and grab the yearbook from art class, bringing it to my bed to browse through it, get my mind off things while I spoon too- hot, too-mushy macaroni into my mouth. The cover of the year- book is an embossed dark red, with silver stamping. *Our Lady of Sorrow, 1998–1999,* it says. Mrs. Jean was right on the date—she'd referred to the funny haircut inside as a nineties style.

I flip through, ripping out photos that look interesting. A floppy-haired freshman throwing peace signs. A girl with big curls, smiling toothily at the camera, her brows pencil thin. A couple slow dancing, the girl wearing platforms and a swishy short skirt, her eyes closed. It makes me think about the dance coming in a few weeks—Spring Fling. Will we be immortalized like these kids were, captured in some book only to be ripped out decades later? I sip my tea, and it crosses my mind—my mom went to high school then, didn't she?

I go to the back of the book and find her name—Lena Sawyer. Then flip to the first listing. On page eighty-six a girl's face stares back at me and my breath catches.

She looks so much like me here at this age. Both our noses a little too long but turned up at the end in a cutesy way; eyes the color of sticky amber. Her hair then was warmer than my natural dishwater brown—before she started highlighting hers and I chose the more-colorful-the-better route—but otherwise we could be sisters. I've seen a couple of photos of her when she was younger: baby pictures, some from childhood, even from her teen years. It's just that . . . here she looks . . . unburdened. Happy. My throat lumps up, my eyes stinging. I could rip her photo out, but I can't bring myself to. I'm not gonna plaster her into a collage. It's too close. Too personal. And I know we look alike—but I hate when other people say it. We may look the same but we aren't the same. I turn the page, moving on. A rumble of thunder from outside. I tear out a photo of a guy in a baggy striped T-shirt doing a cartwheel in the hallway, bystanders laughing, and I add it to my pile.

"Izzy."

I jump, jerking to attention as I look up at my open door. "Mama."

She stares, eyes sharp, zeroed in on the yearbook. "Where did you get that?"

"The book? It's from school. For my art class." I try to smile and tell her, "I just saw your picture in it . . ." *You looked happy. You looked young. You looked like me.*

"What picture?" Her words go a little sharp. She's holding her breath, skin washed out against her black salon outfit.

"This one?" Turning back to it, spinning the book around, I show her the shot of her.

I can actually *see* her body relax in relief.

I eye her, confused. What's the big deal? It's just a photo. Then I remember—she told me once her yearbooks were all lost. Was that the truth? Why on earth would she lie about it, though? "Why are you being weird?" I ask suspiciously.

"I'm not." She shakes her head. Walks in and sets a mug on my nightstand, avoiding my stained rug. Her smile is too bright. "I made you some hot cocoa."

I look at the drink in surprise and see that she didn't fully mix it. I glance back up at her. "Mama? What?"

"Nothing," she answers, averting her eyes.

As she walks away, I flip to the back again, quickly scan the page numbers. On 145 I find a different picture of her and suck in my breath. It takes a second for my brain to catch up to what I'm seeing. *This one.*

"Oh," I hear myself saying. She whirls at the door, coming back to my side, hands wringing. Aware that I've found something.

I stare at the photo of my young mother, standing with a group of girls. The shot is a bit blurry, but I can make out some of them—even though they were teenagers here.

Besides, their names are in the caption.

Camille James, Kate Baptiste, Marisa Oliveira, Lena Sawyer, Beth Baptiste, Sutton McBride.

It's our mothers, all of them, together. All this time. All these years. They've been keeping this from us.

They were friends.

CHAPTER ELEVEN

"**Y**ou were friends," I accuse. "This is what you didn't want me to see?"

She goes still, almost afraid. "It's not . . . we weren't—it doesn't matter."

"Doesn't it? In twenty years will I say *my* friends don't matter?" I ask bitterly.

Wincing, she replies, "I didn't mean it like that. And we weren't even friends, not really. It's just a picture. That's all."

I ignore her protest. Looking back at their arms slung around each other, the happy smiles, how close they're all squeezed in together, I almost can't believe it. I knew they'd each grown up in Sorrow, but all this time, it seemed like they disliked each other, at least some of them. All the years of uncomfortable conversation, when they'd have to drop one of us off for a sleepover, pick one up, when they'd be stuck standing together on a front stoop, avoiding eye contact. Making excuses not to have to talk, even sometimes, some of them, pretending not to know each other. And then, back at the Scouts club when we were searching for

Reuel, how they'd argued in the hallway, then embraced. There was an intimacy in those actions—I *saw* it.

I count them out in wonder once more. "You look like *best* friends."

"Well, we weren't," she snaps. Her face closes, and she busies herself straightening up my dresser, avoiding my gaze. Almost knocking over a candle, her hands trembling. I have a sudden sense she'd like to snatch the yearbook from me.

"What, Mama?" I get off the bed and stand, studying her. "What's wrong with you?"

"It's nothing. It just startled me, I guess." I watch her swallow. Her eyes dart again to the book splayed out on my bed. To the girls on the page. Is that why they don't talk about it? Because it hurts too much—the same way I felt when I lost my own friends? Certainly, I can understand that. I can sympathize.

I soften. "What happened with you all?" I ask.

"It was a bad time in my life, and they were a big reason why." She turns away and sighs, inching closer to leaving. Like she can't wait to get away from me and my questions. "We had a falling-out, I suppose. Most of them moved away not long after—for college, to start their lives. And I thought maybe we'd have a reconciliation when everyone came back—"

I nod, knowing that part, how they all were born in Sorrow but most left. Then returned. She turns back and her eyes hold such sadness it hurts to see. But I look closer, narrowing my gaze. *Is* it sadness, though? It looks almost like paranoia. Like fear.

"Well, you never mentioned you *were* friends." I know I sound wary. I can't help it.

"You're reading into it. Don't romanticize it. We weren't *really* friends. We aren't now."

"Okay," I say, then I have to ask. "Were y'all talking about Reuel that day at the Scouts club?"

"Of course, we were worried about her. What else would we be talking about?" Her tone is slightly cold. But I can hear how her voice wavers.

Then she's done. She hurries back downstairs and I listen carefully. When she puts on her gloomy music playlist, I know she's reaching for her vodka. I know she's making herself forget something. Maybe losing her friends. But it's not that it made her sad, like I initially assumed. It's more than that. Talking about them seemed to scare her. Knowing that *I* know about them scared her.

And her reaction about their conversation in the hallway, I guess it makes sense, if there's some shared dramatic history they were rehashing, because it wasn't just that they seemed worried for Reuel—it seemed like something more personal to them.

I look again at the picture, but what am I supposed to *do* about it? I can't think anymore, so I kick off my skirt and yank my bra through a shirtsleeve, leaving them in a heap on the floor. I'm too uneasy to sleep, but I put pajamas on, and do my best to try. But after a long while, I give up, get out of bed. Then I pick up my sketchbook, hesitate before walking to my balcony door, remembering Solaina's call, the chills that ran over my body at the way she described someone watching her, the way I remember it feeling the other night. Slowly, I unlock and open the door and peer out, the wind already howling, fighting for attention with my mom's playlist downstairs. But there's nobody out there. Nobody but me. I sit in my wicker chair, but I'm too tense to draw, so I set the book aside and instead light a cigarette, keeping my eyes fixed on the dark horizon. Within minutes I see something.

The moon is a scythe slicing through the black night, casting just enough light that I can make out the girl cutting across the lawn toward my house, in a black long-sleeve top and shorts. In disbelief, I unfold my legs, rise from the peeling chair slowly, rustling the potted plant by my knee. I watch her, my surprise turning to anger, heat turned up the closer she gets. I'm mad, so I clamp my lips shut, look up again at the sliver of moon instead of at Reuel, and ask for patience.

The clearing that leads to my house is green and wide open. I'm not worried about anyone jumping out at her, but bad things happen on familiar ground all the time. Good people get hurt all the time, and bad people get away with all kinds of horrible things. I cannot believe she would walk here, in the dark, alone. Not after what happened to both her and Georgina.

The air is perfumed with jasmine and heat, the humid midnight air kisses the uncovered skin on my arms, as if the wind is trying to soothe me. Resting my palms on the twisted rail surrounding the square of balcony, I squeeze the iron, trying to release some of the frustration running through my body. After a deep breath, I look down again, watch her move closer until she's just below me, face tipped up to where I stand on my creaky vantage point.

I open my mouth to ask what she's doing here, *why*, but no words come out.

"Hi," she calls up.

I don't answer for a moment. Then I ask, "Should I come down?"

"No. She's still awake," she says in her low voice, eyes darting to the first floor. There's one window throwing yellow light onto the grass. "It's not that late."

"It's late enough," I mutter. No other light reaches us; the neighbors are too far off to make much of a difference even if their houses weren't all dark. I look again at the brightness streaming from my mama's room. "She's probably passed out by now."

Reuel bites her lip, voice a scratchy whisper. "I'll just climb up. I don't feel like talking to anyone but you."

I peer down as she grips the trellis and digs her black combat boots into the exact right spots to find a foothold and scale the trellis. We have gone up and down together many times, the path is far more familiar than it is treacherous, but tonight, she eases herself up slower than normal. When she reaches the top, I step back, allowing her room to swing her bare legs over the railing. There's bruising, and I swear I can count the veins running along her thighs, a network of bluish lines under her white skin. I can't help staring.

"So?" I finally demand, lifting my chin to glare up at her. "Why are you over here at this hour? Alone?"

"I needed to see you." Her reply is feeble, soft. Maybe apologetic, or maybe I'm just wanting her to sound contrite. And is she breathing faster than she should?

"So you decided to walk over in the middle of the night? After you *literally* almost died?" I stare at her, the anger dissipating as the tears prick my eyes. "How could you risk yourself like that after what just happened to you and Georgina? What if Solaina was right—what if you *were* taken?"

Before she can answer, I push past her and through the green louvered doors into my room. She follows slowly, her expression regretful.

"I'm sorry. You're completely right." She sits on the bed, then says, almost to herself, "I don't wanna be afraid anymore. I just . . . I needed to do something normal, to prove I could."

"I understand," I say, "but I don't care what the police or doctors say, I don't care what you think about this being all tied up and done. I don't think it is. And what will your dad say when he wakes up and you're gone? Didn't you think of that?"

"I was gonna go home before he woke up."

"Walking alone, again?" I shake my head. "Damn, Reuel, have some sense."

She's crying now, and she flops back on my quilt. "I know."

"Listen." I hesitate a moment. "I talked to Solaina tonight— she felt like someone was following her earlier. And I swear I felt something like that too, the night you came back."

Her chapped mouth gapes open, one corner split, flecks of dried blood there. "What?"

"You have to *swear* not to walk anywhere alone anymore. Not until we figure out what's going on. It's too risky."

"I promise not to do it again. I just needed to see you."

"Why?"

"Why do I need a reason?" She brushes at her eyes. "You're my best friend."

Her words soften my anger again. Because obviously it's just fear for her. I say, "As your best friend, I'm gonna kick your ass if you walk across town at night alone again. I'll also tell the other girls, and if you think I'm mad, just wait until there's *five* of us yelling at you."

A little laugh. "Can I stay? We can watch something? Hang out?"

"Sure. I wasn't planning to sleep or anything."

"You weren't sleeping. You were just being all melancholy on your balcony."

I narrow my eyes. "I was . . . drawing."

"Liar."

"Fine. I was smoking and *thinking* about drawing." Scowling, I move to my dresser to light a few candles, the flames throwing shadows around the nearly dark room, then replace the lighter in its spot next to my dish of earrings and my drawing pencils.

I pause, my hand hovering over the lighter, a funny feeling twisting my gut.

The earrings I put there not that long ago are gone. The seashell dish is empty.

"That's weird," I say, low.

"What?"

Frowning at the dish, lifting it to check, I say, "I put my earrings here before, and now they're gone."

"Are you sure?" Reuel asks mildly. Not understanding.

"I'm sure—they were right here." But when I turn from the dish and look at her, something bright catches my eye, on my windowsill.

Swearing, I cross the room and snatch up the neon earrings.

"Those them?" she asks, raising her eyebrows.

I tighten my fingers around them and nod, the posts gouging into my scar. "You don't understand, Reuel," I say. "I set them in that dish. And no—I know what you're thinking. I didn't forget or remember wrong. They were there, and now suddenly they're here, and if I didn't move them . . ." I trail off, hoping she can figure out what I mean.

"You think someone was in your room?" she asks warily.

"I went downstairs to get food . . . so maybe? But I don't know *how*. I locked my balcony doors. And why would they move my earrings?"

"I don't know. Did anything else happen tonight?"

My twinkly lights—the ones I strung from the peaked ceiling—flicker as I remember. The yearbook, waiting on my nightstand. *The picture.* I don't know how it fell out of my mind so quickly.

"What?" Reuel asks. "What's that look on your face? Something else creepy?"

"No, not like that." I drop the earrings and go to grab the book, and I hold it open for her. "I found this earlier. Our mothers . . . they were all friends. I think so, anyway. My mom wouldn't talk about it—swears they weren't close. But here they are."

She stares down at the page, sucking air between her teeth. Looks at me, stunned. "Why would they have kept this from us?"

"I don't know. But it's weird, isn't it? Six friends . . . and their daughters all share a birthday?" Even the words seem to echo in the air of my room. Reuel and I meet eyes, passing silent thoughts back and forth.

"Really weird," she answers slowly. "What did she say?"

"She mentioned a falling-out—something that broke them apart. But she was being sketchy as hell, honestly, so who knows why they don't like each other now."

"I don't care if they don't all like each other," Reuel says, a sharp edge to her words. "I care that they act like they barely *know* each other. Mine never said anything to me. Not once. It feels . . . icky." And she's right—it does. "You tell the other girls yet?" Reuel asks.

"I will right now." She hands me the book and I snap a photo of the picture. I pull up our group chat and send it along. Likely everyone is asleep. I set my phone down and ask, a little helplessly, "Want a midnight snack?"

"Nah," she answers, and looks like she might gag at the thought of food. Then, brighter, she says, "You left your sketchbook outside. It's gonna rain. I can smell it."

"Yeah." I go grab my sketchbook from where I left it on an upturned metal pail. As I turn, lightning flashes and the wind rattles the doors open again, sending chills along my skin, the moon at my back. There's just enough humid, warm air blowing in to push the scent of jasmine through. I lock the doors. Extra sure this time.

I set my art stuff over by my easel, the unfinished portrait on it—poor, neglected girl—I really need to finish it. But it's so hard to focus lately. Reuel generously compliments my work, making me flush, and I give the picture one last glance, promising myself I'll work on it tomorrow.

When I step closer to Reuel I notice goose bumps all over her legs. Sighing, I rummage through my closet, grab a big sweatshirt, and pass it to her without words. She slips it on with a grateful smile, then scoots back, getting comfortable.

"I'll get you some water, at least," I say. "Or some hot tea? It would warm you up. . . ."

"Water is fine, thanks."

While she sprawls out on my bed, I run down to the kitchen to get her the drink. Try to forget about the night she returned, devouring my cigarettes. I left the box upstairs. But when I get to my room, she's reading something on her phone, immersed. My Marlboros undisturbed. I stare at them guiltily. I really should stop smoking.

"I'm gonna brush my teeth," I tell her as I set her water down, and I look around some more, just making sure nothing else is out of place. Everything seems . . . fine. But I can't shake this uneasy feeling. I'm especially grateful Reuel's here—I don't wanna be alone.

She nods and follows me to the bathroom. It's just big enough for a sink and a toilet, and a spare set of toiletries for one frequent visitor. When we were all friends growing up, Reuel was the only one who came over often, Solaina the only other one who stopped by; since our mothers worked together and were such good friends, we grew extra close. But as a group we'd always congregated at Georgina's—it's the biggest, the nicest, the neatest house. Ms. Kate brought in takeout and they had a cleaning lady who came in twice a week and their towels were fluffy and always smelled fresh. If not her house, then August's, which was nearly as fancy and just as clean, and *her* mom actually does bake. Nobody wanted to come to my house. Except Reuel.

She brings up the subject of the dance, and I open my mouth to ask if she'll even be well enough to attend Spring Fling—she got winded just walking here, and she still isn't recovered enough to go to cheerleading—condemned to the bench for the time being, until she works up her strength again. And those bruises all over her body disappear. The hollows in her cheeks. Her hair falling out. But I say nothing. Just squeeze some toothpaste onto my toothbrush.

"I can't believe you still don't have anything to wear," she says, trying to sound easy, light. As though nothing has changed.

"It's fine." I shrug. It's hard to get excited for the dance when all these things are happening that we don't understand. But I know she's looking forward to it. "I mean, I won't be August, but I'm sure I'll be okay," I add.

"Yeah, August is on a whole 'nother level." Her dry, cracked lips turn into a smile. "Did she show you the picture of what she's wearing?"

"Um, I'd look like a roll of tinfoil in that," I say, which makes Reuel snort. "You think you're up for it?" I blurt out.

"Yeah," she answers stubbornly. Then she reaches over,

giving me a big hug, squeezing so tight it takes my breath away, her hair trailing over my shoulder, mingling with my blue. "Are you okay if I stay?"

"Of course you can stay." I break away with a smile. "We'll get up early and stop by your house to get your stuff," I promise, and she nods in gratitude, reaching into the tiny mirrored cabinet and fishing out her toothbrush.

I brush my teeth beside her, stare at us in the reflection, only half of each of our faces visible. Her white skin against my warm ivory, her limp black hair against my blue, her sea eyes, mine a muddy golden hazel, her smile strained beneath the levity.

When she leaves the bathroom, I watch her walk slowly down the hall to my bedroom. She's shivering. I'll have to grab an extra comforter for her from the linen closet. Why'd she walk over here in a pair of shorts if she's always so cold? And it's downright balmy tonight, bordering on hot and sticky—she shouldn't even *be* cold.

When I return to my room, spare blanket heaped in my arms, Reuel's already tucked in on the left side of the bed, her usual spot. She's staring at the movie poster I salvaged from my mom's junk years ago and tacked up on my ceiling along with a couple of others. I count a few cracks in the old plaster, spidering around Romeo and Juliet. What a tragedy that story was. What a tragedy this whole fucking house is. Maybe it's haunted, I suddenly think, only half kidding. Maybe there's a poltergeist who moved my earrings. Maybe that's got nothing to do with . . . everything else.

She points upward. "You start reading it yet?"

"I'm about halfway through Act One, I think." I blow out the candles, climb into my big bed next to her, the fairy lights above us. "I like it, even if I don't understand half of what they're saying."

"It's so cliché, isn't it? Assigning *Romeo and Juliet* for English."

"At least Evan Watts isn't in your English class," I say. "He's *unbearable* about it."

"Yeah." She nods, but there's a heaviness to it.

We keep starting conversations, but they fizzle out. We're both uneasy tonight. Is she thinking about our mothers? Her illness? Something else?

Condensation collects on the side of the water glass I got her, leaving a puddle on the nightstand. She doesn't take a single sip.

Once we say good night and I turn off the lights, Reuel falls asleep easily, but sometime in the night I'm woken by a sharp cry, her thrashing beside me.

"Nooo," she moans. "Don't hurt her—"

"Reuel, wake up," I whisper groggily, and gently shake her. "It's just a nightmare."

She gasps, then jerks away. Curling up into herself, she takes a deep, rasping breath, body shuddering, a sob loosening from her chest. "He was choking her. . . ."

"Hey." I lay a hand on her cool forehead, brush her hair away with the pad of my thumb. "It's okay. It was just a nightmare."

Her eyes narrow. They glint in the dark. Her voice raspy. "Sorry to wake you."

"It's okay." I reach over and pat her, trying to comfort her. She's kicked off the extra blanket, and though she's shivering now, she doesn't complain about the cold. I pull it up for her, and she murmurs a sleepy *Thank you.*

Before long, her breaths fill up the silence once again.

CHAPTER TWELVE

A noise wakes me in the night. Blurry-eyed, I glance beside me; Reuel is bundled up under the covers, asleep, peaceful. I let out a breath of relief—that she's here, safe. That she didn't disappear again. I kick my own blankets off, sweating. There's no air in the room because I've locked up the balcony tight.

Another thump from below, and I cringe, recognizing the sound. My mom dropped something or, worse, maybe fell. I ease out of bed slowly, careful not to disturb Reuel. In the hall I flick on the lights to lead me downstairs, to help my parent into bed, tuck her in like a child. She stayed up all night, drinking alone, I guess. Knocked over a footstool in her room. It's been ages since she's been this bad. And she's gotta work in the morning—she deserves whatever hangover is coming.

As I heave her onto the mattress, helping her out of her house shoes, she slurs, "You're a good girl, Izzy."

I ignore her, when I'd like to scream at her.

"I'm sorry, I'm sorry," she repeats, reaching out with one sloppy hand, tracing the side of my face, my chin. "It's my fault."

I grit my teeth.

When I roll her toward her pillow, she laughs against it, turning her cheek, murmuring, "I'm a mess. You don't gotta take care of me."

I'm tired. It's too early for this shit. "Yes, I do," I say with a sigh. "Sleep well. I'm going upstairs."

Her hand is on my wrist, fast. Her eyes open, and she says, clearer now, "No, not upstairs."

"Mama, what do you mean? I'm going to bed."

"Oh." She relaxes, fingers falling away. "Okay. That's okay."

I pull up her sheet, and she shudders. Her laugh is low and bitter. "That damn book. We never shoulda done it. Shoulda burnt it."

Burnt her yearbook? She told me her yearbooks were all lost.

She looks over at me. Seems to remember I didn't leave yet. Shakes her head, her speech syrupy. "Shh. You don't know. You don't wanna know. You're too good, baby. Love you, my Izzy . . ." She's asleep before she finishes the sentence, mouth gaping open.

Her bedroom smells musty, curtains pulled almost all the way closed, but in the gap between the cotton panels, I can glimpse how gray it is outside, the sky the color of ash, dark clouds hovering. I walk over and tug her window up a little to let some wet air in and the sound of rain fills the room.

Then I leave, the door propped open.

I pee in the downstairs bathroom, then I head back toward the stairs, thoughts reeling. She didn't want me to go upstairs, but where else would I have gone besides my bedroom?

The attic. Stuffed full of old junk, where I never go. Where I'd never willingly go, anyway. A great place to hide something.

She had to have meant the yearbook, and she'd have four years' worth. And people sign yearbooks. The mothers must have signed hers. Maybe if I see what they wrote, everything will be clear.

Back in my room, I settle softly into bed beside Reuel. I'm not going to look for old yearbooks in the attic now—it's barely one a.m. I try to sleep. Lightning cuts through the dark and I jump. Every creak makes me think there's someone coming to get me. But there isn't. Right?

That's not a man's shadow on my wall.

I blink and it's gone.

Pulling up just a sheet, I squeeze my eyes closed, slipping into the world of dreams. Not dreams—nightmares. Violent ones, shattering like glass, foreign voices whispering at me, urging me. But what are they saying? There are words I almost catch—too faint to grasp. I'm not sure I'm dreaming when I hear the sharper urging.

Open your eyes. Open your eyes.

So I do.

Bright light streams in through the windows, and Reuel is nowhere to be found. I'm alone, dressed in my school uniform, sitting placidly on my bed. And my imaginary model is staring at me from her portrait, no longer in three-quarter profile, but facing forward. Her eyes are open, pinned on me, and they're not grayscale any longer, but red.

Bloodred.

I blink myself awake—for real this time. Sit up, staring uneasily across my room, not morning yet, but dawn—no bright light coming in like it was in that nightmare. The patter of rain on the roof, as if God himself is weeping. I was only dreaming, and the portrait is just as I left it on the other side of my room—gray, lifeless. Reuel is beside me, sleeping soundly, her face peaceful, her hand splayed open near her cheek, the tiny scar running across it. I reach out and trace it lightly, and reflexively, like a baby's, her fingers close around mine.

I let my body relax into my pillow, but I'm not going to be able to fall back asleep. I grab my phone—it's only just after five—and push away the memory of the model's red eyes—and read messages that have been sent since I shared the picture from the yearbook. Almost nobody has answered yet, surely still asleep, but there's an "um" and a "that's real weird" from Cori with an exploding brain emoji.

I wait until a generous 5:39 a.m. to wake Reuel, which is as long as I can stand.

"Pghft," she mumbles into the pillow. "Let's skip school today."

"Wake up." I shake her shoulder. "We have to go to my attic."

"Am I dreaming?" She peeks out of the blanket suspiciously.

I crack a smile. "No." Then I explain, "My mom is being funny about things. I want to see if her yearbooks are up there."

"In the attic?" she asks, head tilted.

"Yeah. I mean, I'm curious." I bite my lip in thought. "But I don't want her to know we're looking around."

"Won't she hear us up there?" Reuel asks, stretching. The bruise on her neck has faded to a nasty purple-edged yellow. She catches me looking at it and touches it self-consciously.

"Not if we're quiet. And she's passed out cold. So long as we're done before she's gotta get up for work."

She never misses work, at least that's saying something.

Reuel sits up and rubs her eyes, then freezes, pausing. Staring across the room.

"What?" I ask.

"I just remembered—I had a nightmare."

"Yeah. And?" I wince, realizing that I brushed it off last night, when I was trying to calm her.

"It wasn't a vision—I know I was dreaming," she answers, almost whispering. She clears her rattly throat and points. "I saw her. The girl in your portrait. And I saw hands around her throat. Someone choking her."

Chills run down my arms, up my legs. I tell her what I dreamt—those red eyes. I wasn't scared of the girl, exactly. . . . It almost felt like she was warning me. "Why would we both see the same girl?"

"You dreamt her up, didn't you say?" She wraps her arms around her knees, shivering.

"Yeah. The night of our birthday. The night you disappeared..."

She doesn't say anything for a long time, but I can practically see the gears in her brain turning, working at something. My mind is racing too. Who is this girl—why are we sharing dreams of her? It could be, of course, that it's just because the portrait was here—in our field of vision, the picture tilted toward the bed. That brains do funny things. That you dream of making out with your dentist sometimes, for God's sake.

But I don't think that's it.

Reuel climbs out of my bed and pulls her limp hair into a sleek bun. The black makes her pale scalp stand out more in spots, and the tight way she's slicked it back is only going to stress her hairline, but I say nothing. Even as she gathers some loose strands in her palms and shoves them in my wastebasket, her mouth pinched. I pretend not to notice.

"You still want to go to the attic?" she asks me.

I waver. It seems kind of silly now. But the yearbook sitting out makes up my mind. I'm too curious not to check into our moms' pasts. "Yeah," I say.

Our attic is exactly what you'd expect from an attic—cobwebs and squeaky floor joists and old boxes, totes caked with dust shoved in a corner. A broken rocking chair that's been here since before I was born. The taste of damp heat—the rain has settled into a stifling humidity.

Reuel and I stand together, ready to dig through the junk. I push over an old bicycle wheel with my toe. Who thought that was worth saving?

As we take everything in, Reuel's phone dings. She pulls it out and looks at the screen, mouth turned down slightly. She sighs and swipes away. When she turns to me, she shrugs, though her face is cast in guilt. "Grady. He keeps calling and texting."

"Oh?" I ask, trying to sound casual. "Like what's he saying?"

"Here." She hands over her phone. I read one big block of text.

> Just because we broke up doesn't mean I don't care about you. I can't help but be worried! I just wanna help you reuel please let me. I don't care how mad you get—your worth getting mad I don't even care. i don't care if we even get back together (okay I do) but I'm not gonna just stand by and let you fall apart—

Hastily, I shove the phone back at her without finishing the too-intimate stream of consciousness he has going on there. "I get the idea. So he's worried about you."

"I guess," she says, and then tucks the phone away, as if symbolically ending our conversation about *all that.* She claps her hands together, glancing around. "Where do we start?"

Her skin looks so dry I wonder if it might crack like desert earth—it's obvious she doesn't want to talk about her problems. She wants to worry about something else. For a few minutes I can give her that. Putting aside things I'd like to say, I motion. "Over there, I guess." And I head to the far corner of the room.

We start digging through boxes of my outgrown clothing, one even filled with baby clothes—which my mom always promised she'd sew into a quilt one day. Except she never learned how to sew.

"Aww." Reuel holds up a footed sleeper with pink elephants printed on it. "So cute."

I smile back at her, but it's forced. She's lost muscle—even in the baggy sweatshirt of mine, I can tell. Always lean, now she just looks frail. I'm glad she's had to sit out for cheerleading—there's no way she could keep up.

"You're feeling okay, right?" I blurt out. "It's so hot up here."

"I'm not hot," she answers in a muffled voice, her head down, avoiding my concerned gaze. Her jaw tight. She grabs her phone and puts on a playlist, volume low. To avoid talking? Now I'm probably irritating her as much as Grady. For all our differences, we both care about her. I can't hate him for that.

With a silent sigh, I dig through a new stack of cardboard boxes—all three with framed photos. A sharp sting makes me gasp and I pull my right hand away. A broken piece of glass from a frame sliced me and blood seeps out, running down the heel of my palm.

"What happened?" Reuel's voice sounds funny. "You're bleeding."

"Yeah." I stare down at it. Now I'll have a scar on each palm, I think. It's almost funny. "Just cut it on that glass."

"Did it hurt?" she asks, coming over, reaching with gentle fingers. She takes my hand in hers and I grimace. Her skin is so cold it sends shivers down my spine.

"A little," I say. "It's okay."

Her eyes go unfocused—and for a moment I think she might pass out. I steer her to a clear place to sit.

"Reuel?" I squeeze my fingers into a fist and swallow. There's no air up here, even *I* feel a slight dizziness, but she's gone deathly white—she's sick. I pull off the stretchy headband I'm wearing and wind it around my palm, uncaring about things like germs or pain. Trying to find the words for what I'm feeling. Tightly, I say, "Things aren't . . . right, Reuel."

"I don't wanna talk about it." Her eyes fill with tears. But I'm too worried now to be gentle with her. I hate to even think it—but Grady is right.

"Hey." I blow out a breath and, reaching out to touch her, say, "I'm sorry. You know I'm not mad at you. I'm *scared* for you."

"I know. I'm scared too." Her voice breaks, and she whispers, "I can't eat. I can barely drink. I'm falling apart."

"I won't let you fall apart," I say. "I don't wanna be scared to be honest with you because *you* want to avoid the truth." I force myself to say it: "There's something really wrong with you still, and I think you need to see a doctor again."

"I know," Reuel says, and her eyes are shining, like she's a sentence away from crying again. She adds softly, "And I love how much you care about me."

When she gently slips her hand into mine, matching up our twin scars, my breath hitches. But why? We've held hands so many times. Though maybe it's the look on her face . . . something different. The seconds tick by, and we stare into each other's eyes.

It's so goddamn roasting hot up here. I clear my throat, push my hair off my sweaty forehead. Reuel drops her hand. It's this stuffy attic, making me feel weird.

When I look at her again, she's watching me like she's the one worried now. For me. "You okay?"

"Yeah," I answer, and the dizziness passes. I turn back to the boxes and continue digging.

The next one doesn't turn up anything, and I try not to let it bother me. We still have half the room left, and we're getting through it quickly. We'll have plenty of time to get ready for school and be down before my mom's awake. I cross my fingers we'll find the rest of the yearbooks and whatever it is she didn't want me to find inside them.

The next box is big, and even with Reuel's help, I give up trying to move it, because the cardboard seams are only a few rips away from breaking open. I crouch under the eave and go down to my knees, tearing open the tape and unfolding the flaps.

As she hums along to one of her favorite songs and digs through a bin of newspapers, I pull out a bunch of old periodicals—*Farmers' Almanac*s and junky-looking magazines I'm not sure why anyone would save—I'm guessing a ton of this crap was my grandpa's back when he owned this house, before he escaped to Florida decades ago to make a life out of gambling and dating woman with big hair. I riffle through, unimpressed. I shove aside the last set of magazines to uncover a large book on the bottom.

I stare at the black leather cover, like in some odd way I almost recognize it. But I can't remember ever seeing it. I don't even know what it is. Puzzled, I lift the book from the box, marveling at the weight of it, at the browned edges of papers sticking out the sides, more than one ribbon dangling. It's stuffed full, and I retake a seat on the floor, sitting cross-legged, the book in my lap. I open it, a damp and green smell wafting up, and a language I don't know is scattered across the first several pages. The next page I flip to is yellowed, sewn in after the fact, with a red seam. It has an illustration of a moth, then below that one word stitched into the center in black thread: *Sorrow.*

My whole body erupts in goose bumps, even in this heat.

"Reuel," I say, and my voice sounds unnatural in my ears, tinny.

She drops what she was doing and pushes off from the floor to meet me. Her eyes full of curiosity, the haze from before gone. I stroke the spine and a shiver runs down my own.

"What is it?" She crouches beside me and touches the corner of the book. Her fingernail is chipped. But at least she *has* nails still. Unlike Georgina.

I flip the pages again and again, taking in the words. *A Remedy for Homesickness. To Bring a Lost Cat Home. To Sweeten Affections. To Loosen a Tongue. To Mark a Liar. To Exact Revenge.*

"Spells," I mumble.

I go back to the sewn-in page. *Sorrow.* Skepticism takes over. It couldn't be *hers,* though—Sorrow. This can't be *real.*

Why on earth would my mother have this?

Should've burnt it, she'd said. I thought she meant the year-book. But looking back down at the spell book, I let myself sink into the possibility, because something about it feels real enough to push the skepticism aside. It seems more likely—far more likely—she meant something like this.

That she meant precisely this.

My alarm goes off, and I jump, swearing. Reuel groans, eyes glued to the book. I know exactly what she's thinking. How can we possibly go to school now?

"Come on," I say, standing. Watching how she straightens herself up, wincing. "I can't wait to show this to the girls. I'm going to shower quick, then we'll go. You *are* okay to go to school . . . right? You haven't eaten or drunk anything since you got here."

"I'll try." She sighs. Then, seeing the look on my face, she softens, nodding slowly. "I'll try, okay? I'll try to have something this morning."

"All right." I put the book in one arm and we head down-stairs. I text the others to meet us before school in the courtyard outside the cafeteria. There won't be many—if any—people there then. Not with this miserable weather.

My phone buzzes.

Wtf is going on? August asks. I can almost picture her questioning expression.

I just saw the picture!!! Solaina text-shrieks. *Don't tell me there's more . . .*

I'll show you when you get there is my cryptic answer.

I have something to share too . . . , Cori says. But she doesn't answer any follow-up questions, and I'm deeply apprehensive now.

By seven a.m. I'm showered and dressed for school, and by

five after, Reuel and I are in the kitchen, scavenging for breakfast. I search for something that's palatable to her.

"French toast sticks?" I suggest, digging through the freezer. "Scrambled eggs?"

I swear, her face goes as green as the half avocado spoiling on the counter. Hastily, I offer another option, "Yogurt?"

Reuel politely turns that down as well, sitting at the table like she's out of breath just from the effort to get to the kitchen.

"Toast?" I ask lightly.

When she begrudgingly accepts that, I make us both a piece. I spread them with salted butter and add a liberal dose of cinnamon sugar. Reuel takes her first bite and chews carefully, swallowing and then nodding. "It's good."

She could be appeasing me, but it's still a relief that she seems to enjoy the food. I keep my gratitude quiet—but I feel it all the same—and as we eat, a door groans open. My mama exits her bedroom, dressed head to toe in black, her salon attire somewhat rumpled, just like her. But she's showered and smiling, so there's that.

"Hi, girls." She greets us both, then reaches out a hand and pats Reuel, saying warmly, "I'm glad to see you, honey." Glancing at Reuel's slicked-bun hair, she adds, "Do that color recently? Looks fresh."

She wouldn't be able to see the bald patches the way Reuel's hair is styled. But if she looked closer she'd surely see it's not as thick, not as shining, that there are places near Reuel's temples that are thinning. And doesn't she see how gaunt her cheeks are?

"Yeah," Reuel answers, giving her a sweet smile. Reuel's never weird with my mom, no matter what state she's in. I've seen her carry on a polite conversation with my mother when she was drunk, and then go on like she didn't even mind. For my sake, of course.

"I like it," my mama answers Reuel, pouring herself a cup of coffee from the pot I brewed. I peer over at her, apprehensive, wondering if she'll say something about last night. About the yearbook picture—or anything else. But she just says, in an absent-minded way, "There's cereal, I think." Then goes back to her coffee. She doesn't seem to remember our conversation in her room. Smiling at Reuel, she adds, "You could carry off any color, just like Izzy. I wish some of my clients were that brave. Always the same thing for most of them—"

I jump at the sound of glass breaking and look—the mug in her hand, now broken on the floor, coffee puddling around her feet. "Where did you get that?" she demands in a strangled whisper.

I snap my gaze to where she's staring. On a chair nearest the door, my backpack. And it's open, the corner of the book peeking out—the zipper wouldn't close around it. Shit.

"You said—" I start. Glance at Reuel, who is looking at her, wide-eyed. Reuel gets up from her chair, coming to stand by me, swallowing her bite of toast. I set down my own breakfast, wipe the cinnamon sugar from my fingers.

"Never mind." Mama shakes her head emphatically. She steps over the broken mug—in bare feet—hands outstretched. "Just give it to me."

"Why?" I grab my backpack, clutch it to my chest, and twist out of reach, evading her.

Her mouth goes hard as we face off on either side of the kitchen table. "Isabeau Marie. Give me that. It's dangerous."

"It's just a book," I say without meaning it. Even as I know.

Not just a book. Not *just.* Narrowing my eyes, I ask the smarter question, "Why is it dangerous? What do you mean?"

The look of horror on her face makes me realize it's not the potential for danger that's the issue right now—spells that might do big, scary things. It's a confirmation. I *know* it.

"You did something, didn't you?" I say as it dawns on me. "That's why you're afraid. You did one of the rituals in here."

"No, we didn't," she answers, too quickly. And I hear it. *We.*

She tries to take the book again, but I move away, Reuel at my side, boots clutched in her hand. I don't have to yell at her to follow—she knows without words. I grab her elbow, to help her in case she struggles, and push her out the door, Reuel in her stocking feet, my mom yelling at our backs.

We race through my yard, until Reuel is out of breath and has to stop at the end of the driveway, wincing about a charley horse in her calf. Mama's words echo in my mind the whole time I watch Reuel lace up her boots, even out her breathing.

Not the word *no.*

The word *we.*

We didn't.

And I have a pretty good idea who *we* is.

Backpack against my chest, we continue on, walking now for Reuel's sake, but still just as determined, toward her house first, so she can get ready, then on toward the rest of our friends. To tell them about our mothers. I don't know exactly what they did. But it was something. Something bad.

And I wonder if, in some twisted way, we're paying for whatever that is.

CHAPTER THIRTEEN

At Reuel's house I wait in the living room while Mr. Carson gives her a rightfully earned earful about going out in the night without permission and *insists* she be home for dinner tonight. When she comes out of her room, she's in her uniform, backpack over her shoulder. She throws me a tight smile and whispers, "Let's go."

We head straight to school to meet the girls, and when we arrive everyone is there, assembled in the courtyard.

Cori begins first, her hair chlorine-damp post–sunrise swim. She clears her throat, fidgeting with the yellow SAVE THE BEES key chain hooked on her backpack.

"I was lying in bed this morning—I was drowsy, but awake—I knew my alarm was about to go off, but I wasn't asleep, you know? And I felt a hand touch my face."

Shivers up my spine—shivers *everywhere*—and everyone remains silent.

"I sat up—I bolted up. But there was nobody there."

Then everyone is talking at once, throwing out ideas, words. *Ghost. Hallucinations—the fever?*

I think of my earrings moving. Clear my throat. I don't think it's a ghost. But I do think there's something supernatural at play here.

I'm itching to share the book with them all, but first things first.

"Okay, about the yearbook picture—nobody knew they were friends, right?" I ask, holding my breath a bit. "Nobody ever saw the yearbooks? Or other stuff?"

"Mine never had hers—I think she told me they were lost—"

"—packed away in storage."

"—showed me her class photo, but that's all."

"—never thought to ask, to be honest."

Solaina pulls a paper from her blazer pocket. "When I saw the picture you texted, I couldn't believe it," she says, unfolding the paper, smoothing the creased edges. "And I found *my* mom's yearbook—I wanted to see it for myself."

I thought I had the photo memorized, but I gaze down at the page ripped out from a moment in time, memorializing our mothers, and I learn it all anew.

"I asked mine," Georgina says.

Is it just me or does anyone else notice that there's sweat dripping from her hairline? It's hot out, but still, that's strange—Georgina doesn't even *sweat* normally. She swipes her forehead, her damp upper lip, frowning. Then lets out an enormous, truck-driver-sized belch, making us all flinch.

"Jeez." Cori gapes at her cousin, looking as surprised as the rest of us. I blink. I've never heard Georgina burp in her whole life.

Embarrassed, she pats at her mouth, her fingers freshly bandaged. "I feel better. Excuse me, though," she mumbles, then goes on, "Anyway, she went frozen. And she looked *afraid.* I don't get it."

"We need to just ask them," Cori says, her typical optimism faded—she seems scared, like she can still feel that touch on her face. "We need to *try.* They're hiding more than one thing, I think."

"You're right, Cori," I say. "And I found something that could begin to explain."

They turn to me, waiting. Faces creased in confusion, anticipation, wariness.

"Go on," Reuel says, nodding. "Tell them everything."

"It was bizarre enough that we had the birthday in common," I start, "but now we know our moms were friends. And last night I found proof that there's more. Something magic."

August laughs, loud, and I glance up, meeting her dubious expression.

"I'm serious," I say quietly. Her grin falls and I watch her throat work as she swallows, her eyes going sharp. "I think maybe they somehow cursed us."

I pull my cuff over my hand and wipe the table free of rain, then I pull the book from my bag and lay it out in front of us. "Reuel slept over—she and I found this in my attic."

They stare at the book in silence, then look at me, questions in their eyes.

After a minute, Solaina opens the spellbook, touches the first pages reverently, the metal of her bracelets shining. "It's a book of shadows," she says. "I've heard of these. Do you think . . . uh, it's real?"

"How could it be real?" Cori whispers, almost to herself. Her fingers graze the moth drawn on the page, and she adds uneasily, *"Death's-head."*

"My mom tried to take it. She said it was dangerous," I tell them. "She's been hiding it upstairs in a box of my grandpa's things."

Solaina flips through, staring at the weathered pages. "You think they did a spell?"

"Well, her mom's reaction was *not* normal," Reuel says. "She seemed terrified."

"Yeah," I agree. "And look at yours." I jerk my chin toward Georgina. "You said she was afraid when you asked her if they were friends. They were hiding that, and I'm guessing from how my mom acted that it might have something to do with this book."

"It says Sorrow," Georgina says skeptically. "As in, *the* witch?"

I think of the oil painting of Sorrow that hangs in the library where they keep the special collection related to the myth and history of her. She's thin, with white hair and milky eyes, and looks about a breath away from death—she was *old* when it was painted, even by today's standards. The idea that she was a real witch and had all kinds of powers seems far-fetched.

Suddenly things are clicking into place. And I am decidedly *not okay.*

"It could be the name of the town, and not her," Cori offers, fidgeting. She pulls the hair tie out of her perfectly fine ponytail and completely redoes it.

"Didn't people used to think there was a spell book?" Solaina says. "I remember my great-uncle talking about it. Could this be it?"

We look back at the book.

"But . . ." August hesitates, chews on her lip.

We all meet eyes and I know them well enough to know we're thinking the same thing. The story about Sorrow—the witch, the town. It's *fake.* Nothing but a story. Make-believe. Sure, maybe she was a real person, but a witch?

". . . It's not real," August finishes her thought, adding, "It can't be."

"What if it is." Solaina sets her mouth, today painted a light plum. "And it's all connected—our moms, our birthdays, the nightmares." While they exchange uneasy looks, she waves a hand to Reuel and Georgina. "Whatever is happening now. Maybe we *are* cursed or something, like Iz said."

"But—spells?" Cori helplessly asks. "How can this be real?"

"It can't be." August shakes her head. "Right?"

"There's only one way to find out. We could try one." Georgina's reply is only half joking. Maybe she's right—doing a spell would be one way to tell us if it's real.

"No. No way. We are not doing *shit,*" August replies quickly.

"I didn't mean anything nefarious," Georgina says.

"August, don't worry," Solaina says. "If we do *anything* in here it would be something one hundred percent non-dangerous."

"Solaina," Georgina teases. "Aren't you the one who loves those dark fairy tales?"

"Those are fictional!" Solaina answers.

We smile for a minute before sobering and looking back through the book.

"Why was it at my house, though?" I wonder aloud.

"It should be in a museum," Georgina says thoughtfully. "If only because it's so old."

I take in her appearance. Her puffy face, the smell coming off her breath. Something sickly sweet, almost rotten. I choke down the urge to gag. What is going on with her?

"Um. Have you looked *closely* in here? Shit." Solaina breathes as she flips through the book. Georgina's learned to ignore our cursing by now. Or maybe she doesn't care anymore.

First Solaina glances around, making sure the courtyard is still empty. It's sticky hot, and I thank the weather gods for it because nobody will come out here. *"A Spell for Easing Your Monthly Pains,"* she reads aloud. *"Ritual to Lengthen the Day. To Darn Stockings. To Sharpen Your Kitchen Knife."*

She leans closer, with a look of awe. Then confusion. "This is a strange one. I mean, they're all strange." Her voice rises, sounding tight and funny. August reads over her shoulder.

"But this doesn't look like a spell," Solaina says. "I think it's a recipe." She runs her finger down the page, listing ingredients. *"Stew meat, parsnips, carrots, wild bitter greens, red wine, onion, sea salt, and hemlock."*

She looks wide-eyed at August next to her, then at the rest of us. *"Hemlock.* I've read about that in my botany class. It's really dangerous. This isn't a recipe to feed someone. It's to *poison* someone."

"Wow." August breathes. "What's that note down there?" She points to a different script, slanted near the bottom. I fight the urge to drag the book toward me across the table.

Solaina bends her head, reading out loud, squinting to make out the handwriting. *"Added wine near end to mask the taste and smell—waited until he was half into his ale before feeding. The outcome was as desired."*

Everyone stills, understanding what this is implying.

"So, if this is Sorrow's book, you think she poisoned someone?" I ask, frowning. "I thought she was supposed to be good—she's supposed to be this icon."

"She was said to be powerful, strong," Georgina says. "She may have been iconic, but whoever said she was *good*? And anyway, maybe she *was* good. Just because she wrote this—maybe—it doesn't mean she used it, despite the note at the end. Maybe she never killed anyone."

"Or maybe it was someone who deserved it," Reuel says darkly.

We are silent in our own thoughts.

"I wish we could ditch, so we could keep going through the book," I say wistfully. I can hear more and more people inside—school will be starting soon. "Solaina, wanna read some more of those titles out loud quickly?"

"Some of these are in Latin, I think. I'll read the ones I can, anyway," she mutters. Clears her throat. *"To Still One's Dreams. For a Wish Come True. Blessing for a Good Harvest. Wart Remover. A Tea for Aches in the Teeth."*

"To cure or to cause?" I ask, fully serious.

Solaina cocks an eyebrow, scanning it. "To cure."

"So she mostly wanted to fix things. To make things better," I say. Then add, as if I need to clarify, "Sorrow."

"And a lot of these are simple, everyday things, right?" Reuel gazes at her phone, tapping out a message. She frowns once and turns it back over. "Like she was just trying to make life easier."

"Yeah." Solaina nods and goes on. "Okay, can't read this one. Another tea—this one for quieting the mind . . . Kind of reassuring, knowing even she had anxieties. A spell for easing colic. One simply titled *B.W.* that I can barely read, looks like a binding spell of some sort? Maybe it's French—this word is *Reinette*—sounds like a name. Then there's an incantation to dream of your future lover. More I can't read. This thing is stuffed full." She whistles at the book in admiration, easing it shut when the first warning bell rings.

"But what are we going to *do*?" Cori asks. "We're not really trying a spell, are we? And how can that fix you two, anyhow?" She gestures to her cousin and Reuel.

Georgina chews on her lip. "We need to find out what, exactly, our mothers did first. And maybe we're wrong. Maybe our illnesses have nothing to do with"—she forces herself to say the word—"magic."

"Maybe," I say. But I'm just placating her, and she seems to know it.

"They'll never tell us. Look how freaked out Iz's mom got," August says, scoffing. "And you think mine is gonna tell me about *spells*? Please. She deals in the logical. The real."

"Like you?" Georgina asks, her eyes bright, her face flushed.

"Well. Yeah. But anyway. I know she won't talk."

"And I can't ask mine," Reuel points out. But I can see the sadness in her eyes. We all can. I lean in closer to her, for comfort. "I think the spell book can wait. We need to get answers about what they did . . . if anything."

"Right, we need to force them to admit they were friends and why they hid that from us in the first place. Start at the easiest question and go from there," I suggest right as the second bell rings. "Can we all get together after school? We can look at the book more. My house will be empty."

"Yeah, I'm dying to go through this thing for real." Solaina gives the book an affectionate pat, making us all smile. She grabs her phone and starts to text someone. "I'll ask my mom if I can. I think she wanted me home right after school, but I don't care," she says.

"I actually had swim this morning," Cori says. "Count me in."

Reuel frowns and says, "I won't be able to stay long."

"Oh." I remember. Jolene is making dinner for them tonight. "Your dad said you have to be home, didn't he?"

"By dinner, yeah. He insists I stick close," Reuel says, adding, "I'm not quite grounded . . . but almost."

"That's okay," I reassure her, tucking the book away. "We're just gonna figure out a way to broach the topic. And really get them to talk."

"If anyone is in denial about anything, it's my mom. It's sorta her thing . . . ," Georgina answers breezily, but as easy as her words come out, a second burp follows. She grimaces, lets out a groan, moving a few steps away, clumsily. "It hurts."

"What?" I stare at the way she's clutching her stomach. "Is—"

"I think I should go . . ."

"To the doctor?" August stands up straighter now, alarmed.

"To my house! To my own bathroom!" Georgina cries. She grabs her bag and rushes away, cheeks aflame.

If it were another time, we might've teased her—but she's ill.

We follow behind, stop at the entrance of the courtyard to watch her run to her car. She pauses once only to hack something up and spit it on the ground. We stare after her, stunned.

"She's gonna be late for first hour. She's never late," August says in wonder.

"She won't go in the school bathroom . . . ," Cori says.

"Is she gonna be okay?" I ask as we make our way around to the front of the building, up the steps, to go inside.

August darts a solemn glance at Reuel, who almost trips up the top step, her gait unsteady. Lays a hand on her elbow to guide her, while I take the other. August answers me, "I hope so."

The school day drags on, painfully slow, and all I keep thinking about is Georgina running home because she was so sick and that smell coming off her. And Reuel, bruised and breathless, looking like she could blow away in the next wind, three-quarters of her cinnamon sugar toast left on my counter. And the spell book in my locker, waiting for me, for the girls, when we can bring it back to my house. My mom is working a double, so nobody will bother us.

When I finally see my friends after school, we greet each other, half nervous, half relieved. Georgina made it back in time for second hour, and she brushes the incident off, clearly not wanting to talk about it. She starts her car and we drive toward my house, listening to music, wind in our hair. I can forget about my two sick friends, and the spell book, and the worry sunk like a peach pit in my belly. We're together, and in this moment, we are okay.

When we get to the house, we settle in my living room, pushing aside the coffee table to sit on the floor in a circle, book in the middle on the worn rug. But as I reach forward to open it, Georgina stops me with a gentle hand, her bandaged fingers applying pressure to my wrist. I look at her quizzically.

"I have to say something." Georgina's voice is clear, it's never sounded so authoritative. "Before we get distracted by this thing, I think we should talk about it, since we haven't yet."

We stare at her, puzzled, then I realize what she means and I swallow, my throat dry. "Oh." She's talking about us—our friendships. What happened. Before anyone else can speak, I blurt out the question that's been on my mind for the last three years. "It was because of our thirteenth, wasn't it? Or that was the main thing?"

I still remember it like yesterday. The birthday party.

Georgina's parents rented out the whole floor of Nino's, the swankiest restaurant in Sorrow—not saying much. Our entire families were welcome, which was probably the first mistake.

That meant I brought my mom. She started casually, just a beer to go with her pizza. And then she moved on to vodka tonics. I was savvy enough to catch the looks between the other parents. The way the girls darted eyes at each other. The tight silence around the room, permeating it, overpowering even the garlic and oregano.

She got stupid drunk and made some snide comments. Rolled her eyes and slapped down a fifty to cover our meal even though Georgina's parents said they'd take care of the tab. Stood up, knocked over a glass of water by accident. Slurred, sneering at Mr. and Mrs. Boudreau, and my whole birthday was ruined. It felt like my life was ruined.

I was mortified. Still feel the scratch of embarrassment now, thinking about it. Just one night and Mama and her vodka. Did Georgina's parents pull her aside later and whisper that she should spend less time with me? That my family wasn't one of the good ones? Was it Georgina that had the idea we should all split apart, and everyone else just followed suit? I hold my breath, waiting for her to admit it. Or waiting, I guess, for them to blame my mother for it all.

"No?" Georgina frowns. "What do you mean? The birthday party?"

"Yeah." I nod miserably. My girls had found me, hugged me, wiped my face, the six of us squeezed into the restaurant bathroom. They couldn't really understand, even if they could empathize. Their parents might all have had their faults, but public humiliation by way of intoxication wasn't one of them.

"Don't you remember?" I ask them all, hating how wimpy my voice sounds. "It seemed like the next day we all stopped talking."

"That's not how it happened," Solaina replies thoughtfully,

bringing her knees up to her chest, wrapping her hands around the top of her knee socks. "I remember it being, like, slow. You stopped calling."

"Me?" I can feel my face grow heated as I defensively tap my own chest. "Georgina stopped calling *me*. And Cori did. And August."

"Well, I never did." Solaina holds my gaze from across the spell book. "You stopped talking to *me*—then I guess I didn't talk to you. We gave up on each other."

"That still doesn't explain you—" I start to address Georgina.

She holds up a hand, her chin trembling. Like she might cry. We stare at her, stunned silent—Georgina almost *never* cries. She says, "It's my fault, Iz. It's because of me."

"Why?" I ask, totally lost, still reeling—over my own fault in it with Solaina.

"Because." She takes a breath. "They had an affair."

The room goes silent, the quiet almost brittle. "What?"

Miserably, she nods. "I found out. My mother didn't know I was listening to them fight that night—the night of our party, afterward. All this time I thought he was so perfect, but he was a cheater and a liar." Bitterness clings to her. And I can feel the eyes on me. Blankly I stare back at Georgina, waiting for her to finish, to explain.

"What?" I finally say again.

"Don't you understand?" Georgina looks away with a frown, a tear trailing down her cheek. "My dad had an affair with *your* mom. He cheated on mine—with yours."

My heart is thundering in my chest. I find myself shaking my head, side to side. Side to side. Finally, I form words, my voice cracking with the shock, because this is a bombshell I could never have seen coming. Brant Boudreau and my mom? "What? Why didn't you tell me?"

"I was so upset. At first, I thought he was your father too—"

My inhale comes sharp—even considering that unsettling theory—but Georgina rushes on, "Later I found out that wasn't the case, but still. I was jealous or something—angry. I couldn't even *look* at you. I made excuses to August and Cori not to include you. I couldn't give up those two—and I figured we'd split down the middle. You, Reuel, Solaina. I didn't want to give anyone up, but I wasn't thinking right. Then it just got out of hand. It went on too long, and even when I realized we weren't half sisters, it seemed too late to fix anything."

Solaina's crying too. All the fight I held on to for so long goes out of me as I realize that exactly what Georgina did to me, I did to Solaina, even if I didn't mean to.

Georgina continues, saying, "I know it's such a stupid reason . . . it doesn't even matter, does it? I ruined everything. I'm so sorry I didn't tell you, Isabeau. I'm sorry, everyone." She lets out a sob and clamps her mouth shut. She hates to let anyone see her cry.

Am I angry? I guess. But I crawl over to her, wrap my arms around her swollen body, and she sniffles against my chest. I know she's trying to hide her tears.

I hug Solaina next, telling her I'm sorry. I didn't mean to hurt her. We all cry. We all make up with each other. We apologize. We forgive.

"We should do something now. Actually try it," Georgina suggests as she gazes down at the book, spread open before us, after we have all wiped our eyes and settled down. "Maybe there's a healing spell—or a memory spell we could try for Reuel and me. What if we remembered what happened to us? Why we vanished in the first place?"

"I gotta leave soon," Reuel reminds her. "And I thought you were skeptical?"

"So, what's the harm?" Georgina shrugs out of her blazer. "Kinda willing to try anything at this point to feel better."

I stare into Reuel's tired eyes. Wouldn't I do anything to make her feel better?

Everyone else says no. I don't say yes to Georgina's suggestion. But I don't say no, either. I reach forward, tilting the book my way, and land on a page. There's nothing wrong with at least looking. I read the title:

To Find Something Lost

Georgina says, nodding, "*If* we did something, this one seems like a harmless, easy thing to practice on. I'm sure Iz has something she could think of that we might try to find. Lost keys? Or a school paper? An earring?"

"Unless your ear gets lost with it or something," August says. Only slightly kidding. I wince on two counts—thinking of her words, and also, at the earring suggestion, picturing my lightning bolts upstairs.

"Iz's ears are perfect," Reuel says, reaching over to brush her icy fingertips on my earlobe. "We won't let that happen."

I can't ignore how sick she looks, and instead of playing along, I frown and look back at the page. She drops her hand, and a strange moment of tense silence follows.

I stare down at the spell, reading the instructions silently.

"It might not be so harmless, though. I think August is kinda right," I say, pointing to the page. At my side, Cori reads for everyone.

A plant with roots, ready to be sown
A place of fresh earth to plant it
A red thread for binding
A needle

"Then it says to say these words—" Cori breaks off hesitantly. "I don't think I should say them out loud."

Everyone reads it to themselves, rotating the book so we all get a chance.

Find this lost thing, make it mine again
I bind it to me now, root it to my life
Find this lost thing, make it mine again

Repeat three times, it says, *as you make three knots in the arm's-length worth of thread. When finished knotting and repeating, place the plant in the earth. Say the final words as you picture what it is you wish to find:*

What's been planted, now is true
Return to me where you belong
You are mine again.

"It doesn't even rhyme, but whatever," Georgina says. "So what's the problem, Iz?"

I tap the tiny print on the bottom and read it out loud this time: *"Be certain before you say these words, for finding what you seek shall cause a loss of equal value."*

"Oh." Solaina's eyes widen, and she shudders. "Never mind. Not harmless, then."

"So you'd have to lose something to get back whatever it is you're looking for?" August frowns. "I guess I wasn't *wrong* about your ear."

Nobody corrects her about the equal value thing—that an earring is surely not the same value-wise as a whole-ass ear—because the technicality doesn't really matter. "What's that saying?" I quote, "'All magic comes with a price.'"

"Yeah." Solaina's shaking her head. "Everyone knows that, even if they didn't watch *Once Upon a Time*."

Reuel is about to reply when the front door swings open.

We snap our heads around to see, one at a time, our mothers walking into my house, squeezing inside to crowd the kitchen. Five in total. Everyone's but Reuel's.

"Hi, girls," mine says, voice strained. She locks eyes with me as she steps through the kitchen and into the living room. Her eyes flick to the book laid out on the rug, unsurprised, then back to me, and she says, "We have to talk."

CHAPTER FOURTEEN

My heart is pounding. I'm pretty sure I know what this is about, but still, I ignore my mom and instead ask Marisa, "Why are you here?"

"Solaina said y'all were coming here after school, so I called the others," she answers as she takes a seat at the kitchen table. "It's time to tell you girls the truth."

Our mothers look at each other grimly, and mine says, finding a spot next to Marisa, "We obviously know you have the book. Come here, and we'll talk about it."

Silently, the girls and I stand up from the floor and go into the kitchen, finding spots leaning or perched on counters, while the other moms take seats at the table. I don't miss the way Ms. Kate sits as far away from my mom as she can.

I hold the book close to my chest and lean against the fridge, Reuel beside me.

"We don't feel we can keep things from you any longer, if there's a chance more of you could get hurt," my mother starts.

Her chin trembles. "But first, you have to understand what we did."

My friends and I wait, holding our breath.

My mom takes a long inhale and continues, "It was our sophomore year. We were all friends, as you know now. Best friends." She pauses, maybe thinking of the photo from the yearbook. "You know I grew up in our house, Izzy, and it was about a week before the Day of Sorrow when Grandpa was cleaning things out of the attic to make room for some stuff he was planning to buy at an auction. There was a false window, apparently. No one had noticed it before, but I did that day. He had me helping—I was mad at him for it, I remember. All my friends were at the movies, and I wanted to go too, but he had me cleaning up his junk on a Saturday. I found the book tucked away in the false window, and I almost called him over to show it to him—he could have sold it and made money in the auction, even if it was just a good fake. I could tell that it was old. But I didn't tell him—I kept it."

"You really didn't think it was real?" I ask. I was pretty sure right away that it was. I wonder briefly, why?

Shaking her head, she says, "I thought it was cool. An antique that might be worth something, for the novelty of it. I didn't think anything was real. Until the night we did the spell."

Ms. Kate lets out a choked sob and stares into her lap. Georgina pins her with a hard look, and asks, "Which spell?"

None of them answer for a moment. Marisa hesitates, her black-brown eyes troubled. "We made wishes."

I step forward and lay the book on the table, fumbling through the pages, ignoring the fearful protests from the women—how they visibly recoil. I bet none of them have seen it in years. I remember Solaina listing the names of the spells, and I stop when I find it, jabbing at the title. "This one?"

For a Wish Come True.

"Yes." Marisa winces.

I scan the instructions . . . and again, on the bottom, a warning.

A desire fulfilled for a price—the thing you hold most dear.

A terrible feeling settles inside me. I jerk as Marisa continues.

"We were hanging out at the cemetery, and Lena had brought the book along. We thought it was just for fun, just something silly to do. Everyone asks Sorrow for wishes, you girls know that. We just . . . took it a few steps further."

August's brows rise nearly to her hairline. "What happened? And what does it have to do with *us?*" she asks.

Ms. Camille gives her daughter a pained smile.

Across from her, Mama is silently imploring me, and a sick, horrible feeling nestles in the pit of my stomach. She murmurs, "We just wanted our wishes. We all knew the lore—give something, get something. We didn't think past that."

"What—" I start, in a whisper.

"We didn't know the spell was real," she interrupts miserably. "Not until you were born, and even then, we tried to brush it off as coincidence. But with two of you disappearing and then returning, so sick . . . We talked about it after Reuel—and once Georgina went too, that's when we knew for sure that it was time to face it. That what we'd done was real. That now we're paying for it."

I open my mouth to speak, but all that comes out is a strangled noise. I exchange loaded looks with the other girls, realizing we've all arrived at the same conclusion. None of us ask what our moms wished for. It wouldn't make us feel better anyway.

"It just said, to give up something you hold most dear," my mom pleads to me. "We had no idea it would be something taken from our future."

"You bargained us away?" Georgina gasps, turning to her mother with a hurt look.

"It was just supposed to be for fun." Marisa wipes at her face too, smudging her mascara. "We already had the fire lit, herbs and gifts for Sorrow tossed in. Then we opened the spell book Lena had brought. We cast a circle, using some margarita salt we had."

"And the . . ." Ms. Kate breaks down for a moment. Then sits upright and steels herself, a flash of something across her face—like anger, as if she's mentally reprimanding herself for not keeping herself together. She is much calmer as she re-counts the rest, smoothing the linen of her skirt. "The night was clear, and we started saying the words on the page. We had to cut ourselves—"

I gasp at the same time as Reuel. *We* cut ourselves. My hand throbs and she visibly whitens. I steady her, filled with a sick regret.

"—and the ground sort of shuddered, the air itself seemed to . . . I don't know. *Quiver.*"

Mama shivers, wrapping her arms around herself.

"We were bleeding. And then it started raining." Ms. Kate looks around the room, making her words slow and careful, so that we understand. "The sky was clear one minute, and the next lightning and thunder. We were soaked to the bone. And suddenly so frightened. So we ran away. Later, we laughed. But in that moment, we were all of us afraid."

"Fuck," Reuel breathes beside me. Her hand is freezing but I don't let go.

"Yeah," Mama says, bringing me back to the present. "We didn't finish the spell—we ran, leaving our mess behind. But I took the book back with me."

"When we learned you'd all been born on the same day, I was terrified," Marisa remembers. "But . . . time went on, and nothing happened."

"Still, when you were younger, you can't imagine how strange it was, to see you all together. And we couldn't keep y'all apart. You girls always ended up in classes together, in group projects, on teams," Ms. Camille says.

"I told myself, maybe your births were a blessing," Marisa says. "But now, I haven't slept easy since your birthday."

Ms. Camille remembers, staring off into the past, picking at a nonexistent bit of lint on her pantsuit. She swallows, hesitates. "We talked ourselves out of it. But we can't any longer. There are consequences to what we did—I see that now."

Cori's mom, a plumper, softer version of Ms. Kate, lays her head in her palms, shaking it, finally speaking up. "It actually never said who, or what, was going to grant our wishes," she says, and looks up. "But now we don't think it was the witch."

"What are you saying?" August blinks her long-lashed eyes. "You mean you contacted something else? Something evil?"

She gives her daughter a haunted look; then Ms. Camille says, "Maybe nothing at all. But whatever we did that night must be connected to what is happening now."

"Maybe . . . ," I say, "it's because of us. Me and Reuel. Maybe we woke the spell somehow. Reuel and I cut ourselves the night we were in the cemetery—just a silly thing. But we both got kind of queasy right after—Reuel even fainted. I felt like there was something wrong there."

As everyone starts talking, asking questions, I don't add the terrible thought: *Is this our fault?* I'm still too mad, my blame solely on our mothers.

"What's gonna happen?" I ask. "Reuel and Georgina both disappeared and came back sick. It feels like they're getting worse. What's gonna happen to the rest of us?"

"I don't know." Marisa shakes her head.

"I still don't understand." August frowns. "Why do we share a birthday? How does that connect to the spell or whatever magic was created? And what does it want with *us*?"

"We are owed to it. Right?" Solaina says slowly. "We are payment. But . . . the magic didn't kill anyone," she continues, as though she's thinking out loud. "It took two of us—but they came back. So, what is the point?"

"Maybe it can't kill us at all, or maybe just not yet," Georgina murmurs. She looks up, eyes lit with understanding. "Maybe we can stop it before it *can*."

"Why did you come back to Sorrow?" I change focus for a moment, eyes focused on Marisa, but I don't only mean her. "Why didn't you stay away forever?"

She shakes her head. "I can't explain it," she answers, a touch helplessly. "I just felt like I needed to return. I was drawn back. No other place ever felt right."

"But you didn't tell anyone? You didn't say what happened back in high school?" Solaina asks. "Does Daddy know?"

"No." Fear rests on Marisa's face.

"Some of our memories are fuzzy," Cori's mom says. "I don't really even remember that night." She gives Cori a remorseful smile.

"And it seemed fantastical—too crazy weird to be real," Ms. Camille adds. "The more I thought about it, the more I thought we'd overreacted—that it had to have just been a dark rainy night and our imaginations got the best of us."

"I always believed it was real, deep down," Mama says, voice thin and wispy. To herself, she adds, "I was even too afraid to throw the book out or burn it. I hid it away, put it out of my mind. Or I tried to forget, anyway."

"Like we said, until Reuel went missing," Ms. Kate says. "That's when Marisa started questioning things, started trying to get us all to talk about it. That maybe it wasn't just a random tragedy—but a consequence of what we'd done. You're all in danger."

"That's pretty clear now," Reuel says, shivering. "What can we do, though?"

"We'll do what we can to help—" Ms. Kate starts, putting an arm around her daughter.

"I think you've done enough." Georgina glares at her, pulling away. She gives the rest of us a meaningful look. As if to say, *We're done here.*

"We'll fix this on our own," August says. We all silently agree. There's no other option. Even if it was all unintentional, just a series of mistakes, they got us into this mess. But we'll get ourselves out.

Georgina steps forward and reaches for the book I left on the table, but before she can grab it my mom cuts her off, scoops it up and clutches it to her chest.

"No," she says quickly. "You're not using the book."

I nudge Georgina aside and hold out my hand, temper rising. "Give me that," I demand. "You can't take it from us."

"It's dangerous," she says. Her mouth is tight, a hard line. She will not give it to me. The moms surround her, Ms. Kate stepping in front of her like a bodyguard.

"Give us that book!" Georgina shouts, even stamping a foot in fury.

But they don't budge.

"We walked in on you girls about to do a spell," Marisa says as my mom passes her the book. Her arms lock around it—and she may be dainty but I bet she'd fight to keep us from getting our hands on it again. "We'll protect you from making a mistake, like we did. You can't have it, girls. I'm sorry."

"We weren't going to actually do a spell!" I sputter. "We were only reading it—"

"It's too powerful. We can't risk it."

No matter how much we argue, they don't give in. Too soon, the room starts to clear.

Cori's face is streaked with angry tears, her cheeks beet red with fury, and her mom sighs, pulling her purse up on her shoulder. "Let's go, Cori," she says. "We can sort this out later. I won't have you getting hysterical here over this book. It's for the best. Now, come on."

There's no arguing. Not anymore. Cori pauses to hug us all tight before following her mom out without a word.

Then it's Ms. Kate, steering Georgina out the front door. "We're going home too." Even I flinch at the tone.

"Yes, ma'am," Georgina answers coldly, her eyes flaming. She snatches up her backpack and stalks off with her head held high.

"Wait," Reuel whispers. "I'll need a ride from one of them. I gotta get home. . . ."

I don't want her to leave, but I watch her walk to the door without protest. She looks back once, and her eyes sear into mine. My scar tingles—does hers, too?

How I wish we could go back in time and not do that stupid blood oath. Georgina, August, and Cori had a spa night. And Solaina spent our birthday bingeing *Goblin* and eating a pile of caramel pralines. Those would have been better choices.

The door falls shut behind Reuel, and then it's just me, Solaina, August, and our moms. Mine, crying.

"Solaina . . ." Marisa stops and sighs. "You can stay while we . . . take care of things. We might be a while."

"What do you mean, take care of things?" August asks.

"Don't you worry about it, August," her mother answers cryptically.

The three women stand still, waiting for us to leave the room. That book held like an infant to Marisa's chest. She'll never give it up.

August, Solaina, and I turn without words and go up to my room, hearts and footsteps heavy. While they sit on my bed, stunned, I grab my cigarettes and I light one, drawing in a breath, needing it badly. I wander over to my balcony doors and open them, blowing the smoke out. But it only chokes me, and I curse and stamp the cigarette out right away, watching the cars headed down the long drive, away from my house. I go back into my room, where Solaina is muttering angrily and August is slumped, deflated, on my bed, looking like a feather could blow her over.

"I can't believe they took the book," I say.

"I can't believe any of this." Solaina frowns. "I mean, I believe it. But what they did—I know they didn't *mean* to. But we're still screwed, aren't we?"

"I don't know." I grimace. "What do we do without the book to help us?"

"The book was also a crapshoot," Solaina says. "We didn't know what to do with it anyway."

"You're right," I say. "I guess. But it still sucks. Now, where do we start?"

A door shuts, and the three of us walk to the window. Watch our mothers leave in Marisa's car together. They're taking the book.

"What do you think they're doing with it?" Solaina asks tightly.

"Maybe burning it. Burying it in salt. I don't know." I lean on the windowsill and sigh.

"I think we should write down what we remember from the book," August suggests. "And maybe all our dreams and stuff— then we can cross-reference and see if any of the details can lead us to . . . a conclusion. It may be pointless, but it's all we have now. We should do it before we forget even more than we probably already have."

"That's a great idea." Solaina nods, whipping out her phone to text the other girls. I glance at the notifications popping up on my own phone—our chat is already blown up. Solaina sighs, gesturing uncertainly. "And maybe we can do some research. There's the special collection at the library. They might have leads . . . somehow. I don't know. What else?"

"I'm already googling it—" I say, the internet open on my phone. I type in four words: *Sorrow witch spell book.*

The third hit draws my attention. An older-looking blog— nothing that's been updated in the last ten years, at least—but the headline is *Sorrow, Louisiana & Sorrow, the witch:*

I was visiting Sorrow, Louisiana, back in 2001 when I learned of some of the local lore—that the town had been founded by a witch back in the 17th century. Ever since then I've been something of a collector of anything Sorrow-related. When I went to an estate sale last week in Baton Rouge, I almost passed up this sweet little portrait—it's not in the best of condition, and it doesn't seem like it's worth much. It was only priced at a dollar. But on a whim, I grabbed it, and the man I paid was a talker—he mentioned that he inherited the house from his grandparents—and that they'd always told him it was a woman named Sorrow, and that they'd heard she had powers. It's too similar to be coincidence— and I thought I'd have a heart attack right there on the spot!

When I scroll down to the picture attached at the bottom of the post, I drop my phone. It hits the floor with a thud and I scramble to grab it, my fingers shaking, my eyes locked on the picture of the portrait of a young woman, at her face.

It's the person from my portrait, that I dreamt the night of our birthday. That I thought I'd made up. *From a dream.* And I *did* dream about her, her face.

"Solaina!" I gasp.

I'm almost afraid to show her. I tip my phone toward her, and as she reads, her eyes go saucer round.

"Holy shit," Solaina breathes, then looks across the room at my portrait. "It's her."

August peers at the phone, frowning in confusion, and I pull her gently from the bed and lead her to the easel, gesturing to the paper clipped to it. "You can see that it's her, right? I'm not just being delusional?"

"No," August says slowly, glancing from the blog on the phone to the picture and back again. "It's definitely her. Even that tiny mole . . ."

"I know, right? It's *Sorrow*," I say in wonder. But I should have realized this sooner.

Solaina scrunches her face up, remembering. "I thought your picture was an actress or something—remember? But maybe that was just because she was familiar to me."

"Did you dream her?" I ask. "Reuel did."

"I don't know . . ."

"But you're not sure." I frown as August hands me back my phone. I take it and copy the blog link to send it to the other girls with the message: *Has anyone seen her in a dream or anything?*

My throat feels tight.

August is reading on her own phone now, and tells us, "The blog links to a store in New Orleans. The Dragon and the Bee."

I lean into her and read alongside her. "The woman who writes the blog owns the store, I think. Her name is Melissa Honey."

"It's like, a witchy shop or something," August says.

"Well, that's perfect. Maybe we can pick up some kind of protection spell or something," Solaina suggests. "How do we keep ourselves from being the next one to disappear? We have to protect ourselves—and our homes."

"What are we protecting our homes *from*?" I wonder out loud, pacing. "We still don't really know what is behind all this."

"Well, it's better than sitting around waiting," Solaina says. "What if we can prevent someone else from being stolen from their beds? I, for one, would sleep a little easier knowing we'd tried."

Nodding, I blow out a breath, rub at my face. "I agree. I still wish we had the book, though."

"It would be best if we talked to a living resource. Someone who could help us with this on a general level, at least. Like . . . an expert." Solaina suggests.

"A witch." August isn't quite asking, but the skepticism is written on her face. She adds, "Like Sorrow."

"And this woman who wrote the blog is familiar with Sorrow." I wave my hand toward the portrait. "Maybe she can help us in more than one way."

Noises float up from outside, and Solaina glances at the window. "They're back," she grits out. "And they've got bags of stuff with them."

"The book?" I hold my breath, and she nods.

"Yeah. They still have it."

We can all hear when they come into the house. I go to my bedroom door and open it, listening. I only make out snippets of the three women's' conversation.

—*What else are we missing?*

—*help them!*

—*What about hiring an exorcist*—

I shut my door a little harder than necessary and turn back to the girls. Solaina is looking something up on her phone; August has procured a violet-colored notebook and is jotting stuff down as she sits on the edge of my bed, chewing on one fingernail while she thinks.

"Okay—so we'll go to that shop. Do you think we can do it tomorrow after school? Or should we hit the library first?" I ask.

"The shop is closed tomorrow—every Thursday, it looks

like." Sighing, Solaina sets the phone down on my quilt and loosens her tie. "And the hours are funny—they close early on Friday. We won't make it . . . unless we skip the last few periods at school."

"I'm fine with that," August says decidedly. "But we'll get caught."

"No." I shake my head. "I have an idea."

While they both work on their own, I scroll through my contacts. I have only ever texted with Bridger once or twice, about art class stuff, but I find him in the *B*s right up top.

> Hey sorry to bug you—but I need to ask a favor.
> can we meet tomorrow before school?

> Sure—everything okay?

6:30 at Kel's Café? I ask. Then add *yeah ofc*
Great he answers.

Hours later, someone pulls into the drive—pizza delivery. My mom brings dinner up to the room, her face tired and tight.

"It might be a while yet," she says, eyes on August and Solaina. "You girls may end up staying the night . . ."

"Why?" I take the boxes she hands me, setting them on the floor. "You're trying to destroy the book, aren't you? And it's not working or something?" I challenge.

"Oh, Iz. You don't know what we're doing, and we're gonna keep it that way. Y'all stay up here—eat, study, watch something, sleep, I don't care what. But don't be prying—we're your mothers, and we're handling it."

And with that, she closes my door again.

The girls and I force down dinner, and eventually we slip out of our uniforms and everyone throws on a big T-shirt from my impressive thrift stash. Then we snuggle into my bed, Solaina nestled in the middle. We talk into the night, about nothing, really. We talk until my lids are so heavy I can barely think anymore.

I don't want to think anymore.

And so I shut them.

lz!" Solaina's voice shatters the air.

"What?" I blink, staring into her panicked eyes, her fingers digging into my shoulders.

"What are you doing?"

In an instant I'm aware of multiple things at once: she looks terrified; I'm not sure why we're not in my bed; and we are standing on the balcony—or, more aptly, I have one knee up on the rail, like I was going to pitch myself over.

All of a sudden my legs start quaking and I pull my knee off the railing, gripping the metal tightly, growing dizzy. What was I about to do? What if Solaina hadn't stopped me?

"Were you sleepwalking?" she asks, pulling me back, nudging me toward my balcony chair, staring at me, the oversized T-shirt she borrowed from me floating about her knees. "lz. You look hella messed up right now."

I sit shakily—collapsing, almost. I struggle to inhale and exhale. After a moment I look at her. "I don't know what I was doing. Or why."

A man's voice—no, whisper—in my ear. I shudder, both trying to remember the words and pushing them away, but they're like an oil slick on my skin, too slippery to hold and also refusing to be washed away entirely.

I turn to see August sit up in bed, moonlight kissing her face. "What's going on?" she drowsily asks, and gets up to join us, rubbing at her eyes.

"Iz was sleepwalking or something," Solaina explains. "I woke up and she was out of bed—and about to jump off the railing."

I would have climbed down, I think automatically. *I was gonna climb down . . . to get to him. That's what he wanted me to do.*

I fold over in my chair, shaking from the horrible feeling of losing control. "I was following him." As soon as I say it, the memory fades. But the certainty remains. That it wasn't my idea. That the voice I imagined was real. Even now there's something about it that lingers, calling to me. A faded whisper haunting the edges of my consciousness.

"Him?" August screws up her face. "Who's *him*?"

"I don't know," I whisper. "But I just realized something. I don't think the girls were taken at all. I think they went willingly. And I was almost the third one."

Solaina leans over impulsively and hugs me tight. She doesn't say a thing. But it's exactly what I needed in the moment. August wraps her arms around both of us, and we huddle still, holding each other.

Before I start to cry, my emotions heightened by what just happened—or what could have, if Solaina hadn't found me in time—August tenses, sucking in a breath. The hair on the back of my neck rises even as she whispers, "Do you feel that?"

The wind gusts, rattling the shutters, and the three of us stand, peering out into the dark. The night like a gaping mouth that has us in its teeth.

There is nobody in my backyard. Nobody there. But that

doesn't mean I don't see something. I fall to my knees, the images slamming into my mind.

Dark hair, long and neat, framing a pale face. A long brown coat. Gray eyes, pinned on me, calling me without words. Holding out a hand, fingers outstretched to me. And there's a part of me—a tiny, terrifying part—that wants to go to him.

I gasp and he disappears. Disappears into the darkness of my subconscious.

Struggling to my feet, I grasp at the girls, and ask, "Did you guys see that?"

They both shake their heads, and I explain. Quietly, I add, "He felt close."

"I didn't see anything. But I felt everything in my body like a warning," August admits.

Solaina swears, leaning forward, squinting. "Is he . . . gone now?" Her voice is so low it's barely audible.

We all hold our breath, staring out into my yard.

Gradually we relax and retreat inside. I lock the balcony door and the girls help me scoot my easy chair in front of it—it's heavy. No way any of us could move it on our own. If he tried to lure us out, at least the others would be warned by the sound of it moving.

"I can't believe that," August says. "I'm shaking . . . Iz, you must be too."

"That was fucking scary," Solaina answers. She looks outside again through one of my windows. "I think whatever—or whoever—it is—he's gone now."

I don't say it out loud, but somewhere in the back of my mind the words come:

Maybe he didn't leave. Maybe he's always with us.

CHAPTER FIFTEEN

Downtown isn't anything to write home about. It's about three blocks of businesses, but it's ours, the only thing we've really got here besides marshlands and the narrow strips of white-sand beaches. Most of the second stories of the buildings downtown are living quarters—I glimpse squat plants peeking out from metal railings, a patio chair, even a lazy cat on one balcony, snoozing in the sun. When we arrive at Kel's, a mint-green building with white trim and a sun-bleached tangerine-colored door, Bridger is already sitting on a bench outside. He stands, handing me a whipped mocha, and waves awkwardly to the two girls, who head into the café to buy their own drinks and some sort of goodies for us.

"Thanks," I say to him, surprised. The cup is icy under my warm fingers. "You didn't have to."

"Glad to," he replies easily. "And I figured you like chocolate. You're always sneaking those little candies in art."

I'm still uneasy from last night, but I smile and take a sip, then sit on the bench, and he sits next to me.

"So, what's up?" he asks.

"I need a favor," I explain. "I know it's a lot to ask. But is there any way you can help me and my friends sneak out of school tomorrow afternoon?" His face is curious, not shutting down, so I go on, "If you could make sure we aren't marked as absent. We need to skip the last couple hours of school, but our parents can't find out."

Bridger doesn't hesitate. "Sure. I'll change you to present in the computer. No problem."

"Are you sure? It's a lot to ask. . . ."

"You're not gonna go do something illegal, right?"

"No." I shake my head. "Promise. We just have somewhere important to go—nothing dangerous or illegal—and they keep odd hours. We'll never make it if we have to wait until after three to catch the ferry."

"So you're going off island, then." It's not a question, and he's not really prying.

"Yeah." I'd leave it at that, but because he's so willing to help, I say, "It's just to a shop in New Orleans. It's important for my friends. We really need this. I'm sorry I can't tell you more."

"I got it, and I got you all. We're good." Bridger takes a sip, his knee bouncing. "I gotta ask you something too, a favor, I guess."

I stare at his sneakers. *Please don't ask me out, I don't want to say no to you. I don't want to hurt you. And I don't know exactly why but I can't can't can't go out with you.*

"Would you be willing to look at my portfolio?" he asks. "I'm close to something I think I'm finally proud of, but it still feels unfinished, or unbalanced or something. I'd love your perspective on it."

"Oh." I straighten in relief. I find myself smiling wide. His smile is even wider. "I'm flattered you thought of me. I'd love to look at it," I say.

"Awesome, thanks. I really appreciate it."

"Of course!" Then, impulsively, I ask, "Hey, Bridger? Um, do you wanna go to the dance with me and my girls? Just as friends," I add. "It could be fun."

He hesitates. "Well, Grady and Reuel—"

"Oh, yeah."

"I can't ditch him," he says apologetically.

"No, I get it," I quickly say. "You're a good friend, Bridger."

"You too, Iz." He pauses. "Find me at the dance if you wanna say hi, though. Maybe we can dance." Another pause, a little humorous smile. "As friends, of course."

I laugh a little, nodding. "Great." I stand before I make it weird, tugging down the hem of my skirt awkwardly. "And for the drink. I owe ya one."

He gets to his feet as the girls come back out, cups and paper bags in hand. Bridger smiles at us all, then says to me, "Well, save me some of your trash, okay?" He seems to realize what he just said, and he mumbles about his art project while I try not to laugh.

"You got it." I smile at Bridger, grateful for him. Impulsively, I lean forward and give him a quick hug, and he squeezes me back before nodding goodbye at the three of us.

"All good? He's on board?" Solaina asks, sipping her iced latte and watching him walk down the sidewalk, toward school.

Nodding, I reach into the bag she holds out and pull out a blueberry scone, thanking them both. After a bite, I swallow and then say, "Yeah, we're good for tomorrow."

August hooks each of her arms in ours, careful not to spill our drinks, and the three of us follow Bridger to school.

The first few hours of the day actually fly by—thankfully—and I walk into the cafeteria eager to compare our notes and fill the other girls in on the research plan August and Solaina and I came up with. This is the only period the six of us have together.

August is quick to ask Louis to go find his friends under the guise of us girls discussing dance details, and he kisses the top of her head and crutches off into the crowded courtyard.

"Now . . . about yesterday . . . ," Cori starts, looking disturbed.

But I have to stop her to tell everyone what happened to me last night. As I catch them up, I watch the fear flit across their faces. Beside me, Reuel is stiff and jittery, and she inches closer to me. The topic turns to the visions, the voice in our heads, the way he tried to pull me out of my own bed. Whoever *he* is.

Reuel leans her head on my shoulder in a sweet, almost protective way.

I reach between us, lay one thumb on her wrist. I tell myself I'm not counting her pulse, but maybe I am. She's just so delicate now, and I'm scared. So much more than I was before we found out what our moms did. We still don't understand what the magic will do—what being owed to this spell or whoever created it means. But we know it's not good.

"Who *is* the man you saw, Iz? What does he want?" Solaina asks. "Maybe it's Sorrow sending us these visions and things—maybe she's trying to help us or something. It was her book."

August pushes aside her tray and says thoughtfully, "Yeah. Maybe she's sending us the dreams. . . ."

"But I saw them both. They feel connected, only I don't know how." I shake my head.

"Besides. Even if it's Sorrow sending us visions, how does that help us?" Georgina says glumly.

Solaina tells them about the shop we found, the blog post, and the woman who ties it all together. Her eyes glitter even more than the gunmetal liner she swiped on her lids this morning. "If we have to ask someone about a spell, why not another witch? Someone who has apparently made a business out of supernatural stuff."

"Huh?" Cori asks, dropping her Tater Tot and wiping her hands on her napkin.

"It's like a crystal shop or what—" Reuel starts, then stops to cough into her napkin. She folds it up hastily—but my stomach twists at the flecks of blood I caught a glimpse of.

"The Dragon and the Bee," Solaina answers. "From what I could tell on the website bio, this lady knows about Sorrow. Iz showed you the picture, right?" When everyone nods, she adds, "If we cut out around fifth hour tomorrow, we can make the ferry and still be home in time to appease our parents."

"Oh." Cori's face creases in thought. "I have swim today *and* tomorrow. I can't miss it."

"And I'm going to the doctor tomorrow," Reuel tells us quietly, her lunch uneaten. "My dad said either I go to the doctor or I miss Spring Fling Saturday night. My choice."

I don't think she should be dancing in the state she's in anyway, but I squeeze her hand, give her a sympathetic smile.

"It's for the best," August says gently.

"Today, though—" Solaina waves her fork in the air, a clump of chicken about to fall off. "We thought we'd go to the public library—I already checked our school library, but the one there should actually have *something*. We can dig into the Sorrow collection."

But Georgina and Reuel have cheerleading—even though they're not allowed to participate, they are supposed to go and watch from the bleachers. Cori has swim. And August has plans with Louis and his parents and his grandparents. No way she can flake out now.

"That's fine," I say. "I don't think it's a good idea to wait. Anyone who can go, we're going after school."

Reuel scratches at her scalp. Strands of hair fall onto her lap. She sweeps them into her hand and looks up, frowning. "I agree with Iz."

"We're going to figure this out," Solaina says. "We have to. But until then everyone needs to protect themselves as best they can—put something in front of your bedroom door, booby-trap yourself in your bed, whatever. Iz and I will do the library today, and tomorrow, those of us who can will go to New Orleans."

I pull up some kind of confidence and nod. "I'll get the ferry tickets."

"What about the moms?" Georgina asks doubtfully. "Mine seems scared to even let me sleep down the hall from her, alone. How do we get permission to go off the island?"

"Easy," I tell her. "We don't ask for it."

August and I make it to English as the bell rings, sliding into our seats.

Our teacher starts waving impatiently, calling out to quiet down and get our books open. Evan Watts groans. I open my worn-out copy of *Romeo and Juliet* and glare at him. So obnoxious.

"All right, everyone," our teacher says. "Today I want to talk to you about our favorite star-crossed lovers, what we are discovering now about them, before the impending tragedy that befalls them."

Evan Watts groans *again* and I shoot him another daggerlike look, because I can, because I hate his smug face. What does he know about tragedy? About love? Then again, these are just words on a page, and the guy who wrote them has been dead so long his bones have turned to dust ten times over. Reuel. Georgina. What's happening. This is a tragedy *now.* Who cares about a stupid old story?

I can't stop thinking about Reuel, but even on the way to biology she barely talks to me, and I can tell she's feeling worse and worse by the minute. She leaves class early to go to the bathroom and she doesn't return. As soon as the bell rings, I try to track her down, darting into two bathrooms before I slip into the one closest to the basement staircase, the one that, unlike the rest of the facilities, hasn't been updated since the seventies, with two broken toilets and a burnt-out light. Almost no one uses it. It's kinda like people forget it's here. When I get inside, I can hear someone crying in a stall.

"Reuel?" I whisper into the echoey room. "Is that you?"

She quiets instantly, sniffles. Her voice is light but firm. "Go away."

"No," I say, just as firmly. Hesitate. "Did you get sick again?"

With a heavy, rattling inhale of breath, she pushes the door open, stepping out in her school uniform, her black boots and jewelry giving it personality. Her blue eyes are tinged red. She nods, swiping at her mouth. "It looked strange."

Everything in me wants to flinch, but I hold her gaze. "Have you eaten lately?"

Her face breaks. "I t-tried last night. I—I was just so hungry," she stammers. "I was so hungry it *hurt.* I needed something." She cries now. "But I don't know what—and nothing stays down. I just want this to be over—I want to be better, and I'm scared I won't be."

Her throaty voice drives that point home, the twisted ache in it, the tone of it, even. She sounds unrecognizable as the old Reuel. The old Reuel looked healthy—*was* healthy. Had glowing skin and bright eyes, had hair like a crown.

"I'm so sorry." I want to ask a hundred questions. I try one. "I—"

"Look, I will go to the nurse, and I'll tell them I'm sick. You can walk me there, but for now, just give me a minute, okay? Go away, please, Isabeau." She adds, voice dropping, meeting my eyes in the mirror, lips painted red as my heart, pleading, "Go away."

This time, I listen. But it takes everything in me to walk away from her. I wait in the hallway, slumped against the painted concrete block wall.

When she comes out of the bathroom, it's clear she's been crying. I zero in on a trail of blood trickling out of her nose and run back into the bathroom to grab some toilet paper, handing it over, gesturing to her nose

I walk her to the nurse in silence. Before she goes into the office, she turns to me, whispering, "Sorry."

"Shhh." I embrace her, smelling her sweet shampoo, feeling her cold skin. Squeeze my eyes shut and gently release her.

The rest of the day I feel like crying.

It's my fear for her, this horrible, gnawing fear that my best friend will be taken from me. That I'm already losing her. The only bright side is that she's got an appointment already scheduled for tomorrow. I keep checking my phone, but there are no updates. I take that as a good sign.

As soon as school is over, Solaina and I head to the library together, and the only reason she's allowed to go is because we are just a block from the salon and Marisa is picking us up in two hours sharp to take me home and drive Solaina back to the salon to answer phones until she closes up.

Sorrow Public Library is actually a house somebody switched over decades ago. We walk up to the turquoise building with the chartreuse shutters and trim, corbels painted bone white, and push open the heavy wooden door.

Nobody is here, but a sign on the desk says OUT TO LUNCH.

"It's nearly four," Solaina huffs.

"Now what?" I ask, waving a hand around at the shelves full of books. "Do we even know where to look? I haven't been here in a while. . . ."

"Sorrow's stuff is this way." Solaina steps forward and veers to the right. And I'm grateful I'm here with the biggest book nerd of our group. Even if there's nothing in the special collection, she'll probably know where to look in other sections— history, folklore, etc.

She stops in front of a back wall, and we both look up at the same time.

Sorrow's portrait—the ancient old biddy version.

"See," Solaina says, pointing. "She's got a little mole here, too."

It's just one more confirmation in a long line, but I can't help the decidedly unsettling belly flip that occurs within me at the sight of it.

"So where do we start?" I ask, looking at the books and cabinets in front of us.

Solaina begins scanning the spines, pulling promising books out, handing me enough to fill my arms; then she takes her own stack. The dust caked on top of some of the books makes my nose tingle, and there's a musty smell about a few of them, but Solaina seems to enjoy it, sighing contentedly.

We make our way to a long wooden table—one of only two, smooshed off into a side room. There's even a green lamp like in the movies, though it's unlit. Sunshine pours into the tall windows and paints the room in amber warmth, particles of dust dancing in the shafts of light. It almost gives everything a magical air, and I don't know . . . it makes me feel better, somehow.

"I kinda thought we'd be digging through one of those film things," I say as I pick through my stack. I pull out a slim folder with some loose papers inside, which surprises me—I didn't realize the library also had papers. I thought they only dealt in books.

"Microfiche, I think it's called. And Sorrow's not that advanced," Solaina says lightly. "But there's actual newspapers in here we can look through."

The librarian doesn't return, even after over an hour. We read to ourselves, setting aside book after book, each turning out to not be so helpful. The smaller my stack gets, the more defeated I could feel—could let myself feel—but Solaina seems to be growing more optimistic, even humming under her breath.

"Here—this one looks promising. It was donated by the historical society—it looks like a self-published pamphlet, about unsolved mysteries in Sorrow."

"Really?" I lean forward, interested, shifting my body, my legs getting sore. And since nobody's here anyway, I kick off my loafers and tuck one stockinged foot beneath my other leg.

"Mostly it seems gossipy, and this page is just a description," Solaina says. "But then there's a photocopy of an old book cover. Here's what it says below the image:

```
Sorrow Children's Primer, fair condition,
with
minor tearing along the edges of pages,
black leather book,
dated 1721, handwritten inscription in the
upper inside
back cover: long live the witch, long
buried the bones
```

"Long buried the bones," she repeats under her breath. "Not sure how that helps us, but okay." She sets the paper aside, picking up the next and reading it while I lift a paper from my own stack. My breath catches when I scan it.

"Oh, here's a news article from the fifties. And it mentions the cemetery!" I say in excitement. Solaina's eyes widen, and I unfold the creased edge of the paper and read, *"July 1952 Sorrow Morning Chronicle by J. D. Limbren.*

"Efforts from the city to raze Greenbrier Cemetery—the only one in Sorrow—and rebuild on the north side of town have been met with plenty of protest—but it is the cemetery itself which seems to be causing the most problems." I looks up at Solaina, her eyebrows quirked. I gaze back down and continue, *"'Baseless,' city council members say, when asked to comment on the rumors of paranormal activities. But local residents don't find it so.*

"'My own uncle wouldn't even go into the cemetery in his later years—he used to be a gravedigger in the thirties,' one Mrs. Betty Lincoln tells me when I speak with her. Her concern isn't so much the high estimated cost of relocating the occupants of the cemetery, or safety concerns others have after one engineer tripped on the uneven ground and concussed himself on a headstone. It's that some things should stay as they are, especially such hallowed ground. Not

only because it would mean disturbing centuries' worth of graves, but for one very specific reason.

"'Do you believe in the old stories?' I ask her, mostly curious, rather than judgmental. My own paw could recite every fact you ever heard about the witch Sorrow—and some you never did. I'm a man who deals in facts. But even I cannot deny all the strange occurrences.

"'Of course I do,' she answers simply. 'The stories my uncle would tell me solidified any belief I already had. Things happened in that cemetery, where the witch is buried, along with her secrets. It's not only bad luck to tear it down—it's sacrilegious, in my humble opinion.'

"Despite the back-and-forth between council members and the dwindling population of true believers of Sorrow, it seems the arguments are for naught. Whether it's bad luck or something more, any efforts to make headway on the project have been stalled for months. From broken equipment to things going missing, nothing seems to want to work in the cemetery.

"I'm only a quarter of a believer these days, but it's with that quarter that I have to wonder—maybe the witch doesn't want anyone in her resting place."

"Oh," I breathe. We gaze at each other, meaningfully silent.

"Clearly the cemetery is important, right? I mean, that's not a leap. That's where Sorrow was supposedly buried"—Solaina pauses to correct herself—"*is* buried. It's where you and Reuel spilled blood, and our moms, too. It's where they did the spell."

"Right."

Solaina bends over our group notebook, scribbling as she mutters to herself. She looks up, satisfied with her notes. Points with her pen when I pull something from a small case. "What's that?"

I hold out a tiny cassette tape, labeled with a messy hand-written word—*Collins*.

She takes it from me, puzzled. "How are we supposed to listen to it?"

I hate to admit it, but I say, "I have no idea."

"I bet we can buy some kind of an adaptor. It seems familiar to me. I think I've seen them." She thinks for a moment before getting up to use the copy machine, placing the pamphlet down face-first, then the article I read, and running the machine for the bargain cost of a dime. When she gets back to the table, she peeks at her watch, frowning. "My mom will be here to get us in less than forty minutes."

"On that note . . ." I shove the papers back into the folder gently and grab a new book from the stack. "We better get back to it."

We bow our heads and continue separately. The librarian finally does show up—carrying a greasy takeout box from the local oyster shack—when we've got all of fifteen minutes left before Marisa arrives. Solaina takes the opportunity to go up to the desk and politely ask for her help.

"Excuse me, ma'am, do you have any sort of special player that we can play this tape on? It was in the Sorrow collection?" I hear Solaina say in a proper whisper. The round little woman comes from behind her desk, lifting a large key from around her neck, chattering away.

Not two minutes later, Solaina returns with a disappointed look on her face. "She couldn't find the player, and we can't check the tape out—only books are allowed to be checked out from the Sorrow collection."

I eye the rest of the books on the table. There wasn't much left on the shelves.

Solaina divides the pile in half and pushes one stack toward me.

We read until we have to go, and then we evaluate what's left. I catch two of the titles. *The Sweet History of Heirloom Apples in Sorrow, Louisiana* and *Creole Dishes of Our Island.*

"These are probably completely pointless," I say, "but we can check them out to be on the safe side."

After looking around, Solaina whispers, "I'm going to borrow this."

She slips the tape into her blazer pocket, patting it gently and reassuring me in another whisper, "I'll return it as soon as we find something to listen to it on."

"Okay," I say, nodding.

She flourishes a library card along with a smile at the librarian, who, thankfully, is cradling the phone at one ear and is too busy talking to whoever is on the other end to ply us with questions. When we leave, Solaina tucks a couple of books in her bag, and I get stuck with the rest, including the heirloom apple one, which just seems *silly.*

"Let me know if you find anything in your books," I say to Solaina as we walk to her mom's car. Stepping forward faster, I turn once to throw her a real smile. "And shotgun."

CHAPTER SIXTEEN

I should be in class right now, but instead, I'm staring across the water as our ferry pulls into the dock. By my side, Solaina's half-braided hair flutters in the breeze, her gaze forward. It's just the three of us today—August, me, and Solaina. Georgina wasn't feeling well enough to make it, and we already knew Reuel and Cori couldn't join us. Is Reuel doing okay? I find myself fidgeting, worried about how her appointment will go today.

"I hope this is worth it," August says lightly.

"Yeah." I nod as the boat stops with a jerk, pulling up behind the much-grander steamboat *Natchez*.

The hot, sweet, bitter smells of beignets and chicory coffee greet us as we step off the ferry and onto Toulouse Street. August motions for us to follow, ducking under a green-and-white-striped awning, where she stops in the shade to pull up the map on her phone. We've all been here before, some more than others, but I know for me, it's been years. I forgot the scent of this place, the musicians on every other corner vying for attention, the tourists moving past, snapping pictures, drop-ping coins, and squeezing into the French market to buy all kinds of goods.

It's blistering hot today, and after only a couple of blocks I'm sweating, and tired. But according to the map, and Solaina's confident directions, we only have a few streets to go.

"—stinks like hot garbage," August mutters as we walk side by side, Solaina right in front of us—the slate sidewalk too nar-row for us all to be together.

I scoot over to sidestep a puddle that could be piss or spiked lemonade—who knows. It's not even two in the afternoon, and there are already people drinking from giant to-go glasses with twisty straws. We move out of the way of a rowdy bachelorette party dancing to the jazz music blaring out of an art gallery.

"It's so much hotter here," Solaina says. She's huffing along.

I like it, even with the oven-baked feeling. Because there's a *life* here we do not have in Sorrow, an electric heat to this place. The air almost sizzles.

"It's right there," she says, blowing out a low breath, tugging off her blazer, the lower back of her blouse damp with sweat. She nods toward a peach-and-lilac building, tall, narrow every way you look.

August catches my eye and shakes her head a little, but I give her an encouraging smile, and tug on her elbow. Solaina leads the way to almost the end of Frenchman Street. We follow to the painted front door.

The brass sign on the siding reads THE DRAGON AND THE BEE EST. 2001.

We step inside, the cold blast of air a welcome respite from the heat, there's a blend of scents—patchouli incense, lavender candles, some sort of spicy blend of oil. It's nice. The three of us pause, taking in the things for sale—boxes of tarot cards, trays full of crystals, blessing candles stacked on the shelves.

A thirtysomething woman behind the counter speaks to someone on an old-fashioned telephone. She adjusts her cat-eye glasses and fixes us with a curious-bordering-on-suspicious look.

Silently, we drop our backpacks by the counter before she can pause her conversation to ask us to.

August pushes to the left, through a curtain to a wall of books at the back of the shop.

"I thought we were here to ask about the picture and get some help? Shouldn't we go back out there and ask?" I hiss as she starts riffling through the shelves.

"We will. But she's on the phone, and maybe that's not the owner, anyway," August whispers back. "We can just browse until she's done."

I shrug, staring at the bookshelves, suddenly feeling over-whelmed. We are in way over our heads.

"Although . . . ," August mutters, going on tiptoe to scan the tallest shelf. She pulls down a book, unimpressed. "I don't think "*Naked Arts: Nudity and the Phases of the Moon* will help us much."

"Come on," Solaina teases August, "you know you wanna dance naked under the full moon."

"I'd rather dance naked in the middle of the cafeteria," August says wryly.

I laugh and then sober, realizing how I let myself forget for a minute. We can't afford to forget what's at risk here. I squat down to peer at the books on a lower shelf, reading the titles, browsing through the topics. Gemstones. Readings: palm; tarot;

crystal ball; pendulum; psychic. Animal communication. Botanical studies. *Fairy-Tale Fabulous: Archetypes of Badass Women in Fairy Tales.* Solaina greedily grabs that one, flipping through the pages.

"We need something about, like, ghost-busting stuff," August says, seeing the book in Solaina's hands. "Something to help us understand the spell they did from *your* book, Iz. How to save us from whatever's after us. Whoever, I mean."

"It's not . . . my book," I say hastily. But isn't it? I feel lost without it. It's probably long gone now, though, now that the moms got their hands on it. A pile of ash. A graveyard of papers. I add, "We don't know if he's a ghost, either."

"Can I help you with something?" a voice says behind us.

We whirl around to find the woman standing in the doorway, curtain pushed aside. I didn't even hear her get close.

"Yeah, are you Melissa Honey?" I ask, cocking my head.

She nods. "I am."

"I . . ." I pause and glance at the other girls. "We're from Sorrow, and we're here because of your blog. We're hoping you can help us with, um . . . a little problem we're having."

"Sorrow, huh?" We've piqued her interest. What remains to be seen is whether or not she can help us.

"What do you know about spells?" August asks.

"Probably more than you three, by the looks of it." She laughs. Then, at our somber faces, stops. "All right. We'll talk upstairs."

When we don't move, she gives us an exasperated look, her eyes twinkling. "What do you think I'm gonna do? Turn y'all into frogs?"

But the way she holds her breath tells me she must want to

help us. I study Melissa. Not the feathered wisps of blond hair that look like an homage to the past—seventies or eighties, I'm honestly not really sure. Not the stacks of rings on her fingers. Not the gemstone necklaces strung about her throat. The confident look in her eyes. And I relax a little, leaning into the opportunity. Maybe she can't help, but she's at least willing to listen.

"All right," I agree, stepping forward, motioning the girls to follow.

We gather our bags while she locks the shop, not bothering to flip the OPEN sign to CLOSED. "Come on," she says, leading us through another door, through what might've been a dining room or parlor once. We go up a wide staircase, the heavily carved banister curved like a snake.

Under her breath, Solaina is saying, ". . . on the nose, isn't it? *Melissa* means honeybee. *Melissa. Honey.* The Dragon and the *Bee.*"

The woman twists around to look at her, giving her an eager smile. "You like etymology?"

Solaina answers, "Yeah, I like words."

"Well, not everyone is as smart as you or I." Melissa moves on.

I grab Solaina's hand and squeeze it, trying not to laugh.

We follow Melissa through the second floor, past closed doors, until she stops at one and opens it. She leads us into a room papered in pale lilac wallpaper peppered with tiny white flowers.

"Sit," she tells us, and gestures.

Solaina perches on the edge of a dreadful yellow velvet chaise, while August and I take a spot on the curved red sofa, complete with tasseled trim. Everything clashes, rife with color and pattern. It's all old, used, and a little tattered. But there's a history here, a richness.

It's the ugliest, coolest room I've ever seen.

Melissa hovers above an overstuffed chair. "I suppose I could offer you girls a drink?"

When we shake our heads, she shrugs, finally sitting, crossing her legs.

We stare at her and she stares back at us. After what feels like forever, I finally break the silence. "So. It appears we're tangled up with a spell . . . or some sort of magical contract. We think Sorrow—the witch—is somehow involved. I dreamt her face—and I'd never seen her like that before, young, like the picture on your blog."

"Oh." She nods. "I know the one."

"Do you still have it?"

"I don't keep it here."

I try not to feel disappointed. . . . It's not like I don't have my own picture of Sorrow. "Anyway, it seemed like this might be a good place to find information. If you have anything."

I know I'm ending on a desperate note, can feel how hard my fingers are gripping each other, one thumb tracing my scar. Hope she believes me.

"I thought something was up the minute you walked through my door," Melissa says. "You girls have an energy about you. You've been touched by magic. And fate has led you to my shop."

"It's just a coincidence," August says, testing her.

The woman pins her with a look. "There are no coincidences. And I know you don't really mean that."

August shifts, clearly uncomfortable. She glances at me, her long-lashed eyes wide.

"It's probably none of my business," Melissa says, then laughs to herself, murmuring, "I mean . . . witchcraft *is* sort of my business, but I digress. . . ." It is muggy in this old room. We should be downstairs with the AC freezing us out. For a long time she studies us, thinking.

Finally, a touch impatient, Solaina says, "Can you help us or not?"

Melissa sits back in her chair. "I'm not sure I can help you, but I'll *try*. Can you please start from the beginning and tell me what I need to know?"

"Well . . . ," August starts slowly. "It began years ago, with our mothers. . . ."

Twenty minutes later, Melissa has all the relevant information and is looking disturbingly calm. She drums her petal-pink fingernails on the arm of her chair, a sun-moon ring on her index finger. "Well," she finally says. "That explains the presence I felt."

"Presence?" Solaina sounds half skeptical, half impressed. "You're not even in Sorrow."

"And? It came on strong—like a jolt. Besides, this isn't the first time I felt it. I just didn't know where that feeling came from before this, but I've felt it for years. It was stuck . . ." She pauses, then says, almost to herself, "I believe that it's *been* stuck."

"But not anymore," August says. Not a question. We all know that. Reuel and I woke it up. I finger the tiny scar on my palm, the regret inside me bottomless.

"Y'all could try a protective spell to keep it away for a while," Melissa says, and we nod—we've at least thought of something practical, or Solaina did, anyway. "I can give you some stuff for that. But the truth is, this thing . . . I don't think it's gonna stop until *you* stop it."

"Do you have any idea how we can do that?" August asks.

"Whatever this thing is has affected us somehow, two of us, anyway. And the more I think about it, the more I worry it's like, two down, four to go."

Her words make me swallow hard. Four to go . . . but then what happens?

Melissa shakes her head. "Here's what I do know about summonings—whether intentional or not. In order to send that thing back to where it came from, you're a step ahead if you first learn the history and conditions under which it was created. Or at least, in my not-so-humble opinion, that'd be the wisest place to start—"

"Well, aren't you a medium?" Solaina interrupts, eagerly leaning forward. "Can you talk to it?"

Melissa's eyes flick to her. She considers this. "That's not exactly what I do. I can tap into the source, but I can't speak to it directly—nor would I want to."

"How does that help us if—" I start, but Melissa shoots me an indignant look and I shut my mouth. After a breath, her expression mellows and she nods, agreeing to do it.

I'm expecting her to put on some sort of witchy show, but the woman just lights a few candles—both white and black—and then casts herself a circle with a piece of white chalk, drawn right on top of the antique rug, surrounding us all. She says some sort of prayer under her breath. When she sits back in her chair, her eyes are closed, and she's quiet for a long time.

"This is not a ghost, or a spirit. Not of a human, at least," she finally says, her brows pinched together in concern. "It's attached itself to you and it will not leave until it gets what it wants."

"What does it want?" I ask with a shudder.

"I don't know," Melissa answers, a note of confusion in her

voice, "but I sense that this thing will not go willingly, and that it *is* gaining strength."

"Strength to do what?" August whispers to the room.

Melissa tips her head, her blond hair falling over one shoulder. She twists her lips in thought. "I get a sense of not being able to move forward until something is completed." She looks up at us, and I swear there is fear in her eyes. "You need to destroy it. You need to separate it from its connection to the earth."

Chills dot my arms, my legs, my entire body.

Her mouth quirks, her hand twitches. She swallows visibly and says, "I get a male energy—but I'm sorry, his name escapes me." Melissa's eyes flutter open. After a long inhale and exhale, she shakes her head. "That's all I got. I'm sorry, girls. But I'm not willing to dig any deeper. Not with this sort of . . . being. Death follows this creature. Death and unnaturalness."

Beside me, at one end of the sofa, August stiffens.

Melissa goes on, a trace of fear on her face, "That thing felt evil."

My stomach tightens, drops. "What kind of evil? From where?"

"From? As in, like, from hell?" Melissa shakes her head again. "Hell is just a bad fairy tale."

"Everything comes from somewhere," Solaina says. "And until a couple days ago we thought magic and the witch and everything else were basically a fairy tale too."

Melissa doesn't argue, but gives us a slightly pitying look— now like she's sad for us. When we thank her, grateful, she waves the words away and says, "You're welcome. Now, come on. Let's go downstairs. I'll find what I can to help you here."

We follow her back down to the shop, and she grabs some

things she says may help us, ringing them up at the register. Even after she has checked us out, we hover at the counter, not quite ready to go back out into the world.

"Is there anything else? Anything you can tell us before we go?" August asks hopefully.

Nodding, Melissa reaches across her counter for a Diet Coke, then pauses to take a thoughtful sip. "All I'll say is this—to finish him you can't just trap him."

I nudge Solaina, remembering her reading a spell in the book, something about binding. Now I really wish we had the book! Though I still don't understand what Sorrow has to do with . . . *him.*

Melissa continues, "This thing will just keep coming back. You have to end him. Destroy whatever's left of him, whatever ties he has to this earth, if you can get your hands on anything. Like, literally, burn his bones if you can find them. Belongings, anything of him, about him, or that he left behind."

"I thought he wasn't human." Solaina frowns. "Are you sure he has bones?"

Long buried the bones, I repeat to myself.

"He may not have been human—exactly—but from the visions you shared with me, and from what I saw, he was corporeal at some point. He was inside a body, and it must have died. Find whatever is left of him and destroy it. You've got some tools now to help you, but all you really need is a hot-enough fire." Melissa shrugs.

"Okay, but . . . ," I start, holding up my hands, like *How are we supposed to do it?* I protest, "We have no powers. We're not witches."

"'There's a little witch in all of us,'" Melissa quotes with a toss of her head. At our lost faces, she rolls her eyes. "*Practical Magic*? Maybe you're not witches. But you're girls and you're friends, and together you are strong. You can figure it out."

I exchange a wary look with the other girls. "We'll try."

"All right," Melissa says brightly, adjusting her glasses. "Don't get got before then."

We leave her store with about a pound of expensive salt, books, rosemary sprigs to tie above our thresholds, and at least three smaller bags stuffed full of crystals that clink against each other as we shove out the door. She doesn't even offer a discount, which I sort of admire. I help carry one of the bags. We'll sort everything later, to make sure everyone is protected at their home.

"That was . . . ," August starts, in awe.

"Yeah," I finish for her. "It was."

"Come on. Let's get back to Sorrow." Solaina takes the lead, not bothering to check directions this time. We just go back the way we came.

The three of us are remarkably sweatier on the return trip, out over a hundred dollars collectively, but it wasn't a wasted visit. I only hope the information Melissa Honey gave us will help us defeat him. Whoever he is. When we arrive in Sorrow, we carefully deposit the girls' protection supplies in their mailboxes, and once I'm back home safely, I hang up my own rosemary sprig above the front door, then hop on FaceTime to talk to my friends—to catch them up, except Reuel doesn't answer. I let Solaina and August do most of the talking—telling Georgina and Cori what happened, what Melissa Honey told us.

"So he could be buried in the cemetery—that would be the

obvious place, right?" Cori says. "And that's where Iz and Reuel spilled blood and our moms did the spell. If his body is resting there, then we need to go, right?"

"Right." I nod, adding, "She told us we have to end all his ties to earth. She suggested something literal—that we burn his bones."

Cori cocks her head, not disagreeing, but answers thoughtfully, "But we don't even know *where* he's buried in the cemetery. We can't just start digging all over. . . ."

The girls start throwing theories out—the idea seems to energize them, while I only feel depleted, worried. Somehow talk moves from curses to dancing. I listen, irritated, to them talking about tomorrow's plans.

"I'm not going to Spring Fling," I say indignantly. "Even if I did have something to wear."

"Well." Georgina eyes me up and down thoughtfully through the screen. "We're still almost the same size. You can wear one of my dresses. I'll ask if I can drop it off tonight for you—or have my mom do it. And before you argue, Iz—the dance is a chance for us all to be together."

"Yeah." Cori frowns. "I'm pretty much banned from going anywhere except school, swim, and Georgina's."

"I can't believe some of your moms would even let you still go," I say in surprise.

"Mine's chaperoning," Georgina explains. "It's the *only* reason she's letting me go, and have you all over after."

I bite my lip. I knew her plans for tomorrow—I just didn't expect we'd still go.

"Mine too." August makes a face. "They signed up together weeks ago. And what are we gonna do, Iz? Sneak out to the cemetery in the middle of the night? It was risky enough to go off the island. If they find out we went to search for a gravesite in the middle of the night—we're toast."

"But . . ." Solaina starts to argue. "I probably won't be able to sleep over. My mom's too afraid something will happen. Parent chaperones or no. And the graveyard—"

"I think it's a good idea," August interrupts gently, "to check for his burial spot. But it's a needle in a haystack until we know where to look. We need more time to plan. And the dance is a good enough place to do it. They're not gonna let us hang out otherwise—trust me, I've asked too."

"Great." I sag, shaking my head. "Perfect. I guess we can try to talk if they don't hover. We can maybe meet in a classroom, dig into stuff somewhere private?"

"Yeah. Like how to de-summon a demon-ghost-creep," Solaina says, ending our chat on a rightfully serious note.

I end the call and schlump to the kitchen table, to try to concentrate on homework. I've gotta be failing at least one class, but how am I supposed to keep grades up under these conditions? Who would expect me to?

If this was a regular Friday night, Reuel and I would be together. On an even more recent night, the rest of the girls would be here too. But nothing is normal now, and I am alone, and I don't care how strange it might be . . . these stupid textbooks are keeping my brain too occupied to worry as much.

I'm jotting down answers to a take-home quiz for English when my phone rings. Reuel.

"I got the stuff you dropped off. How was it?" she asks me, her voice low.

"Um. It was interesting," I tell her, and explain all about the trip and what Melissa Honey shared with us.

"How do you feel?"

"Freaked out," I answer. "What about you, though? How was your appointment?"

"I'm okay," she reassures me. "But my dad is ultraparanoid, after seeing the doctor."

"Why?" I shove my homework aside, giving up. Glance at the clock—my mom should be home soon. I get up from the table and head to my room. I don't want to talk to her tonight. When Reuel doesn't answer right away, I say, "Hello? What'd he say—the doctor?"

"That there's nothing wrong with me." Her laugh is bitter. "Like, that there's no medical reason for it—it's psychosomatic. All in my head. So I've been put on strict bed rest—it's so stupid, but they think if I can rest I can somehow destress and my symptoms will de-escalate. I can walk just fine. But they don't want me to even get up. Let alone dance. So my dad said I can't go."

"Oh. I'm sorry, Reuel." I close my door, lean against it. Try not to sound so sad. *You do need to rest,* I think. I hate that she's missing out on everything. I miss her, I almost ache with it. But I still agree with Mr. Carson.

CHAPTER SEVENTEEN

Even with the protection stuff from Melissa Honey's shop, it is decidedly terrifying to sleep alone, knowing there's some *thing* out there maybe wanting to get me, but I make it through the night unscathed—apart from a slight headache, tired eyes, and a sick anxiety that doesn't settle until all the girls have checked in on our group chat.

Though part of me didn't want to go to the dance tonight, I have to admit to myself that they were right—it's the first time we can all be together—except for Reuel—and talk. Although I'm not sure what we can talk about. I'm still waiting for one big thing to click into place, so we can figure out how to fix this all.

Solaina comes up with a good idea, texting it to the group. *Iz,* she says, *remember that little tape we found at the library? I know where we can get a player for it! The AV dept at school should have them! I've seen them before and I'll borrow one tonight. I've still got the tape.*

I just type back *okay* and set my phone down to finish frying myself an egg.

"Izzy." A voice startles me. Mama's whisper.

I barely spare her a glance.

"You have the dance tonight?" She goes to the coffeepot, leaning one hip against the counter, studying me.

"I guess."

"I'll bring you—"

"I have a ride," I say, cutting her off. Push down the button on the toaster to toast my sourdough. "You don't have to helicopter me. I'll be safe. I'll be smart. I don't need a babysitter."

Her hand pauses over her bag of coffee, tightening on the scooper. "I'm not your babysitter. I'm your *mother*. And I'm trying to take care of you. The others and I, we've been talking—"

"Oh, I know you've been talking."

"I won't apologize. Not for trying to keep you safe."

I sigh, pushing some anger aside. I blow out a breath, and in a softer tone I say, "Please let me go. Georgina rented a big car, and she's picking up all us girls, and her and August's boyfriends. And"—an idea hits me, and I seize it, ignoring the guilt—"I have a date, too. Bridger Leland, he's in my art class. He's a really sweet boy."

"And you're not going anywhere after? Not to a party or anything?"

"No—just to Georgina's with the girls. If you'll let me. We'll stay the night—Ms. Kate won't let anything happen to us. You know that. Not after what happened to Georgina."

Hesitation pulls her brows together. "You'll be with everyone the whole time?"

"I promise." Then add a soft, "Please, Mama. I really wanna go."

And suddenly, I do. I hold my breath until she gives me a slow nod. "Fine. They can pick you up here—you can get ready together another time. But I'll let you go to the dance; I'm glad you have a date to look out for you. I think I know him. I want updates, though. Don't ignore my texts."

I can feel a shameful flush. "All right," I mumble.

The toast pops up. My egg is done. I put it on a plate and take orange juice out of the fridge. As I pour it into a glass, she busies herself making coffee. I wish she'd go to her room, but instead she slides into a chair, looking up at me.

I sit across from her and eat, keeping my eyes on my phone. Nothing new from the girls. No brilliant plans. Nothing from Reuel.

We eat in silence.

But before she goes off to do whatever she's going to do today on her day off work, she calls out to me. "Izzy? Let me know when they get here, so I can see that you're off safely. And the dance? Have fun."

I meet her gaze and say slowly, "I will."

Several hours, one long bubble bath, a hairstyle and makeup application later, I'm sitting on my porch in a peach silk A-line of Georgina's she had Jesse drop at my door last night, a cigarette in one hand and my phone in the other. Reuel still hasn't answered my last text.

> Are you feeling any better after resting? Any chance you can come to Georgina's after the dance if we pick you up and bring you home too?

I can see that she read it, but since she hasn't answered, I press the call button. When she picks up, all I hear is her crying on the other end.

I frown, listen as the line goes silent a moment.

Then a gruff voice: "Isabeau, Reuel's not able to talk right now. She just got sick."

"Oh." I clear my throat. "Thanks, Mr. Carson?"

When I hang up, I stare at the porch ceiling, my heart heavy. Something in me is frightened—sick with it. I could almost throw up too.

A nice black SUV pulls up my gravel drive—compliments of the Boudreaus, apparently—and I holler to my mom that they're here. She steps onto the porch to watch me squeeze in with Cori, Solaina, August, and Georgina. My mom waves at us, her smile strangely tight. Fake. She's worried.

"No Reuel," Georgina says solemnly as I close the door behind me. It's clear she's feeling ill—her chest heaving. She clears her throat, a rattling, wet sound at the back of it. She's sucking a mint now.

I nod. "Yeah. No Reuel."

Next we pick up Louis, who is wearing a navy suit with a silver bow tie to complement August's dress, and then Jesse, who basically just grunts when he slides into the car, and absent-mindedly scrolls his phone while Georgina slides closer to him, and we head to school. It's very obvious Ms. Kate is trailing us, but Georgina pretends not to notice the red convertible behind our car.

We can't talk about anything spell-related, not with the boys here. So we crank up the music and sneak a flask Solaina brought. Cori doesn't drink any of it, and neither does Georgina. She grabs a tissue from her clutch and furtively spits into it. We all pretend not to notice.

The dance is already in full swing when we arrive. I hook Georgina's arm into my own, Jesse off talking to someone, and I help her to a seat at a table on the side of the gym. Pastel streamers and gold balloons hang down around us, a bowl of foil-wrapped candies in the center of the paper-covered table. She arranges her skirt and waits patiently for a good song to dance to. I don't know if she even should be dancing. She's nowhere near as weak as Reuel—but she doesn't seem *great.*

If you didn't look closely at Georgina, you might not know anything is wrong with her. Or if you didn't stand by her, I suppose, though the perfume she's doused herself with, combined with mints, helps mask that faint rotting smell rising up from her. And August somehow procured a pair of vintage satin gloves for Georgina, who pulled them on in delight in the car, covering up her fingers. With her floaty red dress, they complete her look, making her look like a vintage prom girl.

She glances across the room as her mother walks in to greet Ms. Camille. The two of them talk, staring at us from a distance. We both look away, and the rest of our group joins us. I feel Reuel's absence deeply.

The music blares, the bass thrumming through my bones. I'm distracted, my eyes flitting over the crowd of bodies in the middle of the floor before I reach for my phone to see if there are any new texts from Reuel.

"You can keep the dress," Georgina tells me generously. I look up to see her smiling. "It looks better on you than me."

I say thank you, tugging one spaghetti strap that fell off my shoulder back up. I probably just fill it out slightly more on top than she does, not that that's saying much. None of us have boobs like Cori.

Standing next to my chair, Solaina stills, a little breath escaping her, as Luca, the guy she's had a crush on for years, strides up to us as the music eases into a slow song.

He is broad-chested and too good-looking, like a god carved

by some Greek hand, and even I hold my breath when he looks at her and asks, "Wanna dance?"

I'm momentarily struck silent, and so is Solaina. I stealthily reach out and pinch her butt and she jerks to attention, glancing at me wide-eyed. I give her an encouraging smile and put my hand against the small of her back to push up toward him. Telling her silently, *Solaina, yes. Go!*

She takes his hand and walks away, turning back to look at the rest of us at the table with an expression of excited awe. Good for him, for finally seeing her. I spot August, who has drifted away to talk to Louis, and who is steadfastly ignoring her mom watching her with eagle eyes. August is now hovering by the punch bowl, which, as far as I can tell, has sadly not been spiked. Grady walks to her, frowning, looking stupid-handsome, his pretty eyes big and wounded. Seeing her shaking her head, I can easily imagine what he asked her: *Where's Reuel?*

When she answers, his face falls, and he shoves a hand in his pocket, grabbing his phone and stepping back toward Bridger. Grady texts rapidly, obviously trying to get ahold of Reuel. I imagine her lying in bed, his text coming through, her face lighting up.

Are they going to get back together? Maybe she does love him after all.

Someone is talking to me.

I shift my eyes. Cori, a worried smile on her soft face. She tugs at the top of her dark-blue dress a little awkwardly. "You're not dancing," she observes.

I clear my throat, lick my lips before remembering the burgundy lipstick I'm wearing. It's dark—almost a reddish-black. I picked it because it reminded me of something Reuel would choose. I answer Cori, "I know. I usually would. I just can't relax." *I hate that Reuel's not here, not in her sleek black jumpsuit, her hair done up, her lips red and pouty, her face shining as she dances. I wish I could—*

"I know," Cori says sympathetically. "I'm uneasy too."

"Yeah," I say.

We sit and watch the others, my eyes settling on August. She's trying to pull Louis onto the dance floor, despite his busted leg, moving beside Georgina and Jesse, who are dancing now too, people all around. They're having a good enough time, letting themselves sink into this. Why can't I? Is it because I feel like we're just sitting ducks? That any moment something bad is going to happen? And is that my instinct foreshadowing ... or just anxiety?

I turn to Cori. "You're missing Adelaide, I bet," I say. "I can't wait to get to know her more."

Tense as she is, Cori seems to brighten at the mention of her girlfriend. "She's amazing—you'll love her. She'll be back from Germany next week."

Next week. If we're all still okay then. I force a smile and say, "Great."

Cori gives me a look that says she sees right through me. She stands up. "Hold on," she says. "Let me get the girls. It's time we talk, now that we're all in one place."

When she returns, she's got them with her. They all take a seat at the table, and we stare at each other, a little lost.

"Well?" I ask.

"I don't know," Cori admits. "But anyone have anything new to share?"

I don't have anything, but I turn to Solaina. "Are you gonna get that tape player?"

"Yeah, I'll grab it before we go," she promises. "Mr. Simon never locks his door. It should be easy to sneak in."

"Just don't go alone," Georgina says firmly. She winces and rests a hand on her belly.

"You okay?" I ask, leaning closer to her.

"I'm okay," she promises. "But I think I'll take a break from dancing for a little bit."

"You want me to get you some water?" Solaina asks.

Georgina nods. "Thanks, yeah."

"All right, well, I'm gonna run to the bathroom." Cori stands. "Who else needs to go?"

August volunteers, and the two of them make their way out of the gym together, arms linked, buddied up. Safe.

As I'm texting Reuel another check-in, a voice cuts through the music.

"Hey," Bridger says. He asks me, shyly, to dance, and after darting a glance at Georgina and Solaina, who is handing her a water, I agree. "Sure."

"Are you having fun?" he asks as we whirl to the middle of the floor—though whirl is a generous term for his clunky movement. Bridger is an adorably *awful* dancer.

"Not really," I admit. "You?"

"Not really." His dark eyes twinkle. He looks great, dressed up in a navy button-down and trousers. His shoes shine.

"Hey, thanks again for what you did yesterday."

Shrugging it off, he replies, "Sure, it wasn't a problem. You did what you needed to do?"

I nod, swallow. Try to sound more optimistic than I feel. "Yeah."

"Good," he says, smiling.

Then he grows serious, scanning the crowd, the table where Solaina and Georgina sit, heads bent together, whispering. "Grady said Reuel didn't come tonight."

"Right," I say, my voice wavering. "She's too sick."

I wish so badly she were here. At my side.

I'd reach for her hand. To take it in mine. To draw our scarred palms together once more.

I love her.

The realization makes me almost trip over my own feet—and my ears are ringing and I don't know what to do.

Except admit it, finally.

The secret I've been keeping even from myself.

I wasn't jealous of Reuel for having a boyfriend. And I wasn't jealous of her and Grady as a couple. *I was jealous of Grady.*

I wished it were me.

I manage to put a neutral expression on. To steady my breathing. My thoughts.

But Bridger seems to read my mind in a moment. His expression going so knowing, so understanding. "Ah," he whispers, his intelligent eyes studying me. "I thought so."

"I—" I shake my head.

I am in love with Reuel. Maybe I always was. I just didn't know it until this moment, really—or I didn't want to see it. Because it could ruin everything if she doesn't love me back.

Wishful thinking. Nothing more. I can't have her—she's not mine to have. We're *friends.* Only friends.

"Bridger—" I start, then clear my dry throat.

"I won't say anything." He steps on my foot, wincing over his clumsiness. I feel wooden, numb.

I love her and I could lose her, and I am fucking dancing to some shitty country song right now, instead of trying to figure out how to save us all. What am I doing here? Tape player or no tape player—who cares, there might not be anything on that Collins cassette anyway. And seeing my friends here didn't turn up anything new, didn't get us any closer to fixing things. I should be at Reuel's. I'm going to go see her. Now.

I ease out of Bridger's arms and apologize. "Thanks. But I have to go."

He smiles understandingly and releases me. The lights are flashing, the smoke machine making me want to gag. And I need to tell the girls I'm going to leave. My heart is in my throat—will they see it on my face? But I need to see Reuel. I need to just know she's okay. I won't tell her. It won't make a difference anyway. But screw Spring Fling. My eyes sweep the crowd, looking for the girls, to let them know. I'll call my mom, I guess—beg her to pick me up and take me to Reuel's, or see if anyone can give me a ride. But I'm leaving.

The girls are still at the table—some of them. Just Solaina and Georgina, still. But where are Cori and August? They're taking an awfully long time in the bathroom. The hair at the back of my neck prickles and I hold my head very still, a sick feeling settling in my middle, rising up my throat, and before I know it, I'm at the table. I tug Georgina up gently, urge Solaina to stand, with a tinge of panic, "Come on. They're taking too long."

Startled, they walk with me, and we sneak out of the gym, while the mothers are distracted. Instinct and fear driving us forward, through the dark halls, as we pick up the pace until we're running, heels clacking. All the levity and festivity of the gym is gone—the rest of the school is quiet, eerily so. It looks like a horror movie set.

It *feels* like it.

"Split up, but *don't* go far," Solaina says.

The three of us race forward and part to peek into different rooms.

"Not in here," Georgina calls out breathlessly, peering into the closest open room. She spins around and darts to the next door, yanking on the knob. It's locked. She looks at us ominously, one eyelid twitching. "They might not even be in the school anymore. . . ."

We freeze for a second, considering this. Solaina shakes her head. "If we don't find them we'll get help. But we could still catch them if they're here."

I take the nearest bathroom, something in me hurting. There are a couple of freshmen fixing their makeup. They look surprised to see me, the frantic way I check each stall. They're empty. My friends aren't here. I meet the other two in the hall.

"Keep going," Georgina says, face red. "Upstairs. Then we'll try the basement."

We run up the stairs to the second floor—well, Solaina and I run, while Georgina huffs and jogs after us—where almost all the doors are locked, or the rooms are empty. Then we take the staff elevator all the way to the basement. The art room—no. Photography—no. Janitor's closet—no. The dim lighting flickers, giving everything an eerie vibe. Georgina bends over and coughs, something phlegmy-sounding. She wipes her gloved fingers over her lips, patting them, and straightens. "Sorry. I just can't run that much."

"Where are they?" Solaina wails, while I rush past her—for once in my life I'm fastest, with my flattest shoes. I hurry through the open door of the band room while Georgina checks on the other side of the hallway.

I let out a gasp as I round the doorframe. A girl in a silver dress, slumped on the floor, clutching her head in her hands, moaning. I run toward her, and something—someone—drives into me, knocking me off my feet.

I go flying, smacking my chin against the floor, eyes tearing.

I swallow a sharp cry as blood pours down my front, soaking me in its wetness. Even so, I catch a lingering smell—something I know—fresh apples. A woman is screaming—*screaming*—and it takes me a second to realize it's ringing through my mind—just in my head. Not happening. Not real.

I twist in time to see a dark blur moving out of the room. Mostly like a shadow, hazed around the edges, all over. Except for the edge of jawline, a man's face, flash of gray eyes that stare into me in one brief, horrible moment. A smile. And arms, hands. Opening to me. Asking me to take them. To follow it—that *thing*—out the door.

"No," I whisper. Forcing myself not to follow. It takes everything in me not to go after him. Georgina and Solaina scream my name, and I can hear that they're getting closer. He is gone so quickly I wonder if I made it all up.

August whispers, drawing my focus, and I clamber to my feet, rushing to her side, where I drop to my knees. I tug her to me, grip her against my heart. Her stupid sequins scratching my skin, but I could not care less.

"I'm okay," she grits out. "I'm okay." She clutches me, burying her face in my chest.

"August, where's Cori?" I ask calmly, praying to God *and* the witch that whatever just ran from here didn't run into the other girls. "I've got August!" I rasp out a scream, hoping they'll hear me. "She's here! Come quick!"

I shake her gently, asking again, crying, "Cori?"

At the same moment when Solaina, towing Georgina along, comes racing into the room, Cori stumbles from the back of it, knocking over an empty instrument case. I let out a surprised breath.

Georgina runs to her cousin, crying with relief, Solaina not far behind her. They hug each other, and then us. I look up into Cori's wide-set eyes, stunned-looking. Her fair skin has gone ashen and she's blinking like she's confused. But she's okay. I sag over August, my breath shaky, and she squeezes me back— her arms shaking but strong. They're okay. They're here. They didn't disappear.

Solaina glances at me, eyes wide. "You're bleeding, Iz."

I dismiss her concern with a shake of my head. "I'm fine. I just fell," I explain, but really I got knocked into. I sit with that for a moment. I didn't realize the being or whatever it is would be solid. That he would be able to actually touch us.

When August looks up, there is blood squeezing from her eyes, like tears.

I hold back a scream; August blinks up at me, the red matting her mascara-coated lashes. The smell of copper coming off her. And one of her eyes is suddenly a whole two shades lighter than the other.

She is not okay. And Georgina has sunk to the floor, wheezing.

August pants, whimpering, bringing her hands to her temples. I reach over and rub her shoulders as I ask the others, "Who's got a phone on them? We should call an ambulance."

"No." August shakes her head, then repeats, "No."

She struggles to sit up, catching her breath. "That thing didn't have time to do to me or Cori what it did to Reuel and Georgina." She pauses, staring at Cori, stricken. "Why'd you run off? One minute you were in the bathroom with me, the next thing I know I'm chasing you down the hall—"

"He made me go with him," Cori interrupts in a whisper. We stare at her, her body shaking. "I remember."

August moans, reaching for her temples again, massaging them.

Her breath is shallow, but Georgina whispers, "I think Iz is right. We should call for help."

"No!" August is adamant now. She stands up, as if to show us she *can*. "If we waste time getting taken to the hospital, we lose days to fix this! We can't eat up precious time getting fluids or something, damn it." She stomps her strappy shoe on the floor for good measure. "I've got a headache is all!"

We don't tell her about the blood droplets on her lashes.

"Apples—" I blurt out, remembering as I dab at my tender chin with the hem of my dress—it's already ruined. "I smelled apples. Cori? What happened? What did you all see . . . or smell, or whatever?"

"Yeah, what happened?" Georgina says, wrapping an arm around Cori's shoulder protectively.

"I got done in the bathroom first," she whispers, leaning on Georgina, "and August was still in the stall. She was telling me something while I washed my hands. I looked up and there was a hazy form standing behind me in the mirror. I could make out dark hair, light skin. And for just a flash—in my mind—his face was clear. He smiled at me. He looked almost . . . kind."

My skin tingles all over. I reach out and take her clammy hand.

"I wasn't scared," she reassures us, even as she seems to puzzle over it. "I know, in hindsight, it's terrifying. But in that moment I wasn't scared. I just wanted to go with him. When I turned around, I didn't see him . . . but I still knew he was there. I ran after him, but then August started chasing me, and he led me in here. He became real again—a form, and stared into my eyes, whispered something. I guess I started to black out—I got so weak. It seemed like just a second and I heard y'all calling for us."

"August?" I gently ask. "What about you?"

August grimaces. "I ran in here after Cori, like she said, and there was a shadowy figure standing over her. He looked at me, then kind of faded away. I heard a laugh—it sounded like a man's laugh—and I got this memory, almost. It felt like a memory, just not one that belonged to me. I guess that's like the visions y'all described." She takes a breath, face screwing up. "It was a woman in a bath, like an old-fashioned tub. I couldn't see her well—but I could feel him finding her there. She looked up and shook her head. She was angry—" She stops abruptly. "Then it went dark."

"Fuck," Solaina whispers. "Sorrow."

Cori takes a calming breath, then says, "I couldn't move or help August—I was frozen, and starting to black out. But I could see him hovering over her—*becoming*. Forming into a man again—clearer this time."

August nods. "I know that much. He's getting stronger—I was getting weaker and he was getting stronger. He was using me to do it. I could *feel* his intentions. He's using us, our energy or health, or whatever, to gain power. And if he gets enough of us, he can become real. Stay in his body. Who knows what he'll do once he's living again!"

I swallow, but it's difficult. The image she paints is horrifying.

"We've gotta get out of here," Solaina says. "Let's get you home, August." She pauses and looks at Cori, whose pale cheeks are turning bright red, almost purple. "You don't look so hot either."

"I want to *help*," August says. "I just need something for this headache—"

"You can help by resting," I cut in, voice firm. "Don't argue."

"No," she says, just as firmly. "Cori and I are coming. We're *all* going to Georgina's. We are not gonna just lie down and rest."

"Besides," Cori says, glancing at August. "If he gets to the rest of you—it's over. I know it."

The rest of you—she means just me and Solaina. Goose bumps pebble my skin. We are the last two left. I stare at Solaina. She gets it. Maybe this is what Melissa Honey meant about him not being able to move forward until something was completed.

"If he gets the rest of you, I don't think Reuel and I—Cori and August now too—are gonna be sick," Georgina says. "I think we're gonna be *dead*." She finishes her sentence just as her nose starts bleeding. She swipes the back of her gloved hand across her face, smearing red, her lipstick bleeding into the blood.

Even in the midst of all that, Solaina got the tape player.

There's no way August can go up to her mom, to tell her we are leaving, even though she's wiped her blood-crusted lashes and put on some fresh makeup—you can tell she's shaken. My chin is split, an angry gash starting to scab. But Georgina pulls out an inner strength we already knew she had, and when Ms. Camille is busy talking to someone, Georgina tugs Cori—who doesn't look too bad now—along to say goodbye to her mother, to let her know we're all headed to their house now, as planned and approved by the mothers already. I'm thanking everyone when Ms. Kate just gives her an absent nod and waves at us from across the gym.

Georgina could win an Oscar, the way she's righted herself, the way she's walking back to us, her gait smooth, like she's not even leaning on her cousin for help. Like she's not in immense pain. We slip out of the gym and leave the school, trying to avoid talking to anyone—August's head down, Solaina and I on the outer edges as we walk in a clump. Georgina is the slowest, the weakest, and it feels like forever until we make it to the parking lot.

Somehow, the attack on August and Cori tonight has made Georgina even sicker. What she said in the band room echoes in my mind. That if he gets to Solaina and me, they might not just be sick. They might die—we all might. And I think she's right. The spell, the magic—he somehow has limitations. Maybe he can't get to us all at once. But taking us a little at a time, he gets stronger, and when he's stronger . . . Well. I think that's it for us.

Four down now. Two to go.

When we climb into the waiting car, Georgina finally lets out a cry of distress. And she fans herself, sweating. "That was brutal."

Settling into the backseat, I give her a stricken look, which she doesn't see. I dig out my phone to check on Reuel, text her rapidly, asking if she's okay.

I slide my phone away when Reuel doesn't answer, my fingers shaking. Georgina clears her throat a disturbing number of times, then coughs, something wet and sickly coming up. She discreetly turns her head and spits into the rumpled tissue from her purse. Behind her, I reach over and rub her shoulder.

And Cori, the one who seems the least affected, still doesn't look wonderful, but at least her color has gone to a normal-ish shade and she's not bleeding. A little bruised and battered, yes.

August, next to me, is leaning back into her seat, her eyes closed. She's shaking uncontrollably. Like she's in shock. Her mother will find out she was attacked tomorrow—but that's for tomorrow.

I twist to face her, lay my hand across her sequined-covered knees and apply pressure. She's promised she'll tell us if she needs to go to the doctor. I believe her—in a way that I didn't with Reuel. Reuel can be stubborn, to her own detriment. My phone rings just as I think of her.

I answer quickly, whispering her name.

"What happened?" She gasps weakly. "I felt . . . a shift. I just blacked out."

"Reuel—" I pant, my hand leaping to my chest. She sounds *awful.*

"Is your dad there?" I ask, squeezing the phone. "Reuel, is he with you?"

"He's in every half an hour to check on me. But what happened?"

"Uhhh . . . ," I start, staring over at the girls. I tell her, a short version.

"I'll sneak—"

"No," I say to her sharply. Turning away from the others for a moment, my eyes pricking with tears as everything catches up to me. "Please, just stay home in bed. Please, just give your body a break."

She must be able to hear how broken I sound, because I hear a sniffle on the other end, and finally she relents, whispering, "Okay."

"I promise, we'll tell you everything that matters. Just, please, stay home," I say again, getting another, clear promise before we hang up.

Five minutes later, we arrive at Georgina's and tiptoe up the stairs before her dad can get a glimpse of us.

We pile around her bed, in clouds of tulle and silk, sequins and crepe. All of us looking some version of terrified, exhausted, dazed.

"Well, that was not the dance I was hoping for." My attempt at lightening the mood is fruitless. But it's only because I could cry instead. Or maybe I am crying. I taste salt. Smell blood. Catch that terrible, rotting smell coming from Georgina.

She has Cori unzip her dress and changes in the corner, miserably slipping on a loose nightgown and stumbling to the bed to join us.

August kicks out of her high-heeled sandals, wincing and rubbing at her ankle. "I think that fucker made me twist my ankle. . . ." She sniffles in pain while I lean over to check it out—it is tender to the touch.

"I'll get you some ice," Cori says, slipping off the bed. I hear her call, "Hi, Uncle Brant," and a muffled conversation. I turn back to the girls, and we wait, silently, for Cori to return. When she does, she hands August an ice pack. Cori's fingers are quivering, but at least her face has returned to its almost-normal shade.

August gives Cori a ghost of a smile, even though her lips look bluish. Solaina clucks at her, tossing over the blanket thrown on the end of the bed. "You're cold?"

"Any fever?" I ask, moving to touch her forehead, then Cori's. They're only a little cool. Not ice-cold. Not burning-hot. Nothing as bad as Reuel was.

"I'm okay," August insists, and Cori nods. "Promise."

I calm myself down, and we get comfortable, settling in to discuss things. August and Georgina and Cori, too, have been bullied into leaning on the pillows, sipping electrolytes. I myself could use a cigarette or a stiff drink, though I take neither, even though Georgina has a bottle or two of wine for the post-dance sleepover. None of us drink it.

"Let's try the tape now," Solaina says.

She gets up, walking over to the pile of stuff we dropped when we came in, and grabs something from the sparkly purse she brought to the dance. She holds up a retro tape deck and the tape she "borrowed" from the library.

As Solaina walks back to the bed, she pops the tape into the deck and it whirs for a minute, sounding staticky. We hold our breath, listening as a voice comes over it. A man's gentle whisper, then a short cough.

He speaks, annunciating into the microphone, "Nineteen ninety-four, interview with Nana Pierce."

A woman's soft laugh of amusement, her whisper, "Oh, Hunter, you make me feel so official."

His teasing reply, accent clearly Northern—maybe Midwestern. "Nana, you *are* official. Now, just relax. Get comfortable, and just tell me what you said before. It's only me you're talking to, okay?"

Her inhalation. I picture her nodding. "When I was eleven or so I remember my mother had her sister—my aunt Lily—over for lunch. I was busy, cutting out some paper dolls she'd made me—my aunt was so creative and I looked up to her," she muses. "Anyway, it was hotter than a mud-suckin' fence, and I was on the floor where it was cooler, with my scissors and all those paper dolls spread before me. The women were talking and their voices got real low. I listened more carefully and I heard Aunt Lily telling a story that someone had told her—about Sorrow. Everyone knew the story about the woman founding the little island of Sorrow somewhere in the late sixteen hundreds, but she told a different version—that there was a man, too. Or a demon, depending on who you heard it from."

Georgina squeaks out a breath and grabs at my hand. I squeeze back, careful of her bandages, understanding. What this might mean. A missing piece.

"Nana, what do you know about him?" the man asks his grandmother.

The old woman goes on. "Well, Lily said quite a lot. The thing I remember is that they'd lived together, existing beyond the bounds of society. Not as lovers—but as teacher and student. He taught her magic, and she became powerful because of him. Because she'd made a deal with him—a deal with the devil, so to speak. As time went on, he became strangely obsessed with her as she got strong—stronger than him, even, and eventually his jealousy drove him to harm her, so she killed him. Then she burned his body and buried his bones. There was talk that the area had been marked, somehow, the land connected to him. It was the only thing they could not erase about him—besides the name—Bayard. It seems a grim tale, if it's true. I don't know what your fascination is with these stories, Hunter." Another soft laugh. "You're just like Lily."

"I like mysteries, Nana. And you're the one who got me hooked on them, remember? Telling me all the stories when I was a kid."

"Well, it was just part of life in Sorrow," she answers, with a hint of amused nostalgia. "We liked our stories."

"Now, can you remember anything else? Anything that might be of interest," he says. "I don't want to forget anything."

"That's what the tape is for, no?" she says saucily. "No, I don't think there's anything else. Not anything other than what I already told ya."

"Thank you, Nana. That will be all for now."

And the tape ends.

The four of us stare at each other for all of thirty seconds before we start shouting excitedly, talking all at once.

"—My God, do you think she really killed him? How?" August asks as Solaina cries out, "Hemlock!"

"She poisoned his dinner!" I squeal. I remember the first vision I had—that was the stew Sorrow made him that I saw. It all makes sense now. "That has to be it! And now we know his name."

"Bayard." A troubled whisper. Georgina shakes her head and swigs from a bottle of Pepto that she had on her nightstand. Her teeth chalky and pink. She groans a little as she pulls bobby pins from her updo, her waves cascading down her pink shoulders, the veins in her skin standing out, dark. Like there's poison running through her.

I gulp and trade looks with the others. Everyone can see how sick she is.

Cori shakes her head. "Let's not think about this now. Let's pick back up tomorrow."

"I think Cori's right." Georgina nods weakly. "Right now, we need sleep." But just as easily as her suggestion comes, a cough forms, and she almost starts to choke.

August reaches over and thwacks her on the back a few times, and Georgina holds up a hand, cough easing. She leans forward and spits something into her palm. We all stare down into it.

One of her teeth, decayed and wet, slick with the pink medicine she was chugging.

"Ohhh." She exhales a whoosh of breath, her mouth gaping open. One bleeding hole where the tooth fell out. The stench coming up her throat reminds me of rotting sugar. Sweet and cloying.

Like death.

CHAPTER EIGHTEEN

B etween Ms. Camille learning that August had been attacked and Georgina's emergency trip to the dentist this morning, the mothers are beside themselves.

And that's not even to mention Reuel and how bad she's doing now. The updates are few and far between and getting more disturbing.

I just ate dinner, she'd texted, roughly after Georgina's tooth incident.

But then not an hour later, *I threw up again . . . lots of it.*

> Not doing good. I keep seeing things, Iz.
>
> I'm scared, Iz.
>
> Love you.

That was the last one—at three this afternoon. It is now six. I try calling as I wait in the passenger seat of our car for my mom to get in, but no answer. I set my phone down, dread pooling through me.

The driver's-side door swings open and my mom slips in. She buckles the seat belt quietly. I sit in protest, arms folded against my chest. It's not that I don't want to go to Solaina's. It's that the moms will be there too. It's that they want to talk to us. It's that they have ideas for what to do.

All I keep thinking is that this is a last-ditch effort.

That they're fucking terrified, and willing to admit they don't know what to do.

That they need *our* help.

The thought scares me.

We drive in silence, apart from the radio, and not even the music can break the tension between my mom and me. I want to ask her a million things—I want to say a million things. But I don't. I close my fingers around my scarred palm, and I think of Reuel until we pull up to the curb. My mom shuts off the car, and I don't wait for her. I climb out into the hot night and let myself into the house. We were always welcome to do that here.

I've always loved Solaina's home—it is small and cozy, an old shotgun with tons of houseplants and a brick fireplace that goes all the way to the ceiling and cuts through the middle of the house. Nobody's there yet, so it's just me and Solaina, and our moms standing in the entryway. For a second, Marisa and I lock eyes, and I hope she can see the softness in mine. Maybe I can't forgive my own mother yet. But I can forgive her.

"Solaina," she says, looking to her daughter. "You and Isabeau can go watch TV or something till the others get here."

With that, she and my mom go off to the kitchen, which has a comforting, pleasant aroma of garlic and yellow onions and bell peppers.

Nobody else is home—not Solaina's dad, grandma, or little sister, Esperanza, and I feel a sense of missing them all, wishing this were just a normal dinner. But it's not. And right when I follow Solaina into the living room, the doorbell rings, and it's August, Cori, Georgina, and their moms. There's no time for TV or pleasant chitchat. We eat a rushed dinner together—there is a thick tension between my mom and Georgina's mom. How will they work toward a solution if every time my mother looks at her, Ms. Kate pretends she's not there? Not that I blame her.

"We can show you the stuff we have so far," Solaina offers to our moms after we've cleared the dishes, looking at me and the other girls. "We brought everything we have."

"Yes, we have things too." Ms. Kate's hand is shaking, her mouth pulled taut. They're too distracted right now to even listen. "First, can you give us a few minutes to go over something?"

My friends and I escape the table to hide away in Solaina's bedroom while the women talk. As we claim spots around the room, it strikes me again—the aching missing I feel for Reuel. She should be here with us. And the ones who've been attacked are looking worse and worse. I'm shocked Georgina was even allowed to come.

"G—you doing okay?" I ask.

"Fine," she murmurs, curled up in Solaina's beanbag. She's started reading through our violet notebook again, brows raised. I can hear her breathing—her chest sounds rattly, full of fluid.

Uneasily, the rest of us sit down in silence.

"What do we know about this Bayard guy?" August asks, with a worried glance at Georgina before she starts digging through her bag, the salt from Melissa Honey peeking out the top.

"He taught Sorrow, then Sorrow killed him," I answer.

"We didn't see anything about him in the library when we

went," Solaina says, "but that pamphlet did say something about bones, remember, Iz?" She's already sorting through her notes from the library.

Pulling out the copy she made, she reads, *"Long live the witch, long buried bones,"* then adds, "I wonder if this was referencing her being buried there, or *him.*"

"Or both." I sit and reach for my tote bag, checking my phone—nothing from Reuel.

"You brought home books from Sorrow's collection, right? These are them?" Cori glances at the small pile on the floor. I reach into my bag and set my own between us.

Solaina shrugs. "Yeah, but nothing too promising. We can go through them now. Here." She fans them out on the floor between us. I nudge off the heirloom apple one to Georgina.

"Can I trade you?" I ask her, motioning to the shared notebook. I haven't looked at it since I wrote my own entry.

"One minute," she answers, eyes glued to the page she's reading. Her freshly bandaged fingertips are oozing blood. When she doesn't hand over the notebook to take the apple book, I set it on the floor instead.

I lean against the wall and settle more comfortably, and outwardly I look chill, but Georgina's lungs are rattling and now August is scratching at the hives creeping up the side of her jaw, and Cori has started to blink incessantly, her eyes watering nonstop, and inside, all I can think of is Reuel. The poetry book she gave me is in my tote bag—I never took it out the night of our birthday. Something in me hurts. The terrible unbidden wondering—what if she dies and I never even read this book she gave me? That she so wanted me to read?

I'm grateful the girls' eyes are all cast down, busy with their reading, so nobody notices my tears. I furtively brush them away and take up the poetry book, flipping through. Christina Rosetti. Rumi. Mary Oliver. Maya Angelou.

"Here, Iz, you can take it now. I've read it all twice over, and nothing new hit me." Georgina pats my toe, but I'm busy reading now, lines of a poem blurring in my mind.

> A thousand Dreams within me softly burn:
> From time to time my heart is like some oak
> Whose blood runs golden where a branch is torn.
> —Arthur Rimbaud

I read it again, even as Georgina repeats my name and everyone is looking at me—I can *feel* them staring, curious as to what has me so still.

"What is it?" Solaina asks, setting her stuff down and coming closer. "That's not one of our library books."

Slowly, I say, "Remember, on the tape Nana Pierce said something about him being tied to the land, right? And we realized the graveyard was important even before that. Obviously."

"Yeah?" Her midnight eyes study me. Waiting for me to work out whatever this thing is that's hooked me.

"It's probably nothing." I hesitate. I don't want to leap to conclusions, and maybe this is a big leap, except something in that poem caught me—the idea of the oak unfolding something for me. "We didn't know *where* in the cemetery he might be, and I just wondered—what if he's buried under the apple tree?"

"There's an apple tree?" August sits back on her heels, her mind untangling my idea.

"Yes—and it really creeped me out when I saw it." I shudder, just picturing the tree in the cemetery.

August's face lights up. "Well, apples have always been tied to Sorrow. And you smelled apples when Cori and I were attacked."

"Yeah, and plus, that tree . . . I don't know why we didn't connect it before."

I stare over at the apple book—Solaina is already hurriedly flipping through it, and she slams it shut with an excited "Aha!" She goes on, "Remember that binding spell in the book? I said it was a French word, and I was right, damn it! Reinette is a variety of apple tree—a *Reine de Reinette.* Iz, you are brilliant."

"We need to go there. Tonight. We need to dig up his bones and burn them," August says. "And now we know where to dig. Or at least, we have a place to start."

"Yes! In order to destroy him, we have to destroy the bones—Melissa Honey said that, basically, right?" Solaina says, shutting her book and setting it aside. "We think we know where he is now. The only question is, how do we get out without *them* knowing?" She jerks her head to her bedroom door. I'm surprised our moms haven't fetched us yet, though by the sounds coming from across the hall, it may be because they're arguing now. Voices ring out from Solaina's living room, and they sound hostile.

Georgina burps quietly behind her hand, and then hiccups, her long exhale coming out sounding asthmatic. She frowns as she presses her fingers against her temples. "All right, let's get us some shovels, I guess."

I laugh at her deadpan tone. I can't help it.

"We have shovels in my garage; my parents were just using them in the garden today," Solaina says. "I'll take them when I sneak out and meet you all in the cemetery tonight. The sooner, the better."

Marisa raps on the open door. "All right, girls. Time to go," she says.

"Mama—"

"Solaina." Marisa cuts her off, her eyes narrowing. "They're going home now. And you are staying here. You think my ears don't work? I know what your plan is, and there's no way I'm gonna allow that. No." She takes a breath and squeezes her hand on the doorknob, her gold wedding ring shining. "No, I'm keeping you safe the only way I know how. You'll stay under my roof and with me until I figure out how to get rid of this thing."

"You're not gonna get rid of it unless you know—"

"Girls." Marisa's voice goes soft, but there's a steel spine in it. "Later."

"What about my mom? The others?" I ask. "I thought we were all gonna make a plan? Talk?"

"We're still figuring it out," she answers with a sniff. "We don't want to involve you yet."

"Then what was the point of all this?" Solaina cries out, exasperated.

Marisa sighs. "Please trust us, okay? We're in disagreement as to the level of involvement we want from you girls. Georgina, your mama said you can take the car and give everyone a ride. She'll go home with Beth once we sort this out. Nobody is walking, and I don't want anyone going off on their own. Are we in agreement about that?"

"Okay." Georgina nods, glancing at us all.

"Can you drive everyone home? Are you comfortable with that?" Marisa asks her seriously.

"Yes, I can do it," she answers.

"Then it's time you girls head home. And I do mean *home.*

Your mothers will be there shortly. Don't give us any reason not to trust you. You want to be involved in our ideas—you prove to us you can be mature."

But we close our mouths and sigh, not arguing. Solaina is crying, mad, but she wipes her tears away, folds her arms. As I pass her, heading out of the room, I cast one more meaningful glance her way.

Solaina nods, understanding the look I give her.

We'll sneak out and meet up later at the graveyard. As planned.

Home is just a detour.

When August, Georgina, Cori, and I pass the closed bedroom door, whispers are audible. Less angry now. More urgent. It sounds like things have calmed down enough for there to be a conversation. But what exactly is *their* plan?

We pile into Georgina's car, but she fumbles with the keys, dropping them.

"Are you okay to drive?" August asks her, concern etched on her features.

Georgina's hands waver and then she leans her head back on the seat. "No. I don't think I should, actually. I'm dizzy."

August looks at me, mouth twisted. She looks like she might be dizzy too. Her mismatched eyes are glassy. And Cori won't stop blinking. I don't trust her to drive.

"I'll drive," I offer. I'll just take Georgina's car home. It's the safest option. As I get out of the car to switch places, I reach for my phone to check on Reuel. But it's not in my pocket and I realize that I left it in Solaina's room, along with the rest of my things.

"Shit," I hiss, turning to gaze across the street. "I left my phone, my bag. And the books and stuff. I need to go back."

"I'm not going back in there," Cori says. "Marisa was ma-ad. . . ."

I nod. "I can go to Solaina's window and she can hand it all out. I don't wanna not have my phone, in case Reuel calls."

I want to cry. Georgina moves to the front seat, dabbing at her sweaty forehead, chewing her gum furiously now, though it does little to mask that eerie-sweet smell coming off her. The heat is only making it worse.

I hurry through the dark and, crouching, make my way to the side of the house—Solaina's room is in the back left corner. I say a prayer of thanks that the moms are still arguing—that they won't hear me rap on the windowpane.

When I peek my head over the sill and lift my hand to knock, to get her attention, my breath catches.

Her window is flung wide open, the curtains fluttering. And inside the room, her door is closed. Solaina is gone. The smell of apples lingers in the air.

Bayard was here.

CHAPTER NINETEEN

He's got her, he's got her.

We're speeding toward Greenbrier Cemetery, panicked, the girls in the car tight-lipped and fearful, when Cori clears her throat. "Iz," she whispers, glancing down at my phone. "You got a text about Reuel. She's on her way to the hospital."

From the backseat, the other girls cry out in alarm at the update. I nearly swerve into a parked car, my hands numb. My words come out strangled. "What did she say?"

She clutches my phone, her fingers bone white, voice strained. "It's from Colton—he sent it from her phone, said she told him if anything happened to let us know. Mr. Carson is taking her into the ER right now. . . ."

I'm crying as I drive us to the cemetery, wishing I could split myself in two—one part to go to Solaina, one part to go to Reuel. I squeeze my eyes closed for a half second before I open them again. This is all still real. "Tell him," I say, over the din of the girls all talking at once now, freaking the hell out, as I pull up to the cemetery, put the car in park. "Tell him she'll be okay."

But it's a lie because I know it in my heart—Reuel is dying.

And Solaina and I are the only thing between her and death now.

And then the others will follow. I will too.

We get out of the car, slamming the doors in the quiet night.

The moon hangs in the sky, bloated and white. The wind whistles through the trees. The headstones stick up like jagged teeth in a black maw. We grab the shovels I snuck out of Solaina's garage in a thankful moment of clarity, then hurry through the cemetery gate.

We grip our tools and race through the cemetery, up the hill, and gather around the trunk of the apple tree.

"Th-this was a t-terrible idea," August stutters out, eyes wide, looking like she's hyperventilating or something. "We shoulda locked Iz in a safe room or something—a vault! We're weak, Georgina, Cori—what if he comes and we can't stop him from getting to her?"

Too late, the sense of what she says settles over us. We should have told our mothers. Our grimaces are identical, and fear makes me almost drop my shovel. But I heft it up and jerk my head. "He's not here, and maybe he won't come."

Too busy hurting Solaina, I don't say. But we're all thinking it.

Heaving my shovel into the ground, I say, "Come on, start digging."

The work is backbreaking, and the three of them are already tired. Georgina keeps getting faint and finally has to sit down with her head cradled in her palms. "Sorry," she murmurs from behind her dirt-caked bandages, blood leaking out the tips. "Just need a moment."

I dump a load of soil out of the trench surrounding the trunk and grunt. When Georgina looks up at me, she smiles, a dark trail of blood coming out of her nose. She shakily gets to her knees, bracing one hand on the trunk.

"Sit back down," I tell her firmly. "I can do it."

"I don't know how much longer *I* can," August says, and spits, the saliva flecked with blood. Her jaw is tight in a way that tells me she's hurting, her head pounding.

"Keep going, August, Cori." I struggle to get the words out, my arms and back screaming. I wish I could tell them to rest, but they're not as sick as Georgina. "We can do it. We're so close."

"What about Solaina?" Georgina's face is ghostly white and she's rocking herself back and forth, back and forth. "We need to find her. She could be anywhere."

"The sooner we find the bones, the sooner we find her." I only hope that's true. I slam the shovel into the ground again, but it's harder—almost impenetrable.

"I hit something. . . ." August sounds as surprised as I feel. Her eyes lock on mine, and I rush to her side, to help her dig in that spot, praying it's bone she hit. As I stick the blade of the shovel into the claylike soil, someone steps from the shadows. And Georgina lets out a pinched scream.

A body. Face, gray eyes, the familiar eyes of a stranger. Not a shadow. A man.

Heart in my throat, I stare at him in shock. Like a real man, crystal clear, every eyelash, every button on his coat formed with precision—in every way a stronger, cleaner, more colorful version than I've seen before. I didn't think he'd look this real. Not yet. Not until he had all of us. He fades, flickering in and out of focus. But for a long minute he's a man—and we all see him.

I reach out and grasp August's hand, wishing I had a knife, a gun, a bomb—something to keep him from us all. Behind

August, and Cori, and me, Georgina's breath comes out wet, gurgling. She's running out of time too. Maybe she should already be in the ER with Reuel.

I turn back to face Bayard, steel myself. I'll face him, for them.

"We know who you are," I say as he disappears again.

"Do you?" The words are singsong. Eerie. He comes into focus once more. Pins his gaze on me. A soft turn of a smile teases his mouth.

That's when it hits me—he didn't actually open his mouth. I only heard his voice in my mind.

"You're . . . not a man. You're a demon?" I try not to sound so uncertain. What if we've got this all wrong?

He smiles, almost politely. And fades away again—and again, I don't *hear* him. But I know what he's thinking. His thoughts are in my mind, and they are loud, and they are clear. I know that he's been here, waiting for a chance. I hear her name in my head—the thoughts break off and I swallow. The way he said *"Sorrow"* . . . staring at her statue. In a hard, dangerous, obsessive way. Like he'd like her back again—but only to hurt her.

"Sorrow," I breathe. And I lock eyes with him.

Then almost fall to the ground as pain hits me. My head aches, and images threaten to split my skull. And I see it . . . so much of it.

She summoned him—for power. Made a bargain. But she didn't know the price of the magic he helped her cultivate, the book he helped her write—not how his obsession for her—the twisted jealousy in him—would drive him mad. Bent toward his own destruction, his hands wrapped around Sorrow's throat. And then later—Sorrow reaching out, talking him down, soothing him. *One meal—perhaps you're hungry. Then we shall talk. I will do whatever you want, Bayard. We can make a new deal,*

Bayard. I shall give up my power—give it all to you. I do not want it any longer. I shudder, listening to the voices, seeing the pictures flash through my mind.

"Iz?" Someone grabs me by the shoulders, and I open my eyes, tears streaming down my cheeks. I stare into August's face.

Bayard comes closer, and I sidestep around the trunk of the tree. He's not desperate—he's confident, certain that he'll get me, that the bargain will finally be completed.

"What do you want us for?" I ask.

He shimmers out of view, but even though I can't see him, it's like a cord, connecting us. Just as he is in my thoughts, my memories, in a way inside me, I am all those for him. Not only did I understand what he was thinking, I *felt* what he was feeling, too. And still the thoughts come. I'm no longer in the cemetery, really. Or I am, but I'm back in time, with him. I feel trapped with him. And I feel a sick hope with him too.

He had to be patient, to wait. It was only a matter of time before he saw a book he recognized, in the hands of some girls he did not, until he saw an opportunity and snatched it—but before he could step forth into this world, before he could be free again, to live powerfully as a man once more, the chance faded—the spell incomplete—and he was stuck yet again.

Until one night, he watched two girls. One with hair as black as Sorrow's. Our blood, which he already knew, which he'd tasted before from our mothers. It was enough to give him strength, even for a moment, to find this new girl, to draw her out. She came to him willingly. She was owed to him anyway. He knew it. And something in her soul knew it, too.

The smile he flashes at me as I run through this leaves me shaken. It's almost warm, kind.

I hate the idea of Reuel lying in her bed. Being taken over.

That warm smile is there, but Bayard's eyes are on me and he's hungry. So hungry. I bite the inside of my cheek to keep from crying out, because I finally understand. I won't be able to outrun him.

Maybe I don't even want to. Maybe he is right—something in me knows I'm already his. My mother gave me to him, even if she didn't mean to. I'm already dead—I was before I was born.

I'm going to die—we all are—and he is going to live. That's what he wants.

Bayard inclines his head. His fingers brush toward me. And . . . and I reach . . . Georgina jumps up with a surge of strength and lashes out at him, smacking his hand before he can get to me.

"Don't fucking touch her," she growls.

Before I can have a second thought, he fades again, and August yells, "Solaina!"

I whirl around to see Solaina, stumbling forward from the trees. I watch her crumple to the ground. Cori flings herself at Solaina, hands fluttering at her face, helplessly, blood pouring into her palms, streaming from Solaina's ears, from her nose. Even, horribly, from her eyes, but it's worse than August's bleeding eyes—it's a faucet, red streaming, unending.

"No!" Cori croaks. I stand frozen. I scream, I can't help it. Is Solaina hemorrhaging?

The ground beneath her plumes up in mushrooms, soaked in her blood, white as bone on the underside. The air stinks of rot. And Bayard is gone. But not. He's waiting. For me.

Georgina's eyes roll to the back of her head and she falls to the ground, not far from Solaina. Her body jerking, seizing. I finally come to my senses and run toward them, waking up my body and my brain, but August yells, stopping me.

"I got it." Her voice is clear, steady, as she looks from Solaina to Georgina. Solaina's eyes are open again now. "She just fainted. The blood . . . I don't know what it is, but I'll take care of it. And Georgina, *God, we have to hurry*. You," she says to Cori, "do *not* let Iz out of your sight. Go back to the tree, Iz. You two keep digging. Go!"

I don't hesitate. I turn and race back to the tree, but someone calls at my back. Whirling around, I feel panicked, because I was too quick, and Cori has tripped on a headstone and is curled up, grabbing at her knee, whimpering, and I'm too far away from the others, and suddenly I'm alone. The night too loud, the sky too dark, and *I'm alone alone I'm alone and he's gonna get me.*

The sharp smell of apples. A laugh behind me. Or in front of me. Where is Bayard? There is no one there. But I know he's watching. Everything in my body tells me this is true. And I should rush away, run back to the girls. But I don't. I don't even try.

The moonlight shines and he comes into view. He looks down and he stares at me, the veins in his skin going black, like poison. But still, that smile. So warm, so gentle. Such longing. I should let him have me. . . . Doesn't he just want to live again? To have a body again? To be human again, for a while? Who am I to stand in the way of that? Why would I want to?

"Dig, Iz!" August yells breathlessly. "Get the bones! Cori, hurry!"

Cori limps back to my side and picks up her shovel again, brandishing it before her. When Bayard steps closer, she swings it—hard—whacking him, the blade connecting with his skull with a sickening crack. I don't understand how he's made of bones, but we are looking for bones, and he's dead and he's alive. I'm hysterical now, gasping for breath, and there is blood pouring from the side of Bayard's dented head, but still he stands, flickering in and out of form, in and out.

August runs to us, leaving the other girls on the ground, waving a trowel, screaming. I think I scream too, as he whispers her name and she drops her weapon and goes to him. Just drops it and goes. He wraps his arms around her, and she closes her eyes so I can't even look at her. His hands encircle her slim waist, so gently, so easily, and as he nuzzles against her neck, I take my shovel and swing it down into the ground while Cori tries to find a way to attack him without hurting August.

Crying, I hit something with a solid thud. In the same spot August hit before. I drop the shovel and start frantically digging into the earth with my hands, digging and sobbing, flinging dirt behind me. My fingers graze something and I swallow down a sob. Roots. Cori and I hold our breath, time stilling.

No bones. A terrible realization. Maybe it comes from me or maybe it comes from the triumphant feeling pouring off Bayard.

There are no bones.

The wind is blowing, throwing my hair in my face, whipping it around, pushing the sweet scent of apples from him toward me. He releases August. She falters, then falls over, faints. And I cannot get to her. I can't save her. I can't save them. I can't even see where Cori is now, where the others are. I can only see Bayard.

And he is only steps away, and if I look at him close, I know it will be over. Already he whispers to me in my mind, already he has won, already my heart breaks. We're not strong enough. There are six of us. Our births were fucking magical. We defied destiny. We love each other so much. But it's not enough.

The sharp fear of that realization leaches into me and I can feel my own spirit weaken, resisting the pull of his magic. My body starts to grow cold. I can feel the wind more strongly the more the doubt fills me. I want to go with him.

I want to help my friends, though . . . I want—

Come to me, come to me, he is crooning in my mind. Time slows, and I wait. For him to take me.

Except—one thought snags at me. Maybe it's something Melissa Honey said about power. We are not just daughters or friends or enemies. We are love. Found family. Power. Forgiveness. We may be flawed, but we are *good,* and he is not. He should burn for what he did to Sorrow. To us.

I place one hand on the bark of the tree in the exact second his eyes flick to it—just a pause, enough for me to see his fear— and I understand.

That one spell mentioned something about binding. We thought his bones were under the tree. But what if Sorrow tied his existence to the tree itself?

I recall what the tape of Nana Pierce said—that he was tied to the land. Sorrow bound him—his bones are buried beneath the apple tree—and it grew from that. I need to destroy the tree. I pray to all the witches in all of history that I am right, and I shove my hand into my pocket for my lighter. I light one of the blossom-laden branches on fire. And my voice is clearer, not as timid, when I speak to Bayard this time. I stare into his face. It's not a spell, maybe, but I say it loud and clear: "I wish you'd burn."

The fire catches quick, withering the blossoms, blackening them. The tree erupts into greenish-yellow flames, a feral, poisoned thing, in the middle of the new circle we've made.

And at some point, Bayard stops moving in and out of focus. He doesn't struggle. He doesn't cry as he catches fire. He doesn't even move. He stands there, that bleeding dent in the side of his skull, those unblinking gray eyes. He fades until I can't see him any longer.

But I can still hear the screams.

"What's happening?" I whisper, helping August rise as she comes to, then Georgina, who is slowly regaining her color, her breath coming even, steady. Cori is helping Solaina push herself up, and Solaina is blinking, swiping her hand over her bloody face. Staring down at the stinking mushrooms on the ground around her before turning her gaze upward to the tree, muttering a prayer beneath her breath.

"He's burning . . . the demon. It's burning as the tree burns," Georgina says. The five of us stand there, take hands, staring at the blaze.

I can feel that human part of me—afraid of this fire. But I stay still. Those flames golden green, acid bright, licking up the trunk, along the branches, plumes of smoke unfurling into the black sky.

We stand there until the fire dies out, clouds of inky smoke coming off the tree, steam as well, fumes of something sickly sweet, until it, too, dies out, evaporating on the air. The whole graveyard goes quiet. At peace, the evil thing here destroyed.

"He's gone," August whispers. "Did you feel it?"

I nod. We all do.

Georgina lifts her chin. She wipes her eyes and says, "Everyone all right?"

I must be imagining it—her skin looks positively dewy. She smells as bad as the rest of us—like smoke and ash. But nothing else.

She kicks at the charred ashes of Bayard's remains. Then takes the salt from August's tote bag and pours it on top of the pile until it's emptied, the whole pound or so of it. Georgina shrugs. "Just in case."

"The tree is, uh, barbecue," August says, her face covered in soot. "And so is he."

"Yeah. He's gone," I say, stunned. Almost not believing it. We did it.

We saved ourselves.

And I know it in my heart—we saved Reuel, too.

We wait, just to be safe, until the sun comes up. When we are sure—absolutely sure—there is no presence left, we leave. "We've got to tell our moms," Georgina says, her face clear of any resentment. "They'll be looking for us. I'm surprised they're not already here."

We drive down the street, early-morning light spilling shadows onto the pavement, battered and bruised. But smiling. We survived. And we heard the news, that Reuel is already on her way home—or there already. The hospital saw no reason to admit her, a healthy teenage girl who was just a bit dehydrated.

Georgina drives straight to Reuel's house. And when Reuel comes running out, my eyes fill with tears. She's *running.* She hugs all of us, crying. "I felt when it all changed. You did it," she whispers.

"We did it," Solaina, says, voice full of wonder, still, hours later.

"I knew you could," Reuel agrees. She squeezes my hand, a question in her eyes, the dark circles beneath them already faded. Her hair will grow in again, I suspect. Healthy and glossy.

I hold her gaze a second before facing ahead, my heart

climbing its way into my throat, her fingers threaded into mine. I know how I feel about her.

But the way she looks at me now? Maybe I was wrong that it was pointless. All of our history floods me. Buying tissue paper in the same shade as my hair. Bringing my favorite candy. Staring at my mouth for a long minute. Grazing my ear with her fingers—saying it's perfect. Reading me poetry as if she meant it for me. Her unspoken questions. The words she didn't say and the words she did. All that and more—so much more.

I shyly return her smile and clear my throat to keep from saying something. Not yet. Not right now.

"Do you think he's *really* gone?" I ask the girls. Which is a little ridiculous. We all saw what happened—but more than that, we felt it.

Georgina's nod is so sure, so confident, it settles into my bones and makes me relax as we pause on Reuel's porch. "Yes. He's really gone."

"How can you be sure?" I ask her, but it's really a question for us all.

She looks at each one of us, then says, even more certain, "Because. This is our happy ending. Love overcame . . . whatever that was."

"I almost didn't think we would survive it," Solaina admits as our phones all blow up—the moms are trying to get ahold of us. "I'm glad I was wrong."

"Come on," Georgina says, texting one quick thing, then nodding toward her car. "I'll give you girls rides. We're probably grounded for the rest of the year, but I'm oddly fine with that."

They all hug Reuel, and I'm about to follow them off the porch when she blurts out, "Iz? Will you stay a minute?"

A nervous confusion flutters in my middle, but I nod, ignoring the buzzing of my phone in my back pocket. I can't talk to my mom right now. The girls give us quizzical looks but don't ask. I hug them all once more, the most grateful, hardest hugs of my life. Solaina's hair smells of smoke and mushrooms, her arms around me weak but steady.

"Good luck," she whispers. I pull away, blushing. What does she know?

She smirks before glancing at Reuel and tugging her in for a hug of her own. "Bye, girls," Solaina says, turning with a smile and jogging down the porch steps to meet the others at Georgina's car.

And then, it is just us. Reuel and I.

"Wanna walk?" she asks me as the others drive off.

"Sure?" My heart beats in my ears. We move off the porch and down the sidewalk. A whole block goes by without us speaking. I count my steps and try to formulate words. Or maybe a question.

"Reuel," I say as we cross the street and circle around the block the other way. "Are you sure you feel okay? You know, after everything."

She stops now, at someone else's mailbox. Faces me, letting her hand fall from mine. "I feel like I got hit by a tank. But you know, otherwise, I'm grand."

I laugh at her wry smile and then hesitate. I realize what it is I want to ask but struggle to articulate it. Biting my lip, I finally try, "What's this thing going on? Am I imagining—"

"Are you imagining that there's something between us?" she asks softly. Searching my face.

I can feel my cheeks darken and heat. As if the sun just lit me like a spotlight. "Yeah," I answer, in an even quieter tone.

Her fingers reach out, tentatively, tracing the lines of my

jaw, my chin, cupping it, her thumb brushing ever so gently against my bottom lip, smudging something away—soot or blood, I try not to think about which. With her hands settling on my hips now, not pulling me in. But inviting me.

"You're not," she says, blue eyes bright and soft all at once.

"Oh?" It comes out as a squeak.

A laugh as she gazes at me fondly. "I've wanted to tell you for a long time." Now she's the one who looks nervous, looking away as she adds, admits, maybe, "A really long time. I wished for *you*, Iz. That night at the cemetery. You're what I wished for."

It's only a second later that I act. I'm the one who steps closer, pulling her face into my hands, tugging her down a little to meet me in a kiss.

"Oh—" she starts to say, one breath against my lips, and then I've got her. One breath and she's mine. Her soft mouth, her tongue, our teeth bump once and it's fine. It's more than fine.

Time melts together, the world spins around us, going on in slow motion, quick motion. We are a beacon, two wrapped into one, kissing and kissing and laughing, her whispering to me, poetry, words. *Love's light wings . . .*

When Reuel pulls back, ever so slightly, she wipes at my eye. "You're crying."

My voice breaks as I nod against her, as she pulls me in for an embrace, comforting me. My cheek laid against her neck. I whisper, "I'm happy."

"I'm happy too."

The sky is lavender, the birds just beginning to sing. All is right. All is more than right.

I'm in love. And the girl I love is leaning down to kiss me again.

CHAPTER TWENTY

When we finally pull apart, Reuel says, her lips swollen from my kisses, "I have something." After digging in her back pocket, she pulls out a piece of paper, folded into a square, and hands it to me.

"It's for you," she whispers.

I take a peek—but the first line is different. This isn't the poem I started reading when she went missing.

"I got jealous," I tell her, explaining with a soft laugh. "I read the poem you wrote for Grady, and I didn't realize it at the time, but it made me so jealous."

"I never wrote a poem about Grady," she tells me. "All of them were for you."

One last kiss, a shared breath of joyous laughter. Then she turns and runs up the block, to her house, up the sidewalk to her front door. The boys probably still in bed. Mr. Carson, surely waiting for her, making sure she's still okay. Maybe they'll talk about her mama this morning, about Jolene, or maybe they won't. But she'll be okay. We all will be.

I continue on my own, to my home. I unfold the paper, taking my time reading.

> *I tangle my fingers into your hair,*
> *You sleep at my side, your chest rises and falls, my*
> > *heart falls, falls under,*
> *Drowns.*
> *This is what I want to say, this is what I can't,*
> *Lock my tongue away, treasure chest buried deep*
> *With my feelings, let the siren cry out, unrequited,*
> > *let the color of you fade*
> *From my need, let us be what we can be and only*
> > *that,*
> *Let me capsize this love, wreck it for what it wants*
> > *to be,*
> *Call you my girl, call you my*
> *mermaid,*
> *Call you my*
> *Everything.*
> *I go out like a light, and you light the way for me*
> *The sea is as blue as your waves, my heart, this shal-*
> > *low feeling spilling*
> *into my lungs and up out my empty mouth.*
> *Light the way for me, and I will follow.*

It's not until I get my phone much later from Solaina's that I can text her.

My heart is so full. I say to her. *I love it. It's about me?*

Of course. She answers. *Always.*

*　*　*

Later, my mama and I pick at a meal Ms. Camille had delivered to us from the local diner, and we talk about what I just went through. The swing outside bangs against the tree as the wind picks up, and she jerks her gaze out, startled. She seems to notice the swing and frowns, turning back to her plate. Her mouth opens, then closes. There is so much I can tell she wants to say—not only about what we all just did. She's mad, she's relieved, she's racked with a terrible guilt, because the mothers couldn't do anything to save us—not that we gave them a chance, really. But there is more to it. More in her unspoken words.

"What?" I wait, putting my water glass aside.

Hesitating, she says, "I was thinking about your father."

My fork stills, hovered above my plate. I set it down and wipe my clammy hands on my thighs.

"You were two," she says, pushing her plate away. "God, I hated him for leaving. I still do."

"Did you love him?" I don't mean my sperm donor. I clarify, softly, saying Mr. Boudreau's name: "Brant."

This seems to catch her off guard. I explain, "Georgina told me about the two of you. I know he's not my biological father, but did you love him?"

She thinks a minute, then gives me a sort of helpless shrug before resting her chin on her palms. "You know, I'm not sure. We were so young, and sometimes I think maybe we ended up together because we couldn't be, do you know what I mean?"

"Is he what you wished for?" I ask, unable to stifle the question. I want to know, despite myself.

Her mouth tugs down, and she says, "No. It was more general than that—I wished for true love."

And she got her wish eventually, but at a price—love, except with a man she couldn't keep. My father left her after only a couple of years—with me, to raise alone. And then there was Brant Boudreau—another woman's man.

"Ms. Kate was your friend." It's not a question, not even a judgment, really. I'm trying to understand. I imagine stealing away Louis, for instance—how much it would hurt August.

"I liked him before they even started dating. I kept quiet—never, ever would have acted on it. And then, after that night . . ." She hesitates. "Something changed, and we all started fighting, nitpicking at each other. It was small things, ways we couldn't get along. But when I lost most of my friends, I felt lost. I got reckless. Marisa was the only person I could count on, and she went off to college. So I started acting out. I guess somehow I decided to wreck my own life. I ripped up all my college applications. I screwed around. And Brant was there one night when I was in a bar, stood up by my dirtbag boyfriend at the time. In that moment I forgot he was Kate's. Or I didn't forget. But I just didn't *care*."

I nod, as if I can really understand, but I didn't live it, and I didn't choose any of it. I lean in, elbows on the table, our forgotten dinner between us, as she goes on.

"Kate and I didn't talk anymore. The girls and I had already drifted apart by then, except Marisa and me—and things were strained between us, with her having left a couple years before. But Brant, he was so full of life, and handsome, and funny. He made me laugh. So we started a thing up. It lasted for years." She swallows. "We broke it off about a week before I met Beau—your father."

I can't hold back a frown—I kind of hate that she named me after him.

Her voice is clear as she recounts: "At first it seemed like he was the answer to everything—he was steady and soft-spoken, worked hard, ya know? I felt safe with him, could push the memory of Brant away. But after I got pregnant, and he had proposed by then, I ran into Kate one day in town—Brant with her—and I could see her belly, realized she was pregnant too. I remembered that promise we'd made. To give up what we held most dear. I was terrified, and it only got worse, when I eventually learned that Kate's sister, Beth, was pregnant at the same time as us. And Marisa. I didn't know about Sutton or Camille yet—I'd lost touch with both. But it was enough to send me into a spiral. And Beau—we fought all the time. I couldn't tell him what I'd done—it sounded crazy to me, to even worry about such a thing." She takes a deep breath, and a pained smile comes across her face. "After you were born, I thought things would improve. Only they didn't—and it wasn't all his fault. We let it die, together. I knew he was gonna leave long before he left. I just assumed one day maybe he'd be back. I hate that about myself. I hate that I waited."

"I did too," I whisper. "Maybe I still am waiting. I know he's in California. I googled him last year. Did he know about Brant?"

"Nobody did—we'd ended it before I met Beau, remember. Or I thought nobody knew. Until Kate confronted me. When you and Georgina were born . . . and we were at the hospital— them and me. I must have looked at him some kinda way, or she noticed something. Maybe she talked to him about it. Kate put it together—must have realized the way I avoided Brant, and her. I apologized, but it was too late."

Mr. Boudreau never treated me any differently than any of the other girls. Except, now that I recall it, maybe there was a look, in the back of his eyes. An avoidance. I'm just a reminder of my mama, a reminder of his infidelity.

And my father—Beau. Why would I want him? Why do I still care? "I think I hate him, my dad," I say, with a half laugh.

She smiles, sad. "You're stronger than me, Izzy. But I know it's my fault you had to be." Her eyes are tired, so tired. So I'm suddenly afraid of what she's going to say. I hold my breath while she goes on. "I never meant to hurt you. I only wanted to hide. I know I drink too much now. I know. I'm an alcoholic." She swallows, like she's trying to get the word back down even though it's out now. "I did well when you were younger—your birth straightened me out for years, but it didn't last. I feel awful about that, and it's my fault—what we just went through. You know me and the others—we were planning our own little ritual?"

I blink, hearing this.

She goes on, smiling a little. "But you beat us to it. I'm sorry we couldn't be there for you the way we all wanted to be. We wanted to fix what we'd done, and it kills me that we almost lost you all. I thank God you are okay. And I want to say I'm sorry. I want to tell you I know I have a problem."

I don't know what to say exactly. But she's admitting it. Isn't that a big thing?

"Talk to me, honey. I can handle it."

I lift my shoulders helplessly. "I'm still mad and hurt. And scared for you, Mama. I'm scared you're gonna kill yourself by drinking."

Her hands shake, but she stretches across the table to take mine and holds them tight. "I can't promise I'm not gonna make a mistake. I can't promise to be perfect. But I'm signed up for a group. I tried to call so many times before. But this time I actually called. I could never forgive myself if something happened to you because of me. And it's not fair, what I've done to you."

"What if you change your mind about the group?" I bite my lip.

"I know. I already thought of that. But this time I want to go. Really. And Marisa promised to take me, so I can't back out."

My mouth twists to the side, because she still could back out. This could all be empty words on empty air. But I let her come around the table. Let her take me in her arms. I tip my head down against her chest. She strokes my hair, like she did when I was a little girl, before things got really hard for her. Curling her fingers around my ears, and I count the beat of her heart.

On Monday, Reuel and I walk to school, holding hands. We're late—but what else is new?

Turns out, lots.

Together, we pause at the top step.

"Ready?" I ask. Not because I'm scared, for the bigger implications. Sorrow, for all that it's small and secluded, is kind. But for the details. Will this change the group dynamic? Will the other girls accept us? Not just accept us—Cori is gay, and obviously we accept and love her—and they know Reuel and I aren't straight, but root for us together? Will this work out the way I so badly want it to?

When we step over to our lockers, they are waiting, and they feel like love. I relax into Reuel, melting with the relief.

"You two . . ." August straightens from where she was

slouching glamorously against my locker. She has a huge grin on her face and slips her phone into her backpack. "You look different."

"Hold on—" Solaina starts before bursting into laughter. "What happened?"

Reuel and I meet eyes before breaking into smiles. I can't help it any more than she can. Casually, Reuel answers, "So, we're together now—"

A muffled shriek of joy and someone throws their weight against me, and before I know it we are all hugging and I hear Cori's warm, triumphant exclamation of "I knew it!"

Solaina laughs again, squeezing my elbow. She whispers, "I knew it too."

"So did I," August says.

"Did you all know?" I ask in wonder, staring at each friend's face. They nod. I say, "I barely knew my own feelings." Reuel laughs at my side.

"I had a feeling," Georgina says. "I kinda thought you two were secretly together this whole time, like even when we weren't talking. . . ."

I smile, shaking my head. "No, we weren't, but no more secrets. I love Reuel."

Reuel sighs happily and tugs me in closer, kissing my cheek chastely—we are in school, after all. "And I love you." It's not the first time we've said it. But it feels just as amazing.

"It's about damn time," Solaina teases.

"And Adelaide comes home today!" Cori exclaims gleefully. "This is the best day ever!"

We all cheer together, until a boy walks down the hall.

Grady, looking too damn good in his uniform, his sharp blazer, his sharp cheekbones, those eyes, green as apples.

"Hi," he says. He smiles in surprise, watches the way Reuel and I lean into each other without even realizing it. His face lights in recognition, and he graciously says, "I see it. I don't know how I didn't before." Grady laughs, but not unkindly. "Hey, good for you. She's a great catch." He looks at me, meaning Reuel, of course. Because I was just a dark shadow in a corner at a party. And that's how it should be.

Then he turns and goes, slinging his backpack on one shoulder, nodding as he passes someone in the hall before meeting up with Bridger down the way—sweet Bridger, who I'll have to catch up one day . . . at least about the highlights. He's the kind of boy who will believe me, no matter how strange my story is. Because that's what good friends do.

I'm so very lucky to have so many.

CHAPTER TWENTY-ONE

II MONTHS LATER

Today, I am seventeen. We are seventeen. And this birthday we are celebrating in style, together. Where it all began. At least some of our story.

We stand in a cluster at the forgotten top of Greenbrier Cemetery, not far from the statue, staring at the surprise laid out in front of us.

Set in the middle of the grassy area free of headstones, very close to where Reuel and I sat a year ago, the long table is draped with dark-as-night lace, topped with a dozen black candles that flicker in the perfect light of the golden hour. The sun sets in the distance over our town, dripping down the sky until it hangs like a yolk in the horizon. And in front of us, silver domed trays lie across the surface. On a separate table there are two uncovered platters, one piled with sweets, the other neatly lined with acid-pink cocktails that are smoking—the only thing that will be tonight, since I've kicked my nasty habit—and of course, there is water, for Cori, and honestly, probably for me as well; I don't drink as much these days. Beyond, the town lights of Sorrow twinkle, as if this spectacle were made for us and us alone. I'm not sure what's more impressive—the table setting or the view.

Cori gasps in delight, her fair skin flushing pink as her ladybug-print shirt.

"Wow." I blink at the table, at the sight beyond. It takes my breath away, the sunset—everything. From the looks on the other girls' faces, they feel the same. I turn to Georgina in wonder. "How'd you do this?"

"I have my ways." She flicks a glossy lock of hair over one shoulder, her smile pleased, uncannily bright. She looks even better these days—an unfair glow-up for junior year. I don't even resent her for it. Not after what she went through. And she's single now too. More popular than ever.

"I'll say." August's voice is tinged with awe as she stares at the lights cast across town, then back at us. Later, she will meet Louis, and we are happy for it—their futures are bright together. But for now, she is here. A breeze catches her new chin-length curls, framing her luminous skin. That one eye— still just a shade lighter than the other, which she's embraced. "I never really knew about this view. . . ."

"I did." Reuel smirks, meeting my gaze. Taking my hand. "But I guess Georgina outdid my birthday picnic, huh?"

I laugh, leaning into her. She brushes her lips against my temple, and I close my eyes, content.

"See. I told you all it would be special," Georgina says triumphantly, right as usual. I open my eyes to find her smoothing the front of her floaty pink minidress. Her flawless manicure matching it perfectly—her fingernails grew in even stronger than before. "It's not weird being here after everything, is it?"

Maybe it should be. But somehow, it feels right. We survived; we are thriving. And we want to celebrate ourselves. Each other. And we want to celebrate her, too—Sorrow. But it wasn't just her. It was us.

"You've outdone yourself, G." Solaina whistles and shakes her head, her new haircut—a sleek, blunt bob—swinging, tiny minimalist earrings mirroring her metallic liner, her expression soft, open.

None of us are guarded anymore. Not with each other.

"Should we?" Reuel motions to what she brought from the florist. She already dropped yellow roses off, down near the front of the cemetery. What's left is a bouquet full of blues and whites. Forget-me-nots. Daisies. Things we thought Sorrow might like, though there is still so much we will never know about the woman or the witch she was.

We all nod. "Yes," Georgina says. "Before we start our party. It only seems right."

Quietly, we walk together, Reuel still holding my hand, and she reverently places the flowers down, her eyes gentle, a little sad. For what happened to our mothers, though they've formed their own truce, awkward as it may be at times. For what happened to my friends, even though they're healed—their bodies, anyway. Sometimes August still gets migraines. Georgina's stomach is still touchy. We all still have nightmares, but that's part of just living, honestly.

We gaze down at the bouquet, laid on the ground, leaning against the statue. Solaina whispers a prayer beneath her breath, for Sorrow. For her peace. August touches the feet of the statue, almost in a holy way. I stare up at Sorrow, finding the solemn look on her face—she looks nothing like the real Sorrow, this statue, but that's okay. My heart is so full of love, I send some out into the universe, for whatever is left of the woman. We will never, ever forget her, because I do believe in my heart she had a hand in helping lead us to the answers we needed. That she wanted Bayard beaten as much as we wanted to beat him. And we'll make sure nobody else does either. Georgina's been fundraising for a museum for Sorrow for the last six months—Melissa Honey is thrilled to be on the board, even though she's not a Sorrow resident. I know that with their passion, grand things will happen. And maybe nobody will believe in Sorrow's powers, in her legacy. Maybe it'll be a joke, the museum. But we'll know the truth. Our mothers know. Melissa Honey knows.

I tip up my chin, almost feel her magic lingering in the air, the ground, in our bones, our blood, woven into our very being, threaded into our friendships. The wind shifts the trees, magnolias nearby giving off their delicate lemon scent, the light casting its way down to us, the last rays of sun hitting my skin, warm and golden. Golden like Reuel's real hair, although I'm partial to the black. The sky blue, ocean blue, like her eyes. I know that color. I'll see it in my dreams for the rest of my lives. If I were a poet, I'd write about it. But it's enough in this moment just to take her hand, bring it up to my lips, kiss the back of it as gently as she kissed my temple minutes ago.

We stand still another couple of breaths, feeling the weight of our emotions caught up with us now. We slowly turn, going back to the tables Georgina set up, her in the lead in her pink suede high-heeled Mary Janes. We take our seats—place cards set out for us. Georgina has me between her and Reuel. I give her a smile and settle into my spot, facing the view of town. Behind me, only feet away, is the corpse of the tree we burned. Nobody seemed to notice the fire that night, or the smoke, or even wonder about what happened to the apple tree.

Georgina instructs us to *Eat!* We lift the domes and dig into the meal, all our favorites: pizza and carnitas and steak with burgundy sauce and fried shrimp and fried pickles and mashed potatoes and French fries and jalapeño corn bread with honey butter and cheeses and fresh fruit on a silver platter. I don't even know how she managed to do all this, but it was well worth whatever effort she put in. Everything is delicious and her thoughtful touch is everywhere—even if it's all clearly catered in.

"So," Solaina starts, dunking a fried pickle in ranch dressing. "I was thinking. Seventeen. We have a whole year to plan matching tattoos for our next birthday."

"I'm in," Georgina says, reaching for a carrot stick. She notices us watching, mouths dropped open, and shrugs. "What?"

"You are the most non-tattoo person I've ever met." I laugh. "I thought you never were into that."

"Well." She munches her carrot and swallows. "I figure you girls are already tattooed on my heart. What's the difference if it's on my skin?"

"Aww!" August cries dramatically. Placing her hand over her heart. The body glitter she swiped on her cheekbones and collarbones makes her already-glowing skin twinkle. We all laugh, teasing Georgina for being a softie.

"My parents will hate it," Cori says. "Yours too, August."

"All the more reason to do it," Reuel says, eyes sparkling, lifting a glass, the charms of her bracelets clinking together. I'll give her the newest one later, when we're alone. It's a tiny mermaid. She continues, "But for now, let's just forget about the future. There's time for that."

"Wait, Reuel. Georgina," I say, before we toast. "Tell the story first. I've missed it."

Georgina leans back into her seat with a smile. She recites from memory, "One rainy day, six baby girls were born. The first, at Sorrow General Hospital, was born pink and tiny, at just after five a.m."

The first, of course, was her.

She goes on, "Then the next, a cousin of that first baby girl, whose own mamas were twin sisters, was born by C-section way off in Connecticut. Around noon, one baby finally made her appearance after a two-day-long labor in a small town in Arizona. She came out with a big cry and a full head of black hair."

Solaina grins at the description of her.

Georgina continues, "Next, a skinny little peanut that popped out in a California elevator, but luckily, her daddy was a doctor himself, and he helped her mama get through it." She winks at August. "Finally, born simultaneously that evening, in the same hour, one of them also in Sorrow, born weeks early, and breech—"

Someone throws a napkin at me, and I whoosh out a laugh.

"—the other, in Minnesota, born en caul. It's considered auspicious."

"You mean *sus*picious," Solaina teases Reuel, poking her with her finger. Reuel grabs it, half smiling.

Georgina drifts quieter now, her words coming sweet. "Six girls born on a single day, though then they didn't know it. As the years passed, they became classmates, then friends, then best friends, held together not just by love, but by fate."

"The end," Cori finishes, eyes shining. She looks around. "But not really. Not for us."

Never for us.

Best friends forever, we promise again. And this time, no blood.

We meet eyes, lifting our own glasses in a toast, to celebrate our births and our love, and our survival. That's all we need for now. Reuel's right—there is time for the future and all its challenges.

"Happy birthday, loves," Georgina says as she passes out boxes wrapped in white linen. We weren't going to exchange presents. She overdid it, but that's okay. I adore her for it.

"Happy birthday," the rest of us echo.

Then once more, I say the words, "I love you."

You can never say it enough. Life is fragile, and it goes fast. Seventeen years and we almost lost each other, twice over. Yet here we are. Together. In this moment, in this cemetery, everything is right. Sorrow at peace. All the spirits quiet, resting.

Just as they should be.

ACKNOWLEDGMENTS

Ah, the sophomore novel—the thing of urban legends and horror stories! Nothing I've written has had to be wrestled to the ground as aggressively as *Six of Sorrow,* and there were times while revising this that I wondered what I'd gotten myself into. In other versions there were seven friends (sorry, Cori, for killing off your twin sister), a girl named Jenny who had a sad ending but not much of a purpose, a rotting cherry pie, two funerals, and zombie cheerleaders. Those things all needed to go to make this the story it is now (though I'm saving that zombie idea!), and it has been a great learning process—a bit painful, as any growth can be, but incredibly fulfilling—to see how an idea can grow and take shape into something you never expected. If only you are open to it. And, of course, if you have the right support.

Without my editor, Krista Marino, I would still be in the ring with this thing, I think. Thank you for helping me tame this beast into something I'm so proud of now! What a wild ride this was, but worth it in the end, and I couldn't have done it without you.

Lydia Gregovic, working with you on my second novel was a delight—I love what you brought to the table again. Thank you so much for all you did, and cheers to our 2024 books!

Juliana, my agent—as always, immense gratitude for your dedication, your positive outlook, and your grounding words whenever I'm spiraling. I'm thrilled to have you. So much more to come! (And by that, I mean good career things, not spiraling, although I suppose . . .)

To the entire Delacorte and PRH team, especially Colleen Fellingham and Barbara Perris, Tamar Schwartz, Sarah Lawrenson, Shannon Pender, and Michelle Campbell, endless thanks for all the work you did to make this story an actual *book*. And it is beautiful! I've been blessed by the cover gods again—a generous thanks to talented artist Kei-Ella Loewe for making the bright pink cover of my dreams. I believe this was fated.

Writing friends—where do I even begin? I belong to a most amazing community, and many of you helped shape early drafts of this story, back when it was called *Bloody Buried Things* (and a few had their eyes on later drafts). Thank you to the following skillful and generous writing pals: To Book Besties Jamie McLachlan and Cathie Armstrong for your support and encouragement, not just with this book but all my work, and to my other Book Besties, Kelly Cain and Bianca M. Schwarz, who not only read early versions but also blurbed later on, along with Britney S. Lewis and Keshe Chow. You all had lovely things to say about this book, and I'm immensely flattered to have such talented authors read and enjoy my work. I appreciate you all! To Storybeast Ghabiba Weston, Kalie Cassidy, Emily Wilson, and Autumn Lindsay for reading and providing excellent feedback. To Jennie Grace James, Amanda Murphy, Alexa Manz, and Anna Leighton for encouraging me during tough rounds of revision. Finally, to Rachel Jenkins, who is the best brainstormer I've ever known, and who was instrumental in helping guide me when I was lost in the thick of the plot. Heart eyes to you all!

Loving gratitude to Madeline yet again for your insight and enthusiasm, and to your mother and her weirdo friends, who are truly soul mates of my heart: Theresa, Melissa, Lindsay. I couldn't have better people in my corner.

Thank you to Larissa Roby-Brown for your kindness and time, and to Linda for reconnecting us and for being generally wonderful!

Thank you to all the readers returning to my work after my first book, *Starlings,* and to those discovering my words for the first time. I hope you'll stick around to see what's next! I am honored when anyone picks up my work, and even more when you connect with it.

Thank you to friends, new, old. The ones who get the memes, the ones who get the tears, the ones who know all my life stories, the ones who helped write them. The ones who were there for a moment, the ones who've left my life for various reasons but changed me in some way. The ones who rock my boat, and the ones who keep me steady. As Iz says near the end of the book, I am so very lucky to have so many (friends). Thank you for being mine.

When my editor said to me that *Six of Sorrow* felt like "an ode to being a teenage girl," that struck me hard. I connected very deeply to my teen self while writing it (although let's be honest, most of the time I feel like I'm still seventeen), to delve into how I felt and who I was and who I wasn't and who I wanted to be. This is all just a poetic and clumsy attempt to say I think she's right, and I hope you feel the same way while reading.

And, of course, to my family: the love of many lives, my husband, and our children. Thank you.

ABOUT THE AUTHOR

Amanda Linsmeier has been a book nerd for as long as she can remember, and it was that great love of reading that led her to write her own stories. She lives in a small blue house surrounded by trees and cornfields with her husband, their three wonderfully wild children, and, somehow, five pets. She is the author of *Starlings* and *Six of Sorrow*.

amandalinsmeier.com